Forza!

A Tribute to a 1970s Italian-American Upbringing

By Michael Sorabella

Dedicated to my family and friends, who have always been so encouraging and supportive. A special thank you and appreciation for the first generations of family and neighbors, who instilled the distinct and ever-present sense of community throughout our early years. For those who have now been gone for far too long, you will always be missed.

Especially you, Dad.

Indice
(Table of Contents)

Giovedì 1 Luglio 1976
(Thursday, July 1, 1976)

Venerdì 2 Luglio (1976)
(Friday, July 2, 1976)

Sabato 3 Luglio (1976)
(Saturday, July 3, 1976)

- Continued -

Domenica 4 Luglio (1976)
(Sunday, July 4, 1976)

Lunedi 5 Luglio (1976
(Monday, July 5, 1976)

Inspired by a True Story

Giovedì 1 Luglio (1976)
(Thursday, July 1, 1976)

I - Sveglia Presto
(Early to Rise)

At exactly 7am, my mom crept into my room and gently woke me. "Michael, time to get up." Still half asleep, I mumbled something and slowly rolled over. "Time to get up and do your route," she said.

Earlier that summer, my mom "surprised" me and my oldest brother Bobby with a neighborhood paper route, a job that she happily secured on our behalf. Bobby and I would share the work, alternating weeks, delivering Boston Globes to about forty homes in the neighborhood. I quietly sprang from bed and, with a tremendous case of bed head, walked to my dresser. I stepped quietly, trying not to wake my youngest brother, Steve. Steve, who is five years younger than me, had moved into the room with me about a year ago. For the first nine years of my life, I shared a room with Bob, but we had been separated a year earlier, after countless battles between us had culminated with the final and massive battle of 1975.

My parents chalked it up to a severe case of sibling rivalry. Bob and I had had hundreds of fights over those first years as roommates. But I'm not sure that you could call something so one-sided a rivalry. Over that span, I'm certain that I never won any of those skirmishes with Bob, who is two years older, a foot taller, thirty-plus pounds heavier than me and a kid who was generally born in a bad mood. Regardless, the room swap was a good one and the fragile peace that settled in the aftermath seemed to be keeping.

I headed to my dresser, opened the second drawer, and pulled out a pair of shorts and my "Jaws" tank top, and then quietly exited the room and headed for the bathroom. There, I swapped the shorts and the tank for my pajamas, tossing those into the hamper, giving my mom even more work to do. I made two quick swipes with my toothbrush, going through the motions, but checking the box that I made the effort, and ensuring that my toothbrush would now pass the dry bristle test that Mom would undoubtedly be running moments later.

As I stood there feigning to brush my teeth, it hit me. Today was the first day of July! July was my favorite month of the year. The first full month of summer break from school. Hot days, beach trips, pool parties and, of course, the Fourth of July holiday and, again, no school! Things were good, especially given that this Fourth of July we'd be celebrating the country's Bicentennial. This was a big deal. A huge deal. And we had big plans of our own to celebrate with a neighborhood block party on the Fourth.

Before heading out on my route, I walked downstairs and into the kitchen. Our kitchen was a classic example of early-to mid-70s home decor. Bright yellow and orange colored flower petals, with lime green leaves and stems, adorned the wallpaper of our kitchen. The style was an undeniable tribute to the 70s and a sight to be seen. It was a thorough representation of my mom's sense of taste, captured in one single ten by ten square-foot area.

On the far countertop, located directly under the yellow wall-hung rotary phone, sat a standard RCA radio that was blaring the morning's latest news updates from a Boston area Italian language AM radio station. Alongside the RCA radio, a small porcelain coffee maker was hard at work brewing a fresh cup that I could smell long before turning the corner into the kitchen.

"Michelino!" my grandfather, after whom I was named, shouted at me. "Buongiorno!" "Morning, Nano," I answered.

Now, the proper word for grandfather in Italian is "Nonno". But somehow, someway my brothers, sister and I "Americanized" it to "Nano," and it stuck. I'm sure, deep inside, our butchering of the pronunciation was a bit of an afront to my grandfather. Especially for such a familiar and endearing word such as grandfather. However, to us, his grand kids, it was, more or less, just his name. And although it was our failed attempt to culturally identify him, he was simply "Nano" to us.

We had lived our whole lives together in the same house as Nano. First with him and our grandmother in a converted two-family home in Somerville, a city just on the outskirts of Boston. And then for the past three years in Stoneham, a small town less than ten miles North of Boston, where we had moved, shortly after my grandmother had passed away.

Nano was up early most mornings, commandeering the kitchen to either construct his lunch each weekday or to get his sauce going for most weekend days. For his weekday lunches, Nano would hollow out a good-sized chunk of Italian bread and forcefully fill it with whatever leftovers he had handy from last night's dinner. He'd pack his lunch to bring to work at his furniture store, Saviano Furniture, which was a small storefront furniture shop located on Canal Street in Boston.

Canal Street is a one-way street that intersects with Boston's Causeway Street and is situated directly across from North Station and the Boston Garden. Canal Street also sits on the very edge of Boston's North End, which is the city's oldest residential community and a predominantly Italian neighborhood. That's if you define predominantly at roughly ninety-nine percent. Those factors are what made Canal Street an ideal venue to house Italian American businesses and, as a result, the street was lined with small, family owned, Italian retail shops, most hocking gaudy furniture like Nano's storefront.

Over the years, his furniture business had proven to be a good provider for him and his family. But nowadays, with Nano in his seventies, it was more of a pastime for him. It provided him a sort of sanctuary, as well as a sense of purpose following my grandmother's passing. It also served to keep him in touch with old friends and stay connected with the community.

I quickly zipped past Nano in the kitchen and headed down to the garage. I was anxious to clear my schedule of my one absolute duty of the day: getting a stack of Boston Globe newspapers from my driveway into the impatient hands of about forty of my neighbors. I sped down the basement stairs, buzzed past Nano's homemade wine cellar, that he had erected a couple years earlier, and straight into the garage. I hit the garage door opener and then lifted the bundle of newspapers from the driveway, dragging it behind me into the open garage.

I used a pair of plyers that I kept on a wooden work bench, also built by Nano, that I used to lean my bicycle against. At the time, my bike was my prized possession. It was an orange Schwinn Sting-Ray, complete with high rise handlebars and an orange and white striped banana seat. It was the one and only wicked cool thing that was mine and only mine. However, there was one undeniable buzz kill that sucked nearly all the cool factor out of this masterpiece from Schwinn.

It was the unmistakable steel, wire basket that my dad had attached to the front of my Sting-Ray. Dad had fastened the basket to my bike so that it could hold my newspapers for quick and easy delivery. It made the paper route far easier, but the "look" was a tough pill to swallow. Hanging this trash barrel from the front of my classic Schwinn was like kryptonite to the cool factor.

I quickly folded the papers like my dad had taught me. Collapsing the paper into thirds, like a dress shirt, and folding it into itself and making an optimally sized and shaped projectile that could be tossed twenty feet or more with dead-on accuracy. I loaded the papers into the wire basket fastened to my once cool bike and I was on my way.

II - Quartiere
(The Neighborhood)

My route took me to a bunch of side streets, but most of the homes were located on my block of Fieldstone Drive. Fieldstone was a relatively new neighborhood with a long straight drive and an oval loop at one end. The street was essentially the shape of a lollipop with about seventy homes in total. Our home sat at the top of the loop, or head of the lollipop, and it was from there that I set out on my route.

The neighborhood was a great place to live, especially for young kids. Every home had been built over the last five years or so and nearly every family had two or more kids. Most families had moved to Stoneham from a nearby Boston area city. There were multiple families from Somerville, others from Medford, Everett, and Malden. Those communities were all situated right on the outskirts of Boston, five miles or less from the heart of the city. My dad used to say if you added up the distance that everyone on the street had traveled to move to Stoneham, it wouldn't even total a hundred miles.

But this was everyone's big move to the suburbs and their pursuit of the American dream. There was a shared aspiration of the people from Fieldstone Drive to be able to offer their kids more than they had in their early years. And the move to Stoneham was their reaching for the stars.

As I pedaled from home to home, tossing papers on the front

steps of the homes on my route, it was hard not to notice an unmistakable similarity of the homes in my neighborhood. The homes had a striking likeness to one another.

It wasn't the style of the homes. There were a good mix of splits, ranches, and colonials. It wasn't the paint or the color of the vinyl siding. There was more than a fair mix of colors. And it certainly wasn't the size, scale or positioning of the homes. There wasn't anything cookie cutter about it. Certainly not like what you'd find in the communities where these families had opted to leave behind. It was something more ethnic.

Let's just say that many of the homes, most of the homes, were decorated with a distinct taste. There was plenty of stone-work, bricks, stone statues of Mary, mother of Jesus, and enough wrought iron in the neighborhood to build a decent-sized bridge. That distinct taste meshed with the overwhelming character of the neighborhood. It was a safe bet that nine out of ten family names on our street ended in a vowel. It was a distinctly Italian neighborhood with new homes and young families.

I hit home after home on my route, cruising in and out of driveways and tossing the Globe onto each staircase. It was a great system, never having to get off my bike to make the drop-off. But it was a far easier ride on the way out than on the way home. The last leg of my route took me down a neighboring block, Citation, which is adjacent to Fieldstone. That street has a steep hill not far from where it merges with Fieldstone.

As I head into that leg of my route, it's an easy glide down-hill into the lower side of Citation which, like Fieldstone, is a large oval with similarly built new homes. As I make my way around the oval and start my trek home, I hit the hill from the other side and it's a real grind. To be able to get up the hill, I need to stand while pedaling and sway, shifting my weight from side to side with each push. Thankfully, I've lost three quarters of the weight from the papers that sat in the basket at the front of my bike. Finally, I reach the hilltop, and with a loud exhale, I slide into the last driveway and toss the last paper at the doorstep of number 32 Citation. It's barely after 8:00 a.m. and it's time to punch the clock, done for the day.

The ride home from here is a short one and with a welcomed,

slight decline down the front of Citation. As I head down Citation, I drift left to merge onto Fieldstone. As I rolled towards the intersection, picking up speed, I caught out of the corner of my eye the sight of something shooting across towards me. I hit the brakes hard, skidding a good ten to fifteen feet and sliding into the curb at the corner. In a flash, a bike had shot straight across in front of me, catching air as it lifted off from the raised sidewalk, soaring into the middle of Citation Street.

The bike, spray painted in a deep black shadowy tone, landed on its back wheel, and came to a screeching, fishtailing stop. In the wake of the bike's abrupt stop, a blackened rubber skid mark punctuated its wild ride. The rider whipped his head around and glared back at me. It was my next-door neighbor, Marco Palermo.

Marco was one of the older kids in the neighborhood, a year older than my brother Bob, and he was a tough kid. He was the kind of kid who would look for a fight just because he hadn't been in one for a while. And he could really fight.

He wasn't the biggest guy, but he was wiry and solid. And he had something extra that the average kid walking around didn't have: a complete lack of fear. No fear of getting involved in a scrap with a much bigger kid and, more importantly, no fear or hesitation to throw the first punch. And that first punch might very well be a sucker punch and that characteristic or trait separated him from other kids.

At the same time, he was protective of his own and wouldn't think twice about stepping in and defending someone in the neighborhood. Even if he didn't care much about that someone. Overall, though, he was just a loose cannon, and no one was completely at ease when in his presence. Marco had even gained some notoriety during his first year at the junior high school for his antics. And, for some reason, he had been given the nickname "Rubberhead" by some of the older kids. It was really the perfect label for him, and it seemed to be sticking. But no one in the neighborhood, not a soul, would dare call him Rubberhead to his face. That would be suicide. But we all thought it, and, in our own circles when he wasn't around, all referred to him as Rubberhead.

"Watch it!" he shouted. "What are you looking to get killed?"

I hesitated a second and then stammered, "Uhm, sorry. I guess I didn't see you, Marco."

"What the hell is that?" he asked. "What?" I replied. "That thing on the front of your bike. What is that? Is that a fucking basket?"

My shoulders slumped and I briefly looked away. "Yeah, my dad put it on so I could use it to hold my newspapers," I said. "Well, I would lose it, if I were you. You look like a wuss riding with that thing. And someone's gonna give you a real beating, riding around with that thing on your bike," he paused. "But hey, if anyone gives you shit, you come and see me and let me know. And I'll take care of it. You just let me know, I'm serious. Okay?"

"Sure, thanks", I said quietly. He then changed the subject and asked me if I had heard the big news. "You hear what I'm doing this afternoon?" he asked. "No," I said.

He began to glide over to me on his bike. "You didn't hear? Really?" "No, I don't think so," I answered. He then announced, as if it was breaking headline news, "I'm going to be jumping my bike today. I'm gonna jump over milk crates, twelve of them," he bragged. "Tell all your little friends, and your brothers. I want everyone to see it. It's going to be a wicked jump. Twelve crates. That's a lot of fuckin" crates, you know!" he exclaimed.

"Yeah, that is a lot", I agreed, "And I will. Where are you going to do the jump?" I then asked. "I'm going to set it up in the open lot, right over there," he said pointing back towards our two homes. "Just after lunch," as he began to pedal away. "It's going to be awesome!" he shouted as he headed away from me. "And get rid of that fuckin' thing on the front of your bike, I'm telling you."

III - Ciottoli Gratis
(Free Cobblestones)

I got back to my house, pulling into the driveway just as Nano sped away in his olive green 1967 Dodge Monaco. He was putting in a quick day at the furniture shop before getting home for the long holiday weekend. I parked my bike back in its place and headed upstairs. My mom was in the kitchen when I walked in, she was in the middle of taking clean dishes out of the dishwasher. "Michael, remember I need you to clean up your room sometime today. We have company coming," she said. "I know, Ma. I'll do it." "Yeah, well I want it done soon and done well," she replied. "Yep, I got it."

I reached for a cereal bowl from the cabinet and grabbed a box of cereal and began filling my bowl. Mom then grabbed the milk from the fridge and handed it to me. "And your father wants your help after you finish your breakfast. So, don't go anywhere." "Okay. With what?" I asked. I turned the corner with my cereal bowl in hand and headed into the den. "He needs you to take a ride with him, so just be ready," she shouted from the kitchen.

As I turned the corner into the den, I could see my younger brother Steve and my sister Pam sitting in front of the TV. They were watching the early morning cartoons. I took a seat in my grandfather's recliner and dug into my Frosted Flakes. "You know, Nano doesn't want anyone sitting in his chair," Pam said.

"Well, he's not here is he?" I replied.

She turned back towards the TV, and me to my sugar-laced cornflakes. I took another heaping spoonful, as my other younger brother, Dave, walked into the room. "You know, Nano doesn't want anyone sitting there," he said. "I know, I know … everyone knows."

"Well, he's going to know that someone was sitting there. And he's going to think it was one of us." "No, he won't," I said. "Yes, he will," Pam chimed in, as she turned back from the television. "He'll just think it was me. He always does," I countered.

"You know, Dad wants us to go with him," Dave added. "I heard. Where are we going?" I asked. "I don't know. All I know is it's somewhere in Woburn," Dave answered. Just then Dad walked into the room and looked around. He spotted me in the recliner and said, "You know, he's not going to want you on his chair, Michael."

I got up from the recliner, cereal bowl still in hand. "You two meet me out front in five minutes," Dad said. "Okay, where are we going?" I asked. He was halfway back into the kitchen and all I heard him say was "Woburn."

Dave and I headed out the front door to meet Dad in the driveway. Dad had the tailgate open to his two-tone 1972 Oldsmobile Vista Cruiser station wagon and was loading a tarp into the back of it. I shouted, "Shotgun!" and jumped into the front passenger seat. Dave slid into the back seat, as Dad slammed the tailgate shut and hopped into the front seat. We were on our way to Woburn.

"What are we going to do in Woburn?" I asked. "We're going to a job site," Dad answered. "It's one of Mr. Oliveri's construction sites. He has some scraps lying around that he said we could take."

We pulled out of the development and onto Franklin Street, headed towards Woburn as the car radio blared some "Easy Listening" 70s tunes. It wasn't long before one of Dad's favorites, "Rock the Boat" by The Hues Corporation, came onto the radio, as we sped down Franklin Street.

We pulled into a parking lot near the end of Montvale Ave in Woburn. There was a flurry of activity in the area with dump trunks, backhoes and other construction vehicles whipping around the otherwise empty lot. We drove to the back of the lot and pulled alongside a trailer that had been placed there to serve as an office.

As we parked the wagon, I saw Mr. Oliveri step outside of the trailer and approach our car. "Bobby! I'm glad you could make it," he said to my dad. "Thanks Carmine," Dad answered. "Hello, boys." "Hi Mr. Oliveri," Dave and I answered together. "Looks like you have quite a project going on here," Dad added. "Oh, not too bad, really. We should finish up in the next week or two." Dad looked surprised and just answered with a, "Really?"

"Let me show you what we're looking at, Bob," Mr. Oliveri said, grabbing Dad's arm and pointing to the far corner of the lot. I looked over to Dave and told him that the building on the other side of the lot was the Bowladrome, where I had had my birthday party only a few months earlier. Dad then whistled to us in his patented style and both Dave and I ran back to the car. Of course, I again yelled, "Shotgun!" and leapt back into the front passenger seat.

Back in the car, we headed for the far corner of the parking lot and stopped just in front of a huge pile of old rocks. Dad stopped the car and gave us our instructions, "Okay guys, let's go." We jumped out of the wagon and followed him to the rear of the car. He opened the tailgate and suggested we get started. "All right, let's go through these stones and pick out the good ones."

"What are these?", I asked. "They're cobblestones," Dad answered. "Well, what are we going to do with them?" I continued. "Mr. Oliveri said we can take whatever we wanted. They're just going to be tossed, otherwise. And I thought we could use them for the party this weekend. Plus, you know, waste not, want not. Now look, the best ones will be the ones that are still fully intact. Let's grab as many as we can and put them on the tarp in the back of the wagon."

Dave and I immediately started to wade into the considerable pile. "Okay, now, be careful moving around the pile. Let's find the best ones," Dad continued to guide us. We each slipped once or twice as we navigated through the piled cobblestones. We moved up and down the pile, turning over each stone and judging them as worthy or not. There must have been hundreds of them. One on top of the other.

Some had big chips out of them, others were still covered with mortar from the cement that had once held them in place.

"I can't believe they were just going to throw these out," Dave said. "Typical," Dad answered. "But we're going to save these from the dump. Aren't we, boys?" "Yep," we both answered enthusiastically.

We continued our hunt, loading good cobblestones into the back of the Vista Cruiser. We must have taken over a hundred of them. And I know Dad was pretty happy about it. As we got back into the car and pulled away from the site, Dad gave three quick honks on the horn, and I could see Mr. Oliveri waving at us in the side mirror as we pulled back onto Montvale Ave and headed for home.

IV - Spericolato
(The Daredevil)

After dropping off the cobblestones across the street in the Palermo's driveway, we rushed into the house for a quick lunch. Mom was still running around, cleaning anything that didn't move in advance of our company arriving. Dave and I shot into the kitchen and quickly put a Fluffernutter together for ourselves. We could see someone sitting at the picnic table on the deck, right outside the rear door of the kitchen. We both grabbed a can of soda and headed outside onto the deck with our sandwiches in hand.

Stepping outside, I saw that Bob and Steve were sitting at the table with Pam, and they were nearly done eating their lunch. I slid onto the bench next to Steve. "What have you guys been doing?" I asked. "Nothing," Bob responded. "Just trying to stay clear of Mom and her cleaning," he added. "Did you hear about what Marco's doing just after lunch?" I asked. "Yeah, who hasn't," Bob answered. "Who do you think helped him swipe the milk crates from in back of Friendly's?" Bob shot back.

Friendly's was a local ice cream shop and burger and fries fast food restaurant located on the edge of town. It was only a ten-minute drive from our house, but oddly, also just ten minutes away by bike if we took the path through the woods. Our neighborhood development sat in between the town's Junior High School and the Middlesex Fells Reservation.

The Fells, as it is known, is a State-owned conservation and recreation area of over 2,600 acres and with over 120 miles of trails for hikers, horseback riding, rock climbing and general recreation. To us, it was a paradise of undisturbed woodlands and a place where we often roamed and played into the late hours of the day. We regularly spent hours in the woods, exploring the many trails and paths and imagining just who may have been in this place years, even hundreds of years, before us. Afterall, we're just 8 miles North of Boston and this area undoubtedly was patrolled by British troops during the revolutionary period and, without question, by Native Americans well before them.

Evidently, Bob and Marco had used these trails and paths to get to Friendly's and "borrowed" some of the loose Hood milk crates that were frequently left out back of the restaurant. These would now serve as the "obstacles" in the way of Marco's planned flight path that he intended to take on his bike. The five of us quickly finished lunch and, with great anticipation, made our way to the gate of our fenced yard and headed out to the vacant lot located next door.

We hustled over to the adjacent, vacant land. When we turned the corner, we were shocked to see just how many kids had gathered. It was really a spectacle. There were no less than 30 kids there, all looking anxiously on as Marco worked to set up a makeshift ramp that he had cobbled together. Most of the kids there were from our block, but I could see a few faces of those who had made their way up to Fieldstone from Citation.

I quickly spotted the crew of my closest friends and made my way over to them. There, Lou, and Lisa Limone were standing with Mario, John, and Josie Padovani. They were gathered beside some large boulders that the contractor had left behind to discourage people from driving through the vacant lot. As we approached them, Lou greeted us with, "Can you believe this shit?" Crazy," he shouted. "Yeah, he thinks he's some sort of Evel Knievel," Bob responded. "You think?" Lou added, sarcastically.

I then saw Matteo Palermo, Marco's younger brother, and I walked over to him. He was fast at work in lining up his brother's ramp. Matteo, who was closer to my age, rushed to put some of the milk crates in place. "What are you on the pit crew?" I asked

Matteo. "You can say that, I guess," Matteo answered. "Actually, Marco threatened to 'kick the shit out of me' if I didn't help him," he continued. "Yeah, I guess that means you're on Team Marco," I replied.

"Really, at this point, I'm on Team Milk Crate, but don't tell anyone that I said that," Matteo joked. Just then Marco sped over to us on his bike and came to a fishtail stop, kicking up dust at Matteo and me.

"What are you two doing? Matteo, get your shit together! Why don't you have the milk crates lined up yet?" asked Marco. Matteo quickly dragged two more milk crates, followed by two more to go in front of the eight that were already in place.

"Whoa, are you serious, Matteo? What the hell are you doing?" he asked. "I'm lining up the milk crates just like you told me," Matteo answered. "Not all twelve of them at once, you moron. Just put eight of them to start. I want to do a practice run and see where my bike lands. I'm sure I'll have the distance, but I want to do a test run, just to be sure," Marco said, as he pointed to a measuring tape that he had placed by the side of the sole tree in the cleared lot.

Matteo quickly rearranged the crates, as his brother had directed, and then tossed the others aside. With that, Marco turned and sped away on his bike. He crossed the street and turned around at the foot of his driveway. He shouted at the crowd from across the street. "Everyone, stand back. I need a clear path to the ramp."

Despite his plea, everyone took two steps closer to the ramp. Marco shook his head disapprovingly but got up on his bike anyway and began pedaling frantically toward us and the ramp. He swayed wildly left and right, trying to get every ounce of power from his legs. He gained considerable speed with every thrust of his legs. I could see the strain on his face as he got closer to the lot and the ramp. He actually grunted like an animal as he hit the base of the ramp and with every ounce of energy in his body he pulled up on the bike's handlebars as he took to the air and off from the edge of the ramp. It was a sight to see!

With ease, he cleared the eight milk crates that were lined up from the edge of the ramp and with a thunderous thud he touched down on his rear tire as a plume of dust lifted from the ground where he landed. It was an amazing jump. It looked as if he was traveling a hundred miles an hour and he finished the feat with his patented fishtail sliding stop which kicked up an even greater dust cloud. Everyone was just amazed and rushed forward. Marco immediately leapt off his bike and shouted for everyone to step back.

"Get back, back! All of you, get back!"

Everyone took a step back as Marco rushed in to take a look. "There! Right there! That's where I landed," Marco said, as he pointed to a clear tire mark on the ground. "Matteo, get the measuring tape."

Matteo rushed to comply with his brother's order. "Now, hold it steady to the front of the ramp," Marco instructed his younger brother. Marco then stretched the tape measure to the spot on the ground where his tire hit.

"Just over thirteen and a half feet!", he yelled. "Cleared it! Cleared it by more than half a foot," he declared. "Matteo, set it up again, and add the other crates. We're good to go," he called out.

The excitement from the test jump had barely waned and Marco was already back across the street, gearing up for the real thing. Matteo had just finished lining up the remaining milk crates, and everyone held their breath as Marco readied himself for the jump. I had to give it to the guy, he was really holding all of us captive, as we anxiously waited and looked on. We were all actually rooting for him, hoping he'd clear the dozen crates.

I walked back over to where my brothers and sister were watching on the rocks. Just as I walked over, I heard Lou Limone say, "I hope Rubberhead knows what he's doing. It's gonna be close."

"Is it all set yet, Matteo?" Marco shouted from across the street. "Just about. One sec," Matteo replied. "Hurry up, shit for brains," was Marco's response to that.

One last tap on the corner of the twelfth crate and Matteo gave the all-clear signal. And with no hesitation, Marco stood again and leaned forward on his bike and started towards the crowd. He repeated his swaying stride, one after the other, and quickly gained speed. He had as much speed, if not more, than in his test run. He swiftly crossed from the street and into the lot. We all shuffled a step forward as he hit the ramp.

He pulled back hard on the handlebars, as he did on his first jump, timing it perfectly with the end of the ramp and he was once again airborne! He seemingly had the speed and altitude to carry him all the way, as he navigated the bike through the air, his bike wheels still spinning as he cleared the final crates. And it was right then, at the very last crate, where it happened.

As Marco and the bike descended back to earth, his rear tire clipped the very top, far edge of the last crate. And it was over. In a half second, Marco went from conquering hero to — hopefully — a survivor of a colossal wipeout. Hitting that last crate caused Marco to pitch forward wildly, and then up and over the handlebars he went. He landed face forward with both arms outstretched. It made a massive, smashing sound as he hit the ground.

His bike now followed him to the deck, rotating uncontrollably and bouncing from tire to tire in the aftermath. It looked exactly like that poor ski jumper seen week after week on ABC's "Wide World of Sports," taking that massive header and being tossed like a rag doll off the end of the ski ramp. Except this wasn't in the snow and there was a bike involved. It was simply an epic failure and crash.

"Holy shit! Holy shit!" Lou exclaimed. "Do you think he's all right?" I asked. "Holy shit!" Lou repeated, with his mouth wide open.

As Marco came to a full stop in a hail of dust and debris, Matteo rushed over to him. "Are you all right?" he asked with concern. Marco didn't answer but slowly rose and turned towards the crowd. He was covered with dust, from his head down to his Chuck Taylors. He looked like he had been dusted with flour, and then forcefully fed through the rollers of a pasta maker. He was a mess.

I could make out the scrapes and blood through the dust on both his knees. My eyes glanced up from his knees and, suddenly, it caught my eye. His left arm was bent in a direction that just wasn't natural. It sort of dangled by his side and flapped aimlessly as Marco staggered forward. It was at that moment that Matteo noticed it as well and then the horror sank in.

With absolute shock in his eyes, as if he was in the middle of a horror film double feature, he looked away from Marco and screamed with all his might, "Ma!"

Instantly, Matteo took off for his front door across the street. My brother Bob ran over to Marco and tried to help him brace his arm as he limped back home. It was amazing though. Marco never uttered a word, not a peep. There wasn't any sign of distress from him, other than the cloud of dust that seemed to orbit around him, kind of like the "Pig Pen" character from Charlie Brown.

He had taken a beating, but he wouldn't let on. I always knew he was a tough kid, but now I knew just how tough. As I stood and watched Mrs. Palermo rush out of her house and get into her car to speed Marco off to the hospital, I could hear Lou Limone, one more time, say "Holy shit!".

V - Tutti Impegnati
(Pitching In)

Still shocked by what we had witnessed, my brothers, sister and I walked back into the house. We knew there would be hell to pay later for what had happened. It only made sense to slinker back into the house and clean our rooms, like Mom had asked earlier. You know, get ahead of the news, and earn some goodwill before the inquisition, which was certainly coming later.

I made my way upstairs and headed straight to my room. On first observation, it wasn't all that bad. My bed wasn't made but Mom had already mentioned that she planned to change the sheets on my bed for our guests. So, check that box. Steve and I would be giving up our bedroom and beds for my Aunt Polly and Uncle Phillip, who were staying with us for the long holiday weekend. Although we called them, and thought of them as, our aunt and uncle, they were actually my dad's aunt and uncle, our great aunt and great uncle.

My dad was an only child, and he grew up in the same house in Somerville as Aunt Polly and Uncle Phillip. He also grew up right next door to Aunt Tre and Uncle Frank, again, Dad's aunt and uncle, our great aunt and uncle. Just to cap things off, Uncle Phillip was Nano's brother and Aunt Polly was also my grandmother's sister. So, two brothers had married two sisters, which I guess made them like super aunts and super uncles or more accurately super great aunts and super great uncles.

I couldn't wait for Uncle Phillip to get here. He was the coolest guy in the family, and by a mile. He was like a character straight out of an old fifties movie, kind of like an Italian James Dean. He just had a way about him, a sort of street smart that exuded confidence. And, somehow, I seemed to be his favorite. And that was a welcome change for me. You see, the first born in an Italian family tends to garner more favor and attention, particularly from an old school Italian like Nano. So, having this extra notice from Uncle Phillip was really something special for me.

A year earlier, we were at our cottage on the Cape when Uncle Phillip and Aunt Polly visited with us. We did everything together that week. We were at the beach basically every day, we fished off the jetties, we dove for quahogs just off the shore, and went crabbing from my dad's small wooden skiff. Near the end of the vacation, and after a successful run for blue crabs, my Uncle Phillip had quite a run-in with an angry blue crab. It all happened as we were sailing back to our mooring.

As my dad steered the boat from the stern, Nano and Bob sat upfront at the bow and Uncle Phillip sat with me and Dave amidship. We had six or seven blue crab keepers from our efforts, and they were held in a metal bucket that sat on the floor of our skiff. To entertain me and Dave, Uncle Phillip began to flick his finger in the water of the bucket, agitating the crabs. I remember that Dave and I didn't know what to make of it, but Uncle Phillip was certainly amusing himself.

As he went back in to tease our captives once more, one of the larger blue crabs struck out and latched its claw around Uncle Phillip's finger. Uncle Phillip immediately withdrew his hand and loudly began to curse in Italian. He whipped his hand left and right, trying to get the crab off of his finger. Dave and I had a front row seat to all this, and we quickly spotted blood flowing from Uncle Phillip's finger.

He continued to shake his hand firmly, but the blue crab wasn't having it. And then suddenly, as I witnessed in his eyes the internal debate that he was having with himself, Uncle Phillip brought his hand right up to his face and without hesitation he bit the claw off of the crab. The crab fell to the floor of the boat, still cocking its one good claw, as if it were ready to go for Round 2.

Uncle Phillip removed the claw that was still clutched to his finger and loudly declared to all of us that he would be having that specific crab for dinner later that night. And that, in a nutshell, summed up the celebrity of Uncle Phillip.

Back to cleaning and further assessing my room, it was simply a matter of picking up some clothes that I had scattered around my room, just the way I like it. Of course, most were dirty and needed to go into the wash. Normally, not a problem, except in this case, as I had already waved off my mom a few hours earlier when she asked if I had any dirty clothes that needed to be washed. Now that she was about a dozen loads in, I couldn't show up with another full hamper's worth.

Thinking quickly on my feet, I slid my closet door open and peered deep inside. Perfect. Plenty of room in here. After rearranging a few things on my side of the closet, I gathered the clothes from around the room and made a neat deposit into the deep back of the closet. The chores were now complete and off I went.

I hustled downstairs, whisking past Mom as she continued to work on a pile of laundry. "Done with my room, Mom," I reported. "You're done?" she asked, with a distinct tone of doubt in her voice. "I want that room spotless," she insisted. "Yes, it is," I assured her. "Okay, I'll be checking," she charged.

And I was certain that she would be. I got two steps into the kitchen, when Dad turned the corner. "Oh good, you're here. I need your help," he said. "Okay, what do you need?" I asked. "I need you and your brothers to help me set up the tent out back. They're out there now. But first, I want you to help Nano. He's home and has all the soda. Go help him out and unload it from his car, please."

Ahh, the soda. Every three or four weeks, Nano would bring home a load of soda. Cases of the stuff, usually a dozen cases at a time, twenty-four cans, twelve ounces a can. Every kid in the neighborhood knew to walk into my basement and help themselves to a free can of soda. Usually, a mix of 7 Up and Dr Pepper, but occasionally a wildcard was thrown in there, like the odd case of Moxie. Try to find that one in a vending machine!

But it wasn't bad, it was one of those acquired taste soda

brands. I'm not sure where Nano bought the stuff, whether it came from a vendor at Haymarket, or some distributor who worked Canal Street in Boston, or if he bargained for it every few weeks from somewhere in the North End after it had mysteriously "fallen off a truck". But it was a steady supply and when it came in, we knew to go fetch it out of the trunk of Nano's old Dodge.

I walked from the garage and headed to the rear of Nano's car. The trunk of his car had already been popped but he was nowhere to be found. Sure enough, there it was. The trunk was loaded with cases of soda cans. This was a special load, as it clearly had more than a dozen cases in it. Nano had upped his order ahead of the holiday weekend.

At first glance, I counted sixteen cases. Now, you might think no way can you get sixteen cases of soda into the trunk of a car, but this was the 1969 Dodge Monaco. It was a boat of a car, probably only getting five miles to the gallon in the city. You could fit a small couch into the back seat of a Monaco, so sixteen cases of soda in its trunk? No problem.

As I lifted the first case from the back of the car, Nano appeared on the scene. He approached me, waving his hand as if he were directing traffic and grunting in short successions. The grunts had a primal sound, forcing air from his lungs and exhaling sharply through his nose. I knew this sound. I understood the language. It was the communication method that Nano would employ to signal his orders, while he swilled about some of his potent, homemade wine in his mouth.

His finest red was apparently powerful stuff and could only be fully consumed after repeatedly rinsing it around, by shifting his jaw from left to right and then slowly swallowing. This, of course, reduced him to grunts and gestures as he attempted to direct me on how to do something the "right way."

With one big gulp, Nano swallowed and blurted at me "Heshpetta … Heshpetta!" That's what I heard anyway. And I heard it quite often. At one point, I actually thought it was some form of nickname that he had adopted for me. "Heshpetta," he would call out as I rushed to help him in his garden, or when each fall I, with my brothers, would assist him with his wine making as we processed that year's batch of grapes. I later learned that he was actually barking at me "Aspettare, Aspettare" which translates, to English from Italian, to "Wait, Wait." Which makes perfect sense, given my youthful tendency to speed through any chore or task.

"Put the top two in the wine cellar," he growled at me in his broken English. "The rest can go on the table," he said.

I dutifully unloaded the soda haul, just as I had been instructed. As I dropped the last case on the table, I caught a glimpse of Nano in the wine cellar, taking another full swig of his Zinfandel. I quickly shot out from the basement, hurrying before Nano could think of anything else to have me do. I headed for the backyard, so I could help out with raising the tent.

I opened the fence gate and rushed into the backyard. There, my brothers, Bob and Dave, were goofing around, throwing the tent spikes at the ground, trying to get the revolutions just right so that the spike would stick like a dart into the lawn. Dad had sprawled the tent out on the grass in the lower portion of the yard near Nano's Garden.

Our backyard was set up as any kid's dream. The top portion, nearest the house, was a rectangular section with a thick, rich lawn that Dad took great pride in. For us, it served as a perfect wiffleball stadium where we would play religiously all summer. We had a beautiful kidney shaped, resort style inground swimming pool on the lower left side of the yard. It was the center-piece of the yard and for all our family activities.

On the lower right side, where we were setting up the tent, was another fair-sized section of lawn. And at the very end of the yard, sitting behind a retaining wall that supported the pool patio, was Nano's Garden, which ran the full width of the lot. It was a beautiful spot and essentially a million miles away from the full concrete, small backyard that we had left behind in Somerville just a few years earlier.

The rear of our yard abutted and looked directly into the Padovani's backyard. Our lot stood a couple feet higher in elevation from the Padovani's, which provided a great line of sight into their equally well-manicured lawn and even more impressive garden. Their garden was a masterpiece. Every square foot had been expertly planned and utilized. There were rows set down with military precision lined with strong, developed plants that were full of ripening vegetables. At the back of the garden stood a system of trellises that hung over the last few rows of plants and supported vine-growing vegetables. Even the air above the dark, rich soil was being used to grow their produce.

At the front of the garden, wooden cases, approximately three feet by three feet, had been assembled using odd pieces of scrap materials. On top of the cases sat old, recycled house windows which all together ingeniously served as miniature green houses that the Padovani patriarch, Ray senior, had designed to house next year's fledgling plants over the cold New England winters. It was an incredibly impressive set up, which would provide one of the four basic food groups for their entire family for the full summer and deep into the fall.

I got to the tent just as Dad was ready for us to put the spikes in the ground. The tent was going up so that we could make room in the house for our visiting relatives. Dave, Steve and I were to camp out back for a couple nights. Of course, Bob didn't plan to join us, being too cool to hang with his younger siblings, and would opt to sleep on the couch in the den. In his place, we had arranged for Mario and John Padovani to camp out with us. It was all pretty exciting, being the weekend of the Fourth and all, and we were looking forward to it. We first had to get this tent up and our full attention turned to that task.

The tent was an old-style, heavy canvas shelter that was more than spacious. Raising it went surprisingly well, considering it was just Dad and three misfits. But Dad had spent a couple of years in the Army, in military intelligence, after graduating college and before he and Mom were married. And that is where he had acquired certain life skills, like assembling an oversized, old tent in your backyard.

After his stint in the military, Dad worked in academia, as a school administrator. Presently, he was the headmaster back at Somerville High School, which means he was the head disciplinarian at a pretty large city school. He had a reputation as a tough, but very fair, overseer of the students. He was very well liked by the "good kids" at the school.

For those kids on the other path, they would either come

to appreciate his actions in intervening their course down the "wrong" path or saw him simply as another obstacle in their life and resented him for it. To us, we never saw that side of him, the hardliner, and it was even difficult to imagine him as the disciplinarian, given his genuinely kind and caring demeanor. But I suppose, we never gave him reason to show it, either. As the final rope was tied off to the last spike, Dad declared the job finished. We grabbed the few tools we had on site and headed back to the house feeling pretty good about ourselves.

VI - La Catena di Montaggio
(The Assembly Line)

The four of us headed back into the house and walked into the kitchen. There, Mom was fast at work, her apron on and covered in flour. She had just begun to work on about a dozen piles of dough that had been sitting on the counter since early morning. She greeted us as we entered the kitchen, "Good, you're all here. Go wash up, soap and water, and come back in to help with the dinner. Soap and water, Michael!"

Dad headed straight to the kitchen sink. Bob, Dave, and I rushed out of the kitchen and headed for the bathroom to wash up. We usually had homemade pizzas for dinner on Friday nights, but with company coming, my parents intended to barbecue the next night and shifted pizza night forward one day.

My mom did most of the cooking at home. And as a cook, she was a great seamstress. It wasn't her fault, really. She grew up one hundred percent Irish, and now lived primarily as an Italian. She had tried, and tried hard, to learn from my grandmother. But Nana's untimely death, coupled with our growing young family, caused her to, let's just say, cut corners.

To be fair to her, she was cooking for seven people, every day and on a pretty tight budget. At least, it was only for seven, not eight, as Nano would opt to fend for himself. But pizza night was different. She had actually developed a decent knack of her own style of pizza. It was, by no means, anything that could be mistaken for pizza that you'd find in the North End of Boston or at a fan favorite, authentic Italian pizzeria. But it was good, nonetheless.

She would set dough out in the morning, cover it with a light cloth and allow the dough to rise throughout the day. When it was time, she'd hit each pile with some flour and then we'd get started. We'd all chip in, Mom, Dad and the rest of us, assembly line style. Just as we would tonight.

We'd each have our own task: someone to separate and flour the dough, someone to roll it out, someone to oil the pizza pans, someone ladling out the sauce, someone to spread the mozzarella cheese, someone else on toppings and lastly someone to season. It was a good system. And it produced a very thin crust, almost transparent, pizza. It was incredibly light. Any of us could eat eight to ten slices easily. Which meant we had to make a lot of pies. But it was tasty, and it was kind of our family thing.

We were just about done with our process for the night. Mom had already moved a half dozen of our mid-sized pizzas in and out of the oven, laying the cooked pies on the stove top to cool and sliding the last two pizzas into the oven. Suddenly, we could hear the front screen door swing open and then, in a familiar raspy voice, we heard, "Lou, Louise, you home?" It was Mrs. Palermo.

She and Mom were the closest of friends and Mrs. Palermo would often, essentially daily, walk across the street and directly into our front hallway and shout for my mom, as only she could. Mom answered while still tending to the oven, "Lil, in here."

Mrs. Palermo turned the corner and whipped into the kitchen. She was obviously agitated, and you could clearly hear some stress in her voice. "What am I going to do with that kid, Lou?" she blurted out. Mom, unaware of what had happened earlier that afternoon, asked unknowingly, "What is it, Lil? What happened?" She asked the question and then quickly glanced at me and my brothers, searching for a clue.

"It's Marco! Didn't the boys tell you?" Another glance from Mom at all of us. "No, no one has told me anything. What happened?" Mom continued.

"He's just a wild animal, that one, I tell you. He's some kind of showoff. And he had to jump his bike in front of all these kids, like some kind of Evel Knievel and crashed on some milk crates that he, and your Bobby, stole from Friendly's!" she frantically exclaimed.

This was music to my ears. At least the part implicating Bob in the deed. Mom shot him a look that could kill. Dad followed with an equally menacing glare.

"He broke his arm in two places. He's a maniac! I don't know what I'm going to do with him, I tell you," she finished. "When did you do this?" Mom shot at Bob. "It was a couple of days ago. I didn't know what he was going to do with the crates," Bob explained.

"It's alright", Mrs. Palermo said. "It's not Bobby, it's Marco. That boy could walk into an empty room and break something," she said. My shoulders slumped briefly, sensing Bob's escape. "I'm sure it's what Bobby said. What am I gonna do with him in a cast for the next four to six weeks? That's almost the rest of the summer," she complained. "Well, as long as he's alright. Broken bones heal, Lil," Mom comforted her.

Mrs. Palermo slowly pulled the nearest kitchen chair and sat at the table and sighed softly, punctuating that she had had a difficult day. "I see you're about to eat. I better go," she said.

"Why don't you join us for some pizza, Lil?" Mom offered. Mrs. Palermo paused for a second, and answered, "No. Thank you. I better go. I need to feed my crew. Plus, I better get over there and make sure he doesn't cover his cast in swear words or anything vulgar. He already had the markers out when I was leaving the house," she explained.

With one more sigh, she stood, using the kitchen table to push off. "I'll talk with you tomorrow. I know you have your company coming," she said, as she headed out of the kitchen. "

Okay Lil. Try to relax, if you can," Mom shouted after her.

Mom and Dad once again glared over at Bob. Bob shrugged his shoulders back at them and asked, "Time to eat?"

VII - Cattivo Sangue
(Bad Blood)

There was a lot of chatter at the dinner table, as we dug into one pizza after another. Dad dominated the conversation by hitting us with rapid fire questions about Marco's colossal, failed jump attempt. I don't know if it was the pizza, or just the anticipation of the big holiday weekend, but the mood quickly shifted to a more upbeat tone. Though, it was probably the pizza. It seemed to be a particularly good batch tonight. So much so that even Nano joined in and grabbed a slice, which was not a common occurrence.

As we finished off the last pie, Mom jumped into the conversation and quickly got right to the point, "Now, your Aunt Polly, Uncle Phillip, and Uncle Teodo will be here shortly, and I want you all on your best behavior. Make sure you give them a good greeting when they arrive, and I don't want any fighting while they're here. None. You hear me?" We all acknowledged that we had.

Nano, Uncle Phillip, and Uncle Teodo were three of seven Saviano brothers from Gaeta, Italy. There were also four sisters in the family, for a total of eleven kids. Five of the brothers had emigrated to the U.S. in the 1920s and 1930s. Only one sister, Maria, would follow, but that was a decade later in the 1940s and after World War II.

Nano, who was in the merchant marines at the time, was the first to take the bold step. I had heard stories that Nano had "jumped ship" in New York harbor but I never knew or understood exactly what this meant. But I did know that the brothers hadn't left Italy initially for the bright lights and promises that were offered in America, but rather to escape Fascism, which was running rampant under Mussolini's brutal totalitarian regime. The brothers had each made the difficult decision to leave their homeland and were determined to make a living, and life, here in America, while also sending whatever they could spare back to their family that they had left behind.

This visit over the Fourth of July weekend was kind of a big deal for us. Not just because it was the Fourth, or because Uncle Phillip would be here but, more so, because Zio Teodo was to stay with us as well. For the record, Teodo is short for Teodoro, which translates to Theodore. My brothers, sister and I all pronounced it as "Ta Doh", but I'm pretty sure that that was incorrect.

Similarly, we pronounced Zio as "Si", also wrong. Anyway, we hadn't seen "Si Tado" for over two years. We were all aware that he and Nano had had a falling out of sorts and the two brothers hadn't spoken over that same timeframe. And we, at least the kids, had no idea why. To address the bad blood between them, Dad and Uncle Phillip had conspired to bring the two brothers together in hopes that they would mend fences over the long holiday weekend. It seemed like a good plan and worth a shot. But no one knew whether it would work or go horribly wrong. And we were all on pins and needles waiting to see just how things would play out.

After the last thin slice of pizza disappeared, we then began the after-dinner clean up. We all brought our dishes to the sink and gave them a quick rinse before dropping them into the open dishwasher. Mom took a soapy cloth to the pizza pans and one after another, she handed them over to Dad who had drying duty.

This was the routine in our house and one that was repeated nearly every night. Mom at the sink washing the dirty pots and pans with water so hot that it could have been heated straight from a blast furnace. I could never understand how Mom could tolerate such heat on her bare hands. And Dad was always a trusted partner in the process, standing to Mom's right and drying whatever she handed over to him.

As she picked up the last, dirty pizza pan, she asked Dad, "Oh Bob, did you remember to get the Galliano for Uncle Phillip?"

Dad groaned, indicating no, as she handed him the final pizza pan. "No. I forgot to stop when I was out earlier", he replied. "Well, do you think you could run out quickly before they get here? You know he'll want something to sip on after coffee later," she said. "Yes, I'll run out quickly. What else do we need, if I'm running out?" he asked. "That's it. Just the Galliano," she answered.

Galliano was an Italian made yellow, greenish liqueur that Nano would sometimes drink. It was a nasty looking substance, and, to me, it resembled horrible tasting cough medicines. Earlier that year, on Easter weekend, and when my parents weren't looking, Nano had me try a small taste of his after-dinner cordial. I almost threw up! It had a very strong taste that just seemed to linger in my mouth for what felt like an eternity. It was just terrible and something that I didn't care to ever have again.

As Dad finished drying the last pan, Mom suggested that he take me on his Galliano run. "Michael, why don't you go for a ride with Dad?"

I was now the only one of my siblings sitting at the table, so an obvious choice. "What do you say, Mister?" Dad asked. "Sure, I'll go with you, Dad," I answered. Dad grabbed his wallet and keys, which he always kept on the right, top side of the refrigerator, and we were on our way.

Dad and I hopped into the front seat of the Vista Cruiser, and we backed out of the driveway, headed for McDonough's Liquors in the Town Square. As Dad shifted from reverse and into drive, I caught a glimpse of Bobby across the street on the sidewalk in front of the Palermo's. Bob was there with a small crew, which included Lou Limone and the Ferraro brothers, Ricky, and Tommy. I then realized that the four of them had encircled Marco Palermo, who was seated on his bike and holding court with his audience. His arms were flailing about, including his left arm, which was now noticeably entombed in its cast, as he was clearly telling his captive audience his version of events from earlier today.

Dad didn't let on that he saw the gathering, but I'm pretty

sure that he did. As we headed down Rustic Road, on our way towards Franklin Street, I couldn't help thinking about the situation between Nano and Si Tado. So, I decided to hit it straight on. "Dad, I have a question I want to ask," I began. "Okay, sure. What is it?" he replied.

"What happened between Nano and Si Tado? I mean, why haven't they talked to each other for the last couple years? Did they have a fight, or something?"

Dad took a second and then started, "Well," he paused and then chuckled, somewhat uncomfortably. "You remember Aunt Sylvia, don't you? Uhm, she passed away about five years ago, when you were just five."

"Sure. I remember her," I answered. Dad went on. "Well, she was Si Tado's first wife and they were married for a long time. And, Si Tado is kind of an old-fashioned guy, you know, set in his ways. And Aunt Sylvia was that way too, where the man of the house would traditionally be the provider, the earner in the family, and the woman would often be the homemaker and take care of all the things that the family needed and every-thing around the house. And, you see, Si Tado was one of those "things" around the house that Aunt Sylvia would take care of, something that he was very used to.

So, when Aunt Sylvia passed away, Si Tado was, of course, devastated by her loss, but he was also lost in another sense, as Aunt Sylvia wasn't around to take care of things for him. And to take care of him, specifically."

As we turned onto Franklin Street, Dad glanced over at me to see if I was following along. "So, as families do, everyone tried to help out with Si Tado. Help him adjust to now being on his own. That included help from Uncle Phillip, Aunt Polly, Nana, before she got sick, and even Nano. After a couple years, things seemed to be getting better but Si Tado was still very lonely. So, eventually, Nano introduced Si Tado to a woman he knew. Turns out that woman was Rose, who you might also remember. Well, Rose eventually became Si Tado's second wife." "

Isn't that a good thing, then?" I interrupted.

Dad tilted his head slightly and chuckled awkwardly again, "Well, yeah, you'd think so, but you see, with Rose, Si Tado wasn't lonely anymore, but she really wasn't at all old-fashioned like Si Tado is, or like Aunt Sylvia was. So, Si Tado really wasn't happy, as everyone had hoped he would be," he continued.

"But I don't understand. What does that have to do with Nano?" I interrupted.

Dad smiled coyly and with another shake of his head, he continued, "Well, it was Nano who introduced Si Tado to Rose. And, well, since Rose wasn't more like Aunt Sylvia, things didn't work out and that led them to split up and eventually get divorced. And, for whatever reason, Si Tado kind of blames Nano for all of it."

"But why? How was that Nano's fault, Dad?", I pressed. "It wasn't. But Si Tado blames Nano for having introduced them in the first place. And, well, that's kind of the story behind the bad blood between them," he continued.

"That makes no sense at all to me, Dad," I countered.

As we pulled into the side lot of McDonough's Liquors, Dad pulled the car into a parking space, threw the shift into park, and finished, "No, no it doesn't. But a lot of things from their old-world ways don't make sense to us nowadays, Michael. Now, you wait here. I'll be right out."

And with that, Dad headed from the car towards the entrance of McDonough's. I waited behind in the car and mulled over what I had just learned about the two-year feud between my grandfather and great uncle. It made absolutely no sense to me, but that didn't make it less real of an issue.

VIII - Forse Un'Altra Volta
(Maybe Some Other Time)

When Dad and I got back to the house, Uncle Phillip's car was already parked in the driveway. Dad pulled up alongside the curb in front of the house. As we both got out of the car, with a bag holding the long-necked bottle of Galliano in his hand, Dad said, "All right, let's see how this goes," and we made our way to the front door.

As we entered the front hallway, our eyes were immediately drawn to the noise from the dining room to our left. Nano was sitting at the head of the table, with Mom seated to his right, and Uncle Phillip to his left. Aunt Polly was standing over Uncle Phillip's shoulder as she placed a platter full of desserts onto the table.

"Hello, everyone," Dad said, entering the dining room.

"Bobby!" he was welcomed by the group. "I'm glad you all got here okay. We're all, especially the kids, excited to have you here to celebrate the fourth," Dad added. "And who do you have with you, Bobby?" Aunt Polly asked, as she gestured to me.

"That's Michael, Polly," Uncle Phillip chimed in, my self- esteem rising with his acknowledgement of me. "Oh Michael, look how big you're getting," Aunt Polly declared. "He is, he's had a real growth spurt this year," Mom added. Yeah, about one inch, I thought to myself.

"Come over here, Michael. Give your Uncle Phillip a hug," he said, waving me over.

I sped over to him with my arms extended, but instead of a hug, he came at me like a ninja, reaching out with his right hand, his index and middle fingers slightly curled in toward his palm but extended out a tad. With lightning speed, he had the full, left cheek of my face in between the two knuckles of his fingers and, as only an Italian elder could do, he began to clamp on my cheek with the grip of a vice.

I tried to rally with a smile, but I could feel all the blood in my face collecting to that one area. I thought to myself, this must be how Uncle Phillip felt on the boat last summer, when that blue crab snapped its big claw onto his finger.

Mercifully, he let go and pulled me in close for that hug. "Michael! How have you been?" he asked. "I'm doing great," I said, just as Mom had instructed us to do earlier. As I stood next to my favorite uncle, Dad asked the one hundred-thousand-dollar question, "Where is Tado?"

The room went silent, and I observed my aunt and uncle shoot a quick look back at Dad and then over towards Nano. Nano said nothing, as he continued to look down at the cup of coffee sitting in front of him, as he stirred the steaming hot beverage slowly with his coffee spoon. Uncle Phillip was happy to jump in.

"That son of a bitch!" he asserted forcefully. "Phillip!" Aunt Polly scolded him. "I'm sorry. I'm sorry. But Bobby and I talked to him all week to make these plans and the bastard cancels at the last minute. He is a son of a bitch!" Uncle Phillip answered vehemently.

"When did this happen?", Dad asked. "He called, just as we were getting ready to leave the house," Uncle Phillip responded. "You should have heard the language out of this one", Aunt Polly said, gesturing to Uncle Phillip. "And the screaming! Mannaggia!" Aunt Polly added.

Uncle Phillip reached for his coffee and shook his head in disgust as he sipped from his cup. Nano looked up at all of us and, from his seat at the head of the table, and said, "Forse un'altra volta," which translates to, "Maybe some other time."

Aunt Polly gestured to the platter of Italian desserts and cakes in front of her. "Let's have some pastry. Bobby, we picked up your favorite, Paragina," she said, pointing towards the rum-soaked pastry cakes at the center of the platter.

The oversized serving dish was covered with treats, which included: Italian cookies, mini-cannoli, zeppoles, chiacchieres, bombolinis and was outlined with Struffoli, which are small, deep-fried balls of dough soaked in a smoked honey.

As Dad took a step into the room, Uncle Phillip asked, "Is that Galliano that I see in your hand, Bobby?" Dad nodded his head affirmatively. "Okay! Get the glasses!" Uncle Phillip ordered. "Michael, go tell your brothers and sister that we're going to have dessert now," Mom directed. "Okay Mom", I said, and sped out of the room to announce that dessert was on the table.

IX - Sotto le Stelle
(*Under the Stars*)

The whole family was sitting at the dining room table, enjoying coffee and dessert when the doorbell rang. I shot up to answer it. It was Mario and John Padovani, with pillows and sleeping bags in hand. Earlier in the day, we had invited Mario and John to sleep out in the tent with me, Dave, and Steve.

After begging their parents relentlessly, they got the okay to camp out with us. "Hey, is this too early?" Mario asked, as he and John entered the hallway. "No, we're just finishing up," I answered.

At that point, Mom greeted the two brothers from the dining room table, "Come on in, boys," she instructed. "Hello, Mrs. Saviano," Mario responded. John, who was a very quiet kid, said nothing.

"You remember Uncle Phillip and Aunt Polly," Mom said pointing to each of them. "How are you?" Mario asked, respectfully.

Mom jumped in further. "These are Ray and Tina Padovani's two boys," she added. Uncle Phillip shook his head approvingly. "Hello boys. How is your grandfather, Ray senior?" he asked.

"He's good, thank you. He's home now, fixing something in his workshop," Mario replied. "We look forward to seeing him this weekend. You know, we're originally from the same town in Italy. Gaeta,"Uncle Phillip added.

"I think I heard that," Mario answered, indicating that he had heard this many times before.

"Mom, is it okay if we get ready and go outside now?" I interrupted. She hesitated for a brief second but gave us the green light. "Yes, have fun tonight. But don't stay up too late. We have a busy weekend ahead of us," she said.

That was all the clearance that we needed to hear. Dave, Steve, and I immediately sprinted out of the room and up the stairs to retrieve our own pillows, sleeping bags and a few other necessities, like flashlights, a lantern, an AM/FM radio, a small black and white TV, several long extension cords, walkie talkies, two bags of candy, and a small number of fireworks, namely two dozen bottle rockets.

We ran out back and entered the tent right around 8:30 p.m., just as the sun made its last appearance for the day, slowly dipping beneath the Western horizon. We hustled in and each claimed our spots by laying out our sleeping bags on our respective parcels. Next, we set up the rest of our belongings and made our plans for the night. As the oldest, at ten years old, I took the initiative and set our itinerary.

"Plug the radio in," I directed Dave. Dave and Mario had already run two long extension cords from the house and into the tent. "Put it on AM 1510, the Red Sox game is on," I barked. The Sox were on a road trip for the long weekend and playing the Brewers in Milwaukee.

"John and Steve, can you guys head into the basement and grab a case of Dr Pepper?" I asked. This seemed like a good idea at the time. The two quickly, and dutifully, took off for the house. As they left to retrieve the soda, Dave, Mario, and I continued to set up things in the tent. We made pretty quick work of it and then we each sat on our sleeping bags and started to discuss our plans.

I started, "So, in about an hour, it'll be pitch black by then, we're going to call Lou Limone on the walkie talkies. He's going to sneak out on his deck and we're going to have a bottle rocket battle with him."

"Whoa, cool," Dave and Mario said at the exact same time. Lou's house and yard were right next door to the Padovani's, two homes down and about fifty yards from our backyard, and in direct, unobstructed sight of the tent that we were sitting in.

"I only have a couple dozen bottle rockets left, but at least we can pick up some more when we go see John Coyne tomorrow morning," I reasoned. John had been a fourth-grade classmate of mine from the Colonial Park School, not really a close friend, just a guy from school. He and his brother, Joe, were widely known as the local source for the underground fireworks market.

Joe was already in junior high and a few years older than me and John. The brothers had been selling fireworks out of their basement to other kids in the Colonial Park area for the past few summers. No one knew exactly where they were getting their supply. One rumor was that they had a cousin in the North End of Boston who would sell to them in bulk and then they would distribute here in town at huge markups.

However it came into their possession, one thing was certain: they had it all, including firecrackers, bottle rockets, skyrockets, tanks, Roman candles, jumping jacks and even M80s, which they wouldn't sell to us. I guess even firework bootleggers have their standards.

"Let's ride over on our bikes tomorrow, right after I get done delivering papers," I suggested. We planned to pool our resources and share the bounty. "I have twenty-eight dollars," I said, thanks to my paper route, as I pulled the wad of bills out of my shorts pocket and dropped it on the sleeping bag in front of me. "What do you guys have?" I asked. "I have seven dollars for me and John," Mario chimed in. "I only have four," Dave added.

We piled the cash together near the lantern that we had sitting on the ground in front of us. "That's thirty-nine bucks all together," I confirmed. "What do you think we can get for that much?" Dave wondered. "I'm not sure. We'll just have to wait and see what they have tomorrow. And how much things cost," I answered.

Just then John, with Steve right on his tail, rushed into the tent carrying a case of Dr Peppers. Unfortunately, John was in such a rush that he bobbled the case in his arms and a six pack of soda fell from his hands. A few of those cans landed directly on top of an exposed rock that jutted from the ground at the tent's entrance. The cans instantly detonated, resembling a skyrocket's closing act, into a shower of soda that sprayed directly back at and up into John's face. It was hilarious!

He stood there frozen, unsure of what had just happened as Dave, Mario, and I burst out laughing. We grabbed the remaining soda from his hands and then quietly coaxed him to slip off his now dripping wet T-shirt. With his shirt off, we convinced him to take a quick dip into the pool to rinse off. As John waded into the shallow end of the pool, I snuck into the house to retrieve John a fresh shirt from Dave's bedroom bureau.

At 9:30 on the nose, we made the call to Lou on the walkie talkie. "One Adam 12. One Adam 12, come in, Lou," I called out on the two-way radio. We all leaned in, hoping to hear a response back from Lou. After five or six seconds, I made another call on the radio, "Lou, this is Mike. Come in, Lou. Over."

We gave it a few more seconds and then, in a small storm of hissing static, we heard," This is Papa Bear, come in Goldilocks. Over."

We all broke into giddy laughter, immediately recognizing Lou's response as a regular call-line from the "Hogan Heroes" TV show, coupled with the beaming excitement from the fact that the walkies were actually working.

"This is Amity Police Chief Brody. "We're going to need a bigger boat!" Lou shot back, an obvious reference to the character from the movie "Jaws". We all howled.

"All right, Lou. Can you hear us?" I asked. "That's a big 10-4. What's your 20?" he continued. "We're in the tent, out back. Where are you?" I asked in plain English.

"My 20 is right on my back deck. And, I have your tent right in my sights," he responded. There was a slight pause in correspondence and then Lou jumped back on. "You see, what we have here, is a failure to communicate." Lou was obviously a huge movie buff, as he stole this line from "Cool Hand Luke". "Okay, okay. We're going to fire a test shot. Keep an eye out," I advised.

At that point, we grabbed a hand full of the bottle rockets and brought them to the mouth of the tent, which faced towards the Limone house and at Lou. I grabbed a lighter that I had swiped earlier from Nano's room and placed a bottle rocket into an empty can of Dr Pepper. I took a moment to aim the can, with the firework resting inside it, directly at the Limone's house and lit the wick.

Sparks quickly began to shower from the fuse, and in a flash, the bottle rocket shot from the can and headed straight towards the Limone's. Its flight was true, as the head of the rocket made several revolutions mid-course. As the mini missile crossed over the middle of the fence line that divided the Padovani and Limone property line, it burst with a "bang!", leaving a condensed spray of red sparks in its aftermath.

"Whoa!" we all said aloud and then cackled together. The walkie talkie clicked on with fresh static, and we then heard Lou announce, "Wide right." The five of us, again, broke out in excited laughter. "Let's light another one!" I shouted.

We went through the same process to load up the bottle rocket in the soda can, adjusted our aim slightly and lit the fuse. The rocket took off, much like the first, shooting straight toward the Limone's deck and detonated with a bang just a few feet from the deck where Lou had sheltered himself. As we celebrated, Lou again called out on the radio, "Getting closer!"

We broke out in laughter again and with wild, almost hyper excitement, we began to reload and repeat the process. Suddenly, as we attempted to get another fix on our target, a piercingly loud whistling sound filled the air. The screeching noise grew louder and ended seemingly just feet away from us with an abrupt boom! We all looked at each other and once again mouthed, "Whoa!"

The walkie talkie again came to life. "How'd you like that, you punks?!" Lou asked mockingly. We were thrilled. "Hurry, get the next one!" I shouted.

We quickly set up our next salvo and sent the missile on its way. This latest rocket flew straight toward the Limone house but clipped the top of a pear tree in the Padovani's backyard. "Missed!" Lou taunted back at us over the radio.

Just a second later, another whistling rocket was sent our way but landed short of its target, which was us in the tent, exploding in Nano's garden. Without a second's hesitation and with military precision, we had our next shot set to go. This one was perfectly aligned and soared straight for the Limone's house. We could see the red tail of the rocket as it hit the Limone's deck, skidding across the wooden surface, and bursting with a loud "bang". We lost it, erupting in laughter and pats on the back. Lou came back over the radio, "Awe … you got me!" Then a short pause, followed by, "But I'm not dead yet!"

With that, another whistling rocket was headed our way. But this one was different. It was as if it had a honing device attached to it, and it was coming straight for us. As the whistling grew near, Dave shouted, "Get down!" and we all dove to the ground inside the tent.

The bottle rocket landed at the very mouth of the tent and skipped off the ground and bounced to the back of the tent, barely missing all of us. The rocket let out a last burst of its whistle and then detonated with a deafening, "Boom!"

The tent lit up brightly from the momentary explosion. We slowly got back on our feet, looking around at each other to make sure everyone was okay. Once we realized that everyone was unscathed, Mario shouted, "That was awesome!" "Wicked cool," Dave added.

As I searched for the walkie talkie that had been lost in the sleeping bags during all the excitement, we heard a sharp and very distinct whistle. This whistle was different though and it was coming from behind us, directly from the deck of our house. It was the unmistakable calling card of Dad's.

He had developed this patented whistle that would cause any of us in the family to instantly drop what we were doing and search him out for whatever command he had in store for us. The purpose this time was extremely obvious. He hit us with a second call, never a good sign. And then I heard him shout for me, "Michael!"

I jumped out of the tent and looked back towards the house. Dad had put the spotlight on that lit up most of our backyard. I put my forearm above my eyes to shade the glare from the light.

"Yeah, Dad", I answered. "That's it. No more. I don't want to hear or see another firework out here. You got me?"

"Yes", I answered with my shoulders slumped. "And tell Louis that's it, it's over. Otherwise, everyone's going home, and you and your brothers are coming back in the house," he finished.

I walked back into the tent and called Lou back on the walkie talkie, but he had already gotten the message as soon as the spotlight had turned on and was long gone. We all settled into our sleeping bags and were ready to call it a night. Just as I was about to turn out the lantern, Mario chimed in. "That was wicked awesome." We all grinned and nodded in agreement as the tent went dark.

Venerdì 2 Luglio, 1976
(Friday, July 2, 1976)

X - La Grande Rapina
(The Great Heist)

Just as planned, I was up early the next morning to get the papers delivered. I had had a terrible night's sleep in that tent, just the worst. Maybe it was the three or four late night Dr Peppers, or the lying on the hard, cold ground, but it was rough. At the same time, it was so worth it! We had a blast, literally.

I struggled up the hill on Citation Ave, slowly making my way back to the house. My legs felt heavy, as I strained to crank the pedals on my Stingray. I had a lot of riding ahead of me this morning, as we were planning to head over to the Coyne's house shortly for our fireworks transaction. The Coyne's lived on Isabella Street, which was at the far Eastern edge of the Colonial Park school district. Fieldstone Drive was at the Western edge of the same district, so our two homes were as far away as any two homes could be and still be in the same school district.

The ride to the Coyne's was nearly two miles each way, close to four miles in total. Knowing that I had this ahead of me, I decided to rest my legs and chose to glide the last half-block back to my house. As I turned the final corner, I rode past the vacant lot, the scene of yesterday's failed bike jump, and rolled up into my driveway. Just as I crossed onto our property, Dad was walking from the open garage and headed for his car.

"Hey Dad," I greeted him, not knowing if he was going to read me the riot act over last night's escapades. "Hi", he answered me back quickly. "You going somewhere?" I asked. "Yes, I'm going to pick up your Aunts Gray and May. Then coming right home with them," he answered, as he got into the car. "Oh, okay," I said, realizing that I had escaped the talking-to since he was on the move.

"Why don't you get the boys up and out of the tent. Your mom is making breakfast," he said, as he started the car and began to back out of the driveway. I nodded to him and made my way to the backyard.

I entered the backyard from the gate that was located at the end of the walkway that lined the side of our house. As I took a couple of strides onto the patio, I noticed Nano and Uncle Phillip sitting together on lawn chairs to my right. Uncle Phillip spotted me and waved me over. "Michael," he said, with the distinct Italian pronunciation which came out as "Mee-kehl."

"Good morning," I responded. "Buongiorno!" he replied, with great emphasis.

The two brothers were sitting together enjoying some warm, summer sunshine. Nano had his cigar lit in his right hand, taking the occasional puff on the best that his favorite brand, El Producto, had to offer, and for just ninety-nine cents. In his left hand, he held a mint leave from his garden and, as he often liked to do, he waved it under his nose intermittently between drags on his cigar.

Uncle Phillip, sitting to Nano's left, held a pear in his left hand and a steak knife in his right. He carved good sized chunks of pear and lifted them to his mouth by using the knife's edge to balance the fruit.

"You delivered your papers already this morning?" Uncle Phillip asked. "Yes, just finished," I replied. "Good. Good for you. It's good to take responsibility," he added.

Nano scoffed out loud at this. "What!? You don't think it's good that he's learning responsibility?" Uncle Phillip shot back. "Responsibility? He needs to learn respect! This one shows no respect … Rispetto! … the way he talks back to me," Nano asserted.

Uncle Phillip smirked and jumped to my defense. "Well, maybe it's the way you talk to him, which is why he talks back to you. I hear how you give him such a hard time." "Me!? Bull shit!" Nano shouted with a wry smile on his face. "Bull shit!" he repeated.

Both he and Uncle Phillip smiled and continued with their debate, as I turned towards the tent to go get the guys up for breakfast. "Michael" Uncle Phillip called, again with the distinct Italian pronunciation. "They're all in the house. Having breakfast," he informed me. "Ahh, okay, thank you," I answered and made an about face and headed for the deck stairs and the kitchen.

I took two steps into the kitchen and found Dave, Steve, and the Padovani brothers sitting at the table. Mom was passing out cereal bowls to them when she greeted me.

"Oh good, you're back. Why don't you sit down and have some cereal with the boys?"

I slid around the back of the table and into my seat. Mom brought the milk over to the table and then slid a bowl and spoon over to me.

"What are you boys up to this morning?" she asked. "Well, me, Dave, Mario, and John are going to take our bikes over to a friend's house," I answered.

"Oh yeah, who's that?" she asked. "John Coyne. He's a kid from school," I answered.

"Stephen's not going with you?" she questioned, looking straight at me. "No, I think it's a little far for him to ride," I replied.

"All right, and what are you boys going to do over there?" the questioning continued. "He's just going to show us a new gocart that he and his brother built," I shot back, thinking quickly on my feet. "We won't be there long. We just want to see it and then we'll head home."

Mom then dropped four boxes of cereal onto the table. One of them was an unopened box of Captain Crunch. Dave and I saw it immediately and we both grabbed for it at once, knocking two of the other boxes onto their sides in our rush.

"Whoa! What are you two doing?" Mom asked. "This box has the baking powder mini-submarine in it," I exclaimed. The mini-submarine, which was propelled underwater by some chemical reaction that was fueled by baking powder, was the coolest of all cereal box toys and a new box of Captain Crunch was pretty much the only place you could get one.

"Well, let's see whose turn it is on the schedule," Mom said, as she took the box from us and walked over to the refrigerator. Mom had set-up a schedule of sorts to track and keep a list of who gets the next cereal box toy. At the time, cereal box toys were the single greatest cause for fights between my brothers and sister and me. They were like a spark around a case of old, dry dynamite and had set off many a battle over the past few years. Mom's response was to keep a tally of who got the last item and who had dibs on the next.

"Stephen," she said, as she looked at the fridge. She then took a pencil and placed a checkmark next to his name. "Bobby is next," she declared. Dave and I groaned faintly and handed the box over to Steve.

After finishing breakfast, and depositing Steve in front of the TV, the four of us headed for the garage and our bikes. It was just after 10 a.m. and it would be about a fifteen-minute ride to the Coyne's. We set out down Fieldstone and headed toward Colonial Park. As we pedaled through the development, we began to talk strategy.

"Okay, since I'm the one who knows John, let me do the talking and see if we can get a good deal," I suggested. "Well, do you know his older brother, Joe?" Dave asked. "No, not really. Just from when we bought this stuff from them last year," I answered. "What if John's not there, and it's only Joe?" Mario added. "So, we'll just do a deal with Joe then. But it still makes sense for only one of us to do the talking. We have almost forty bucks, so we should be able to get some good stuff," I reasoned.

John, as usual, stayed silent as we discussed our plan. Clearly, he wouldn't be the one doing the negotiating for us. However, he would be playing a crucial role, as he would be carrying our haul back to the tent on Fieldstone. To transport our prize, John had brought with him a dark colored plastic bag, one that you couldn't see through, tied to the handlebars on his bike.

We got to the Coyne's house just a few minutes before 10:30 a.m., just as we had planned. I left my bike in the Coyne's driveway, leaving Dave, Mario, and John to watch over it, and made my way to the front door of the house. The Coyne's house was in a more developed neighborhood in Stoneham, meaning the homes were much older, and typically smaller, to the homes in our neighborhood. The Coyne's home was no exception. It was a smaller, ranch-style home with red painted shingles and white trim around the doors and windows.

I walked up the stairs of the home's modest stoop and rang the doorbell. The door was halfway open and the only thing separating me from the interior of the home was the front screen door. I could hear some chatter from inside the home but couldn't pinpoint from where it came. I waited another brief second, and then gave the bell another ring. Instantly, a female voice shouted from the second floor of the home.

"John! Get the door!" I then heard the distant humming of a vacuum cleaner click on, just as John Coyne surfaced at the front door. "Hey, man. What's up?" he greeted me from the other side of the screen door.

"Ah, hey. I'm here to buy some fireworks," I answered. He immediately, with his eyes bugged out, waved me off, hushing me as he abruptly stepped outside on the stoop with me.

"Shush, shush! What are you doing?" he exclaimed, in a rattled whisper. "What?" I answered with my own question. "Are you crazy?" John went on, looking back into the house over his shoulder.

"We need to keep this on the QT," John continued. "Okay, got it. Sorry," I responded. "Meet me around the back of the house. I'll open the bulkhead door for you," John instructed. He turned and walked back into the house.

I leapt off the front stoop and headed for the driveway, where I had left Dave and the Padovani boys. I met them in the driveway and shared the plan, "Okay guys, we're going to go around back, and they'll let us in through the bulkhead door. John, why don't you stay here and watch the bikes," I submitted.

Dave, Mario, and I then rushed out back of the house and headed straight for the bulkhead. As we arrived at the doors jutting out from the back of the house, we heard a clanging sound coming from behind the two, barn-style doors. The door on the left was the first to open, releasing upward towards us, followed quickly by the right. John was standing, knee high to us, on the steps of the bulkhead.

"C'mon in guys," he said, and then turned back down the bulkhead steps. The three of us followed him down the stairs and entered the Coyne's finished basement. John walked over to a closet door that was located directly under the staircase that led up to the first floor of the home. He pulled a large cardboard box from inside the closet, turned towards us and placed it on top of a folding table that sat in the middle of the room. He then returned to the closet and grabbed an even bigger box, and again placed it in front of us on the table.

As he turned to make his third trip, we began to look over the contents of the boxes on the table. They were loaded to the brim with fireworks. And almost every variety of fireworks could be found inside one of the boxes. He dropped the third and largest box onto the table, which held even more fireworks.

"Whoa," Mario uttered. "I know, it's a lot," John answered. "Where do you get all these?" I asked. "Ha! Ancient Chinese secret," John replied, cynically.

Just then, the door from the staircase upstairs that led to the basement swung opened loudly. And then, we could hear someone bolting down the staircase. Everyone's eyes quickly shifted to the stairs, but our vision was blocked by the wood paneling that lined the walls of the basement. We all gasped for a moment, not knowing if trouble was heading down the stairs and straight for us. But, in a flash, John's brother Joe appeared at the bottom of the steps.

"What's going on here?" he asked. "These guys are looking for some fireworks," John answered his older brother. "Oh yeah, what are you boys looking for?" asked Joe.

Dave and Mario quickly glanced over to me. "Well, what do you got," I asked. "We have just about everything," Joe answered. "Set'em out on the floor for them," Joe directed his younger brother.

John pulled various types of fireworks from each of the

boxes and spread them out on the carpet. "So, we have bottle rockets, whistling bottle rockets, skyrockets, jumping jacks, Roman candles," John continued as he placed each kind of firework imaginable in front of us. "How much money did you bring with you?" Joe asked abruptly. "We have enough … more than thirty bucks," I answered. "Thirty? That's not going to buy much," Joe stated plainly.

"Well, we got a lot for that amount last year," I shot back. "Yeah well, things are more expensive this year", Joe replied. As he said this, I noticed Joe shoot a quick glance over to his younger brother. "Yeah, that's right. Things are much more expensive this year", John agreed. After a short pause, I added, "Okay, why don't you tell us what some of the things cost?" "Well fellas, I need to be somewhere, but John can walk you through things. You got this, John?" Joe continued, with another suspicious glance towards his brother.

"Yep. I'll go through it all with them," John responded, shooting a matching glance back to his brother Joe. "Okay, that'll do it for me boys. John, just give me a quick hand with something upstairs," Joe finished. "Okay, sure. Take a quick look at what we have guys. I'll be right back," John said, as he followed his older brother up the staircase.

Suddenly, Dave, Mario, and I were alone in the basement with a full assortment of fireworks laid out in front of us. "What do you think? Which ones do you want to buy?" Dave asked.

"What do I think?" I repeated. "I think they're going to try and screw us!"

"I think he's right" Mario chimed in. "I saw how they were looking at one another when you asked them what it cost," he added. "I know! I saw the exact same thing!" I agreed. "What do you want to do?" Dave added.

"I didn't ride all the way over here to get fucked by these two guys," I declared. "Well, what then? You want to leave?" Mario asked.

I took a second to think about the situation and then looked back over my shoulder towards the staircase. "Mario, hand me the shopping bag," I ordered. "What are you going to do?" Mario asked, as he handed me the plastic bag.

"I'm going to make sure we don't get screwed over," I answered, as I began shoving fireworks into the empty container. "You're just going to take those?" Mario asked with concern in his voice.

"I'm just taking some things," I responded. I grabbed about two of everything from the boxes on the table, intentionally not touching anything on the floor. I mostly grabbed an assortment of skyrockets which were packaged in sets of six rockets. I grabbed four packages and quickly stuffed them into the bag. I also grabbed a couple dozen of both the whistling and non-whistling bottle rockets, a handful of jumping jack packs, four or five of the sun flowers, a half brick of Black Cat firecrackers and various other items.

"You're taking all that?", Dave asked. "Yep. We're taking," I said. "Oh boy", Mario added, still concerned.

I quickly folded the top edge of the bag and handed it to Mario. "Here. Take this outside to Johnny. Tell him to take it and ride his bike down to the end of Isabella. Tell him to wait and we'll meet him there."

"Shit," Mario whispered and then headed up the bulkhead steps and disappeared into the backyard. "What if he notices?" Dave asked. "He won't," I said. "How are you so sure?" Dave continued. "I just am," I replied.

But I was clearly bluffing and could actually feel myself start to sweat with anxiety. I made a quick pass at rearranging the remaining fireworks in the boxes on the table. I stood beside the boxes of fireworks hoping that I hadn't been too greedy, too hasty, and that John Coyne wouldn't notice that anything was missing. They had so many fireworks. Surely, he wouldn't be able to notice that a few items, here and there, were missing. We waited for what seemed like an eternity, until the upstairs door finally opened, and John returned to us in the basement.

"Okay, have you guys had enough time to look over everything?" he asked.

Dave and I nodded to him, suggesting we had. "Hey, where'd your friend go?" John asked. "Oh, he ran outside to make sure our bikes weren't in the way," I answered, smoothly. "Oh, okay then, what are you boys interested in? John inquired.

"Probably just bottle rockets," I said, quickly. "How much is a dozen?" "Five bucks", John quickly shot back.

Dave instantly shot me a look, knowing that this was highway robbery. If my memory was right, a dozen bottle rockets last summer was only two dollars. "And the whistling bottle rockets are six bucks for a dozen," he added.

Just then, Mario walked backed into the basement from the bulkhead steps. We all glanced over at him, as he stepped into the room. "Hey, your buddy's back," John declared. "Yep. So, the bottle rockets are five bucks a dozen, and six bucks for the whistlers," I informed Mario. "That seems like a lot," Mario responded. "Yeah, our costs are a bit higher this year, so the price has to be too," John replied.

"We'll give you ten bucks for three dozen of the whistlers," I offered. "Ten bucks for three dozen? You're killing me, Mike. That's eighteen bucks," John exclaimed.

I said nothing and decided to let him throw something back at us. "I tell you what, I'll let you have them for fifteen," he countered. "Twelve bucks," I shot back swiftly. He paused for a couple seconds, "No, I don't think I can do that."

I took a second to evaluate the situation and then recalled how the whistling bottle rockets that Lou had shot at us last night had quickly gained Dad's attention. I then hit back at him with, "Okay then, we'll give you twenty bucks for five dozen of the ones that don't whistle."

He took a second to think this over. And then with a fleeting, cocky grin on his face, you know the one you try to hide when you think you're getting the better of someone, he said, "You know, I shouldn't do this, but you guys came all the way over here and are good customers. So okay, twenty bucks for five dozen of the regular bottle rockets."

I dug into my pocket to pull out the cash as John began to pull five dozen bottle rockets from the middle box on the table. I then swapped him the cash for the goods. "Hey, you guys really shouldn't be riding out of here with those in your hand. Don't you have a bag or something?" he asked. "No. Forgot to bring one," I answered quickly.

John then stepped back over to the closet door and stuck his head in. He reemerged with a medium sized brown paper bag in his hand. "Here, use this," he said, as he handed me the bag. "And next time, make sure you bring one with you," he finished. "Got it," I agreed.

And with that, Dave, Mario, and I made our way back out the bulkhead steps. As we turned the corner of the yard and headed for our bikes in the driveway, I could hear the bulkhead doors slam shut.

We wasted little time getting out of there. The three of us hopped on our bikes and sped off quickly, heading to find Johnny at the end of Isabella. As we neared the Franklin Street intersection, we found Johnny on his bike, seated stationary on the sidewalk.

"You ready to go?" I shouted towards him. He nodded and began to pedal onto Isabella. I could see the plastic bag, holding our loot, hanging from the handlebars of his bike. We said nothing to each other as we made our way across Franklin Street, heading toward the side streets that would lead us back to Colonial Park and Fieldstone Drive. Once we were finally a good way away from the Coyne's and in the clear, we opened up about our shopping spree.

"I cannot believe what just happened! Do you think they'll ever notice?" Mario started.

"I know," I answered, with a huge smile on my face. "I don't think so. They had so much stuff in those boxes. And it was all just thrown in there. I don't know how they'd ever be able to tell," I added.

"Serves them right. They were looking to screw us. Last year, it was only two bucks for a dozen bottle rockets. Now, they want five bucks? Screw that! The only reason they hiked the price on us this year is because Bobby wasn't with us. So, they tried to screw us," I continued.

"How much do you think we got in that bag?" Dave asked. "Not sure", I replied. "I don't know. It's pretty heavy", Johnny chimed in. "Yeah well, I was only trying to even out what we were taking with what they were trying to charge us. Besides, he's back there at his house thinking he robbed us anyway," I said, justifying what had just gone down.

Everyone seemed to agree with that logic anyway, as we turned onto Fieldstone and headed back towards our house. The thrill and fright were now behind us, and it seemed to give us a tail wind of sorts, as we picked up our pace down the last leg of our ride.

XI - I Giudici
(The Judges)

When we got back to my house, Dad's car was already parked in the driveway, which meant my aunts Gray and May had arrived. Gray, May, and Polly were all sisters of my dad's mom, my grandmother, Nana. Their actual names, given at birth, were Grace, Mary, and Palma. Together, with my grandmother Josephine and late aunt Theresa, they were a family of five girls, born and raised in the North End of Boston.

Dad always referred to them as "The Judges." It wasn't clear if it was due to their grey colored bouffant hairdos, that resembled the wigs worn by judges and aristocrats, or if it was meant to be a comment on their judgmental ways. Either way, it worked. I was excited for their visit.

Dad had a close and dynamic relationship with his aunts. It was obvious to all that they thoroughly enjoyed each other's company. And, among their favorite things to do, was to mercilessly rib one another. It was always in jest, and very entertaining.

Dad would often joke that the three aunts would get older, shorter, and louder as they entered a room, single file. And he was always quick to take the first shot at the sisters, usually with a snide comment questioning which number bottle of dye they were currently using to color their hair. They took no offense and would typically snipe right back with a quip about Dad's weight or some reference to his hallmark jowls. It was pretty amusing for everyone to witness, and very clear that it was all in good fun. It was a close and special relationship.

After combining our legitimate merchandise with our ill-gotten gains, the four of us walked out back to greet the aunts. I asked Mario if he could slinker down to the tent and strategically place the plastic bag of goodies amongst the sleeping bags. He did just that, as Dave and I headed for the pool patio where Mom and Dad were hosting Nano, Uncle Phillip, and the aunts.

"Hello Aunt Gray, Aunt May," we greeted them together. "Hello boys," Aunt Gray said warmly. "Look at these two spitfires!" Aunt May chimed in. I'm not sure of its origins, but Aunt May often referred to us as "spitfires."

"Are you two boys up to no good?" Aunt Gray teased. "Nope. Not today, anyway," I answered. "Oh Bobby, this one's got a mouth like you," Aunt Gray said playfully. "Yeah, there's no mistaking that one," Dad responded with a smile.

"He's a good boy," Uncle Phillip asserted, always having my back. "Why don't you two head into the kitchen. Your Aunt Gray and May brought bulkie rolls and cold cuts. Make yourselves a sandwich and you can sit at the picnic table on the patio with your brothers and sister," Mom instructed.

As Dave and I were about to turn for the kitchen, Mario and Johnny walked by the table and stopped to say hello. Dad jumped in to handle the introductions, "These two boys are Ray Padovani's grandsons," he said, pointing towards the Padovani's house directly behind our pool.

"Oh," Polly, Gray and May mouthed together. "Ray's going to stop by later this afternoon to say hello," Dad continued.

"It's nice to see you all. We need to get going and head home for lunch," Mario replied. "See you boys later," Dad added.

Mario and Johnny headed towards the gate, as Dave and I made our way to the kitchen. I could hear Dad explaining to the table, as we walked away, about us all camping out in the tent that was set up less than fifty feet from where they were sitting.

Dave and I plopped down with our paper plates at the picnic table. Bobby, Pam, and Steve were just about done, except for picking at some chips left at the table. "Where were you two?" Bob asked abruptly. "Just out. We went down to the playground at Colonial on our bikes," I answered. "What's down there?" he pressed. "Nothing. Just some other guys goofing around," Dave jumped in.

Bob stared right at me for a good three, four seconds. He seemed to have some sort of radar that was telling him that we had been up to something else. Up to some no good, probably. I tried to change the subject and directed a question to Pam and Steve.

"What have you two been up to?" "We've been in the pool," Pam answered. "Yeah, we were jumping off the board and Dad was grading our dives," Steve added.

This was a common occurrence at our pool. We'd form a line at the diving board and, one after another, we'd look for Dad to score our dives. This would usually last a good twenty or thirty minutes, until Dad would tire of the exercise.

As I took the final bite of my sandwich, Dad approached the table. "We have some work to do when you guys finish up," he said. "What's that?" asked Bobby. "We need to head over to the Palermo's. It's time that we dig the pit and set up the cobblestones," Dad responded.

"What pit?" I asked. "We're setting up for the clambake on the Fourth, so we need to dig a large pit and line the bottom with the cobblestones we got yesterday. What did you think we were doing with those cobblestones, dumb-dumb?" Dad asked, light-heartedly.

I just stared back up at him, my head tilted to my right and squinting to shade the sun from my eyes. "Okay, finish up and let's get over there," he instructed us. We all picked up our paper plates, deposited them into the trash barrel beside the table and hustled off to the Palermo's.

XII - Tutti Scavano!
(Everyone Dig!)

The five of us followed Dad and scurried over to the Palermo's. There, we found a small crowd in the Palermo's driveway, surveying the grassy area between the driveway and the eight-foot fence that wrapped around their backyard.

"Bobby!" Mr. Palermo shouted. "I see you brought some help with you," he noted. "That's right, Cos. I brought the whole crew," Dad replied.

"Okay kids, seriously, stay to the side as the grown-ups get this hole in the ground," Mr. Palermo instructed. We all acquiesced, as he directed, and took a seat on the retaining wall located on the driveway's right side. It was a pretty wild scene in the Palermo's driveway. We had every dad in the neighborhood within a stone's throw of the scene.

The crew included Dad, Mr. Palermo, Mr. Limone, Mr. Ferraro, Mr. Padovani and Mr. Schaefer. They were each dressed in one form or another of 1970s classically styled, plaid Bermuda-length shorts. And each was holding a spade shovel in their hand. The spectacle immediately reminded me of the famous scene from my family's favorite movie, "It's a Mad, Mad, Mad, Mad World", when the legendary cast of characters is involved in a chaotic and frenzied dig under the "Big W," searching for a buried stash of loot. Except, in this case, the dads weren't digging for hidden treasure, rather just a good spot for a clambake pit.

Mr. Limone seemed to take the lead. "Cos," he said, pointing to a plot of ground a few feet from the fence, "I think we're going to want to put it over here. This way, it'll be away from the kids and the foot traffic into the backyard, but close enough to your refrigerator in the garage." The crew nodded in agreement.

"That's as good a place as any, Jimmy," Mr. Palermo agreed, and then stuck the tip of his shovel into the turf right where Mr. Limone had pointed. "Let's dig in!" Mr. Padovani, shouted excitedly. And, with that, the crew got to work. It was a sight to see. I doubt any single job site had this many shovels at work while being plunged into the earth by feet baring gladiator-style sandals.

The team's progress was extremely slow as they had begun to hit more than a few medium-sized rocks, just a few inches under the grass-line. "Jesus!" Mr. Schaefer hollered. "Cos, where'd you get your fill for this lot? An old quarry?" he joked.

"Well Herb, the town is called Stoneham, so none of us should be surprised," Mr. Palermo answered. Just as it looked like this was going to be a long afternoon in the hot sun, Mr. Oliveri walked down the sidewalk and approached the group.

"Carmine how are you?" Dad greeted him warmly. "I'm fine, thanks," he replied. Mr. Oliveri then took a fast look at the shallow six-foot by eight-foot outline in the Palermo's grass. He shook his head for a second, and then looked over his shoulder to the dozen or so of us kids, who were watching along intently. He smiled at us briefly and then turned back to the crew.

"This is going to take you all afternoon this way, fellas," he advised them. "Why don't I go get my machine, and we'll get this pit dug in a flash," he offered. "If you're willing to bring it over, then heck, yeah Carmine," Mr. Palermo answered. "Okay, give me a quick minute," Mr. Oliveri went on. He then turned and smiled again at the pack of kids sitting on the retaining wall. "Try not to laugh at them, kids. It'll hurt their feelings," he said to us, as he walked back up the sidewalk, headed for his house just two doors down.

"Well, kids, looks like we're not going to dig this hole by hand, after all," Mr. Palermo stated, as he turned towards us. Things were now getting interesting. Mr. Oliveri, who is a contractor by trade, left to go get his backhoe and dig this clambake pit. To a young kid of this generation, a backhoe was pretty much at the top of the food chain of cool equipment, right up there with street sweepers. And a dad who operated a Backhoe was pretty much a celebrity.

Sure enough, we could hear the rumble of Mr. Oliveri on his backhoe approaching. "All right, kids, I need all of you to stand back. Stay right over there," Mr. Palermo directed, as he pointed to all of us, who were now standing on the retaining wall. Mr. Oliveri pulled around the corner on his tractor, skillfully coming to a halt and then backed his machine into the Palermo's driveway.

The excavator beeped rhythmically, as Mr. Oliveri steered the machine, bucket first, towards the pit's outline. He then switched gears and threw it into park, set the brakes and lastly lowered the two legs with large metal pads from the rear of the machine and onto the ground. The excavator lifted upward slightly, as the rear pads set on the ground and stabilized the machine. He then swung around in his seat and began to operate the levers that sat directly in front of him.

The bucket of the excavator extended out and then curled, with its teeth exposed, into the hard soil where the dads had been laboring. In an instant, the bucket pulled up a load of rock and soil. We all looked on with amazement as the machine so easily handled the job that just moments earlier had been quite a struggle.

Mr. Oliveri swung his bucket full of material and deposited it at the far edge of the Palermo's property, where the driveway met the street on Karen Drive. He repeated this for seven or eight bucket loads, and, in less than ten minutes, the job was done. He then methodically swung around in his operator's chair to now face the front of the tractor, the side that sported the large bucket extending from its nose.

After manipulating a few knobs and gears on the dash of the machine, he slowly looked back over his shoulder, and caused the stabilizing pads at the rear of the machine to lift and retract back into place. He then quickly drove the backhoe forward onto Karen Drive and turned sharply back towards the pile of debris that he had moments earlier deposited onto the edge of the street.

He made an initial pass at the pile and captured at least half of the material in the machine's expansive bucket. He drove the full bucket of spoils about fifty yards further down Karen Drive and deposited the load at the far end of the dead-end street. He circled back and, in a flash, repeated the task. This time capturing all, but a small quantity of debris, which Mr. Limone and Mr. Padovani quickly and dutifully shoveled into his waiting bucket. He then sped back down the private road and again dispatched the rubble at the far end. He reappeared moments later, gave three short honks of his horn, and sped away, proudly waving to all us kids. The dads, proud of their work, slapped each other on the back, and cheered Mr. Oliveri as he raced away from the Palermo's.

With the hole now in the ground, a couple of the dads jumped in, and with their shovels began to grade the sides and bottom. "Make sure it's nice and level," Mr. Palermo urged. All of us kids rushed forward to get a good look. "Careful, now kids," I heard Mr. Palermo say. "Don't get too close," Dad added, as he tugged a bit on my t-shirt. After the last full shovels of loose dirt were tossed from the hole, Mr. Limone made an observation out loud.

"You know Cos, I think it would be good if we had something to tamp down the stones once we get them in here." "Way ahead of you, Jimmy," Mr. Palermo responded. He took two steps into his garage and then re-emerged with a large, heavy tool in his hand.

"Here you go, Jimmy," he said as he lowered the weighty instrument down to Mr. Limone in the hole. "What's this?" Mr. Limone asked. "It's actually what you asked for. It's a tamp. We used it last summer when we put the walkway in by the pool," Mr. Palermo answered. "Well, what will they think of next?" Mr. Limone said jokingly.

The next task was to place the cobblestones onto the bottom of the pit. The dads at street level handed the stones one by one to Mr. Limone and Mr. Schaefer, who remained in the clambake pit. The cobbles were aligned in a neat pattern across the floor of the pit, and then tamped down to better secure them in place. After a good twenty minutes, the job was complete, and Mr. Limone and Mr. Schaefer were given a helping hand to climb out of the hole.

Looking back at his work, Mr. Limone proudly declared, "I don't think the Romans could have done it any better, Herb." "I don't think the Romans had Carmine's backhoe," Herb responded. "No, they didn't. Can you imagine what it took for them to do all that they did? Amazing," Mr. Limone said. Everyone seemed to agree with that and, after a few more pats on each other's backs, they declared the job done.

XIII - Che I Giochi Abbiano Iniziano!
(Let the Games Begin!)

While the kids looked over the clambake project, Lou Limone had organized a street hockey game. Street hockey was the game of choice for the kids in our neighborhood, and we played often. The Boston area, in the early 70s, was a hotbed for hockey. This all stemmed from the success and popularity of the Boston Bruins, the city's pro team.

The Bruins were one of the best teams in the National Hockey League and had won the Stanley Cup just a few years earlier. The team had stars such as Bobby Orr, Phil Esposito, Johnny Bucyk, Gerry Cheevers and the list went on. So, it was pretty safe to say that this led to the hockey craze in and around Boston at the time. The previous season, though, had been a trying one for Bruins fans, as the Club traded away a number of its stars, including Phil Esposito and Ken Hodge to the New York Rangers and the team's biggest star, Bobby Orr, had battled a knee injury all season long that had limited him to playing only about a dozen games.

Nonetheless, street hockey was our game, and we had enough kids around this day to have a huge game. Lou had arranged that everyone meet back out front with our gear in about thirty minutes. So, the group dispersed from the Palermo's driveway, and we all set out to gather our sticks and equipment.

I walked back to my house and went straight into the backyard. All of my street hockey gear was kept in the garage, so I didn't need much time to fetch it. As I walked into the yard, I saw two separate groups actively engaged. The first group of Mom and my three aunts sat at the picnic table on the deck, and they were working diligently on food prep. They had a large, wooden board with a linoleum top on it, that Nano had fashioned into a massive cutting board. Mom and my aunts were working together to slice onions, potatoes, and carrots into narrow strips.

"Are you boys done digging the clambake pit?" Mom asked, as I walked past. "Yeah, it's done," I answered. "You should wash up, Michael," she added. "I didn't do anything, Mom. I just watched," I responded. I was in a rush to check on our fireworks stash in the tent, so I brushed past the table.

As I turned for the tent, I immediately heard rowdy shouting and cursing, half of it was in Italian and half in English. It was deafening. And it was coming from a card table that was set out on the lawn where Nano and Uncle Phillip were sitting with the senior Mr. Padovani, Mario and Johnny's grandfather, and Mr. Desanto, who lived directly across the street from the Padovani's.

Mr. Desanto was a giant of a man, with a booming voice to match. He was a captain in the Massachusetts State Police and an intimidating character to every kid in the neighborhood, especially when he was all decked out in his military-style uniform. The foursome was seated and shouting at full volume at one another. They were extremely loud, but more spirited than angry. Uncle Phillip spotted me and called me over.

"Michael! Come over here and help me and your grandfather," he shouted. I walked over to him, and he put his hand on my shoulder. "Your grandfather and I are getting killed by these two bums!" he said laughing. "Don't listen to him, Michael," Mr. Desanto responded. "These two are hustlers and they're just trying to reel me and Ray in," he went on. Mr. Padovani shook his head in agreement.

"You're going to be the good luck charm for me and for your grandfather too," Uncle Phillip claimed. "Don't do it, Michael. These two will never give you a share of any winnings anyway!" Mr. Desanto answered. "How about some more of that wine, Mike?" he asked.

Mr. Desanto was the only one in the neighborhood who actually enjoyed Nano's wine. And it was clear that they were both enjoying it to the fullest during their card game.

"What are you playing?" I asked. "It's an old Italian card game. Didn't your grandfather ever teach you?" asked Mr. Padovani. Nano was quick to answer, "Are you kidding me? These kids never want to know anything. They just watch TV and run around in the dirt, like animals. No respect," he asserted. "I don't believe that Mike. What do you say, Michael? Is your grandfather, right?" Mr. Desanto pressed.

"No", I answered. This got a good rise out of the table as they all, even Nano, laughed out loud. "Atta boy, Michael," Uncle Phillip added, emphasizing the Italian pronunciation of my name.

"So, what are you playing?" I asked again. "It's a game called "Scopa." And we're playing teams. Your grandfather and I are on the same team. And these two are taking us to the cleaners," Uncle Phillip explained. "How do you play?" I followed. "You want to learn how to play? I'll teach you this weekend," Uncle Phillip offered.

"Those are different cards. I've never seen cards like that before," I observed. "Yes, it's an Italian deck of cards. And there's only forty cards in the deck. Do you want to watch?" Uncle Phillip continued. "Well, I would … but we're going to play street hockey out front," I said. "I told you!" Nano exclaimed. "Mike? He said he wanted to, but his friends are playing out front. What do you want from him?" Uncle Phillip backed me up. "Yeah, Mike. Let the kid play with his friends. And stop stalling! I know you two are up to something!" Mr. Desanto shouted.

"Go on, Michael," Uncle Phillip said, as he slapped me lightly on the back. I turned from the table and continued on my way to the tent. The vociferous shouting resumed, which included a few of my grandfather's favorite curse words.

After quickly checking that our fireworks plunder was safely hidden in the tent, I made my way to the front of the house. Two of our homemade street hockey nets were already in the middle of the street. They were wooden framed nets, built by Mr. Oliveri, with scrap wood that he had brought home from a job site. The most prominent feature of the nets, however, came compliments from his wife, Mrs. Oliveri. She had repurposed old bed sheets, tacking them across the wooden frame of the net. All in all, they were as good as any street hockey nets that you could find in any sporting goods store.

As I walked into the garage to get my equipment, my three brothers were in front, encircling one of the empty nets and taking shots. Like most kids in town, I played ice hockey throughout the year. For ice hockey, I played forward, but in street hockey I was always one of the goalies. I'm not sure what it was, but it was always my position. Maybe it was that I had gotten a street hockey goalie mask two birthdays ago, and I had used permanent marker to draw stitches marks all over the mask, just as the Bruins goalie, Gerry Cheevers had at the time. I think wearing that mask, that resembled the Bruins goalie's mask, just filled me with confidence. And, as a result, I was very good at it and everyone knew it, which also helped lift my ego.

I walked from the garage with all my gear on or in hand. I headed to the net closest to our driveway. I jumped into position and pulled my mask down over my face. "Let's go!" I shouted, and quickly got into the classic goalie stance. Immediately, an orange hockey ball came flying my way. I stepped forward and confidently turned it aside with my blocker pad. The rebound deflected out and to my left and directly to Bobby. He instantly "one timed" the ball back towards me and the net. My reflexes jumped into action, and I flashed the baseball glove I was wearing on my left hand and snagged the shot. I was ready to go.

Just then, a pack of kids, all carrying street hockey sticks, emerged from the Ferraro's garage, and walked into view. They stopped directly in front of me and began the process of making teams. The group had grown to twelve and included me and my three brothers, Lou Limone, the Padovani brothers, the two Ferraro's, Kevin Oliveri, Matteo Palermo, and Rob Schaefer.

"Perfect, five on five, with two goalies," Lou Limone shouted. Tommy Ferraro and I were the two goalies, and everyone else threw their sticks into a pile. Rick Ferraro then tossed one stick to the left, one to the right and repeated the process until all sticks were either to his right or his left. And this is how the teams were made.

Tommy and I would each take a net for the entire game. He'd take the net in front of his house and me in front of mine, then the teams would swap sides halfway through the game. So, this would have us both play half the game for each side. Everyone looked around to see who was on their team. At quick glance, the teams looked even, with an equal number of older and younger kids on each team.

Just as the two sides moved forward in preparation for the opening faceoff, we heard a voice yelling to us from behind my net. "Hey, what's going on here?" the mystery voice shouted. We all stopped in our tracks and looked to see who was calling to us. It was Marco Palermo.

"What!? You don't ask me to play in your game? What do I smell, or something?"he followed. "No, it's just that your arm's in a cast, so no one thought you could play," Rick Ferraro answered. "Well, you're wrong cus I can play," he shot back.

Walking behind Marco was another, older kid from the neighborhood, Vinny Collazo. Vinny was already in high school and the oldest kid on our block. He was an excellent athlete, playing both soccer and basketball for Stoneham High, and was sort of a folk hero to us younger kids in the neighborhood. He didn't often interact with Marco, but when he did, he seemed to have a calming effect on his friend's otherwise fiery personality. And, although none of us could prove this, the rumor was that Vinny had coined Marco's nickname, Rubberhead.

"Vinny and I want to play. We'll be on opposite sides to even things out," Marco declared. "Fine, we'll take Vinny," Rick responded.

Marco and Vinny walked over to pick up a hockey stick from the backups that had been left on our front lawn. "Let's have one sub aside, so that there's not too many people running around all at once," Rick suggested. So, two of the younger kids, Johnny Padovani and Kevin Oliveri, being low men in the pecking order, took a seat on the curb.

The game got off to a fast start. Most everyone was a bit on edge with Marco playing in the game. The game ebbed and flowed without any major altercations. I was pretty dialed in and didn't let up a goal over the first twenty minutes of play. Vinny was clearly the strongest player and he had created a couple of chances in tight, but I was able to turn them away.

As the play moved down from the far end, the ball squirted free and right to Vinny, who was positioned to my left about fifteen feet from the net. He wound up and took a blast of a shot. I quickly slid to my left, hoping to cover the ground before the ball arrived, but could only get the tip of my glove on it. The ball, which had some spin on it, deflected up and into the net. "Whoa!", the group sounded, "What a blast!"

The play raced up and down the street at an impressive pace. It was now very hot, and I was dripping wet with sweat. The game was also getting a bit chippy with many loose ball battles ending with some stick slashing, hacks and harsh words exchanged. After about forty minutes of play, and immediately following the tying goal scored by my side, it seemed to be a good point to break for the half with the score tied one to one.

Some of the kids ran into their homes to get a drink. Most made their way into our cellar to grab one of Nano's cans of sodas. I sat on the curb with Dave, Mario, and Matteo, as we waited for the second half to start. When, out of the corner of my eye, I noticed my brother Bob and Marco standing in our driveway. They seemed to be up to something, scheming, as they whispered to each other. Immediately, I was suspicious, as I often was when it came to almost anything with my number one rival, Bob. My attention shifted back to the street, as Lou Limone called and gestured for me to get back in the net. He, and a handful of others, were taking shots on the empty net, as it looked like we were about ready to get the game going again.

I stood from the curb and began to get my gear back in order. I shot a glance over to my left, where Bobby and Marco had been standing in the driveway, and noticed it was now vacant, which again gave me pause. Just then, there were more calls for me to get back in net and face some warm-up shots. So, I slid back in front of the goal and began to field shots from the crew in front of me.

"Game on!" Ricky Ferraro shouted. The two teams took their places at opposite ends.

"Who's missing?" Ricky barked, as he took a quick headcount. "Looks like Bobby and Rubberhead," Lou chimed in. We all snickered at that and then took a quick glance around to make sure that Marco wasn't around to have heard it. Lou hunched his shoulders and grimaced, as he quickly realized that he may have narrowly escaped injury following his remark.

"They're coming. I just saw them in my garage," Matteo reported. "Sorry guys, I can't stay anyway. I need to get going. I've got a summer league basketball game up at the high school," Vinny declared. "Good game though. Hope everyone has a great Fourth," he continued. Everyone wished him the same, as he turned and began to walk towards his house.

We were all pretty much in awe of Vinny, so it was super cool that he had played the first half of the game with us. "Matteo, can you go get them for us?" Ricky asked, but it really wasn't a question. Matteo dropped his stick and turned to run back to his house as asked. He had only taken a stride and a half when, suddenly, Marco and Bobby emerged out of the Palermo's house.

Marco approached us waving the arm that was encased in plaster at us and shouting, "Sorry, game over! Sorry, guys. The game's over." Everyone looked at Marco, confused about his declaring the game over. "What's up?" Ricky asked Marco, as Bob trailed a step or two behind. "We're done, can't play anymore. My father just asked me and Bobby to clean up the horseshoe pits for the party on Sunday. So, we gotta do it and so, we can't play," Marco explained.

"Pork Strip, why don't you come too and give us a hand," he continued. "Pork Strip" was Marco's nickname for Ricky, as he had a husky build. Ricky really wasn't a fan of the name and, much like "Rubberhead," you took your chances if you said it in front of him. But that wasn't an issue for Marco, for obvious reasons.

Marco, Bobby, and Ricky peeled off towards Marco's house. The rest of us just dispersed slowly for our own homes, as Kevin Oliveri dragged the two street hockey nets back into his garage. I tossed my goalie gear into the garage and made my way out back to see what was going on there.

I entered the backyard and immediately heard a commotion. I looked over to the card table and, sure enough, the game was still humming along. I noticed that a bottle of Old Grand Dad, Nano's go-to off the shelf liquor, had now made its way onto the table. As I zeroed in on the card sharks, a roar of cheers and jeers erupted to my left. My eyes instantly veered that way, and I spotted Dad through the chain link fence that separated our backyard from the Ferraro's. He was on the Ferraro's bocce court with the other dads, who had earlier worked together to dig the clambake pit.

The bocce court was fairly new. It had been installed earlier that summer, but, until today, I hadn't noticed it getting much use. The dads were, as far as the dads go, very rowdy as they were obviously riveted by their game. I took a few more steps into the yard to get a better look. In my yard, at about mid-court, my three aunts, Polly, Gray and May, were seated in lawn chairs and facing the bocce play. I could tell that my Aunt Gray was enjoying every minute of it and, from the smile on her face, I got the sense that she had been heckling Dad. I stood with them for a minute and watched the match that was ongoing.

"Don't tell your father this, but he's the best one," my Aunt Gray told me. "Really?" I asked. "Oh yeah, he's making all the points for his side," she responded. Aunts Polly and May looked up at me from their chairs and nodded their heads, agreeing with Aunt Gray's assessment.

"Come on, Bobby! Put your weight behind it and roll that ball!" Aunt Gray shouted, her two sisters enjoying every second of it. "Be quiet, you! Or I'll accidentally drop one of these balls over this fence and on top of that Q-tip head of yours!" Dad responded. This response got laughs from both sides of the fence.

Dad picked up the pallino, the small ball that is the object ball, and tossed it out onto the court. The four dads were divided into two teams, with Dad playing with Mr. Palermo and Mr. Limone and Ferraro teaming up. "Good toss, Bobby!" Cos Palermo shouted. Dad had tossed the pallino about thirty feet out. "They'll never have the finesse to put it close over there", he continued. "Oh yeah, just watch us", Mr. Limone replied.

Mr. Limone then bowled his team's first ball toward the pallino. It was headed straight for the smaller ball. Mr. Ferraro shouted out excitedly, "That's it, Jimmy! It's headed straight at it."

The ball careened off the smaller ball, pushing it away a foot further and bumping it up against the rail of the court. "Oh! Good roll, Jimmy. Just some bad luck," Mr. Ferraro exclaimed. "Thanks, Tony. The only luck I'm having today is bad luck," he responded. "Our luck will change. Just wait. You'll see, Jimmy."

Mr. Limone's ball came to rest about a foot or so away from the pallino, which now sat against the rail. "Okay Cos, put it out there, just ease it up on the rail," Dad encouraged Mr. Palermo. As Mr. Palermo made his play and bowled his ball, I felt a tap on my left arm. It was Nano, followed closely behind by Uncle Phillip.

"Can you believe this?" he said. "They don't know how to play the right way," he added, shaking his head. Normally, I'd question Nano's critical review, but I caught Uncle Phillip nodding in agreement with Nano's assessment so, maybe he was right.

"They don't even know the rules. Oh boy, what a racket. Bunch of phonies!" he added with a smile. "Your card game over?"I asked. "Yes, and we won, Michael!", Uncle Phillip chimed in proudly. "Really? It looked like you were losing earlier," I responded. "We were. But, like Yogi Berra said, "it ain't over, till it's over!" Uncle Phillip said, with great emphasis.

We turned our attention back to the bocce court. And as the game went on, Nano and Uncle Phillip's disapproval of the play on the court went on as well. Both shook their heads and gestured critically towards my aunts who were still seated nearby. In return, the aunts quickly dismissed their critique and let Dad know that the two brothers "thought they could do it better". "Oh yeah?", Dad answered. "They're next," he shot back.

XIV - Furto del Furto
(Theft of the Theft)

As the bocce game continued, I suddenly heard the distinct shrieking signature call, followed shortly after by a "pop", consistent with a whistling bottle rocket. The magnitude of the exploding rocket's sound suggested that it was set off nearby. I whirled around trying to locate the rocket's origin, listening intently. Sure enough, within a minute's time, another rocket could be heard taking flight. This "pop" sounded even closer than the first.

I immediately turned away from the game and followed the sound out to the front yard. When I reached the driveway, I spotted Marco with my brother Bob and Ricky Ferraro standing at the foot of the Palermo's driveway. As the three of them came into view, I saw Ricky raise a BIC lighter towards Marco's left arm. Marco had placed a bottle rocket into a finger hole of the cast that wrapped his left arm and, in what looked to be an attempt to mimic Iron Man, Ricky was launching a whistler from Marco's cast.

The rocket took off towards the empty lot next door. Its high-pitched shrill pierced the air, as it soared toward the tree at the corner of the lot. Just as the missile flew past the tree, the third rocket exploded with a loud "bang". The three perpetrators burst into raucous laughter and looked to reload. Fearing the worst, I sprinted for the tent in the backyard to check that our stash of fireworks was safe and secure.

I hurried into the tent and began to sift through the sleeping bags, searching for our prized bag of contraband. I felt panic setting in as I combed through one sleeping bag after another. As if that was not enough, I heard yet another rocket whistling in the distance. Before that rocket could even detonate, I was certain that Bobby and Marco had found our stockpile and had taken it for themselves.

Options and scenarios immediately raced through my mind. Do I run and tell Dad? But how would I explain that they stole fireworks that I'm not supposed to have? How would I explain that my illegal fireworks are missing? Even further, how would I explain that they had stolen my stolen fireworks?

In a split second, I recognized that they had pulled off a near-perfect crime, as I was incapable of reporting the theft. I thought for another frantic second, as one more whistler taunted me from outside the tent. And then it came to me. Instead of running to tell Dad what had happened, I would run to tell the three culprits that their dads, who were all still playing bocce, sent me over to get them. And that they needed to report to the Ferraro's backyard, because they knew what they were up to. This wouldn't get the fireworks back to me, but it would, at least, put a pause to them setting them all off for now.

I raced from the tent and set off for the Palermo's driveway. As I arrived on the scene, Mrs. Palermo, from their house window right above the driveway, was hollering at the three punks. She had caught them in the act and was now dropping the hammer on them. It was, of course, music to my ears. I strolled closer to them as the verbal assault continued and watched with pleasure as each of them glared over at me.

Marco, looking up at his mom, tried to defuse the situation, "Okay Ma. I get it, I get it, already." "Don't give me that, Marco. You're shooting those damn things right across the street. There are kids all over the place. Someone could lose an eye! Then, how would you feel? Would you like that? No!" she answered her own question.

"For Christ sakes, Ma. I heard you already," Marco went on. "Don't give me that back talk, Marco. Boys, that's it. You got to go home now. No more fireworks show," she finished.

Bobby and Ricky stepped away from the Palermo's driveway and walked towards me. I showed Bob a big grin to let him know that I was on to him. And also that I had just enjoyed the scene with Mrs. Palermo. And to pour some fresh salt on the wound, I told Bob that Dad wanted to see him right away. Although this wasn't true, it would at least cause him some agita as I game planned on how to get my fireworks back.

I walked back to my house and into the backyard. I wanted to quickly seek out Dave and let him know what had happened. I also wanted to figure out a way to get our fireworks back. As I crossed the patio, I noticed that the bocce game next door had ended, and Dad was now getting the grill prepped for a barbeque.

Mom intercepted me, just as I spotted Dave down by the pool. "Michael don't roam far from here. We're having a cookout and we'll be eating in less than an hour," she directed. "Okay, Mom," I answered and sped towards the deep end of the pool.

I walked past Nano and my aunts and uncle, who were sitting together on the patio furniture under the umbrella by the shallow end of the pool. They were engaged in a lively debate, but it was in Italian, which was foreign to me, so I just rushed by.

Although I grew up in the same home as Nano and Nana, whose first language was Italian, we were separated by a single floor in our "two-family" home in Somerville. I think that's the major reason why my brothers, sister, and I never picked up the language. That, coupled with my dad's insistence that my grandfather only speak to him in English, were the likely reasons that none of us picked it up.

Dad's reasoning to only speak English to Nano was well placed. Dad figured that, as a proprietor of a retail furniture shop in Boston, Nano would need to be capable of greeting and selling to customers who might only speak English. So, his plan and determination to only converse in English with Nano was founded with good intentions.

But, for me, it meant my Italian language skills were limited to only a few crude curse words, as well as knowing when I was generally in trouble and needed to leave the room. As for the conversation that was going on pool side, I picked up a swear or two but nothing else.

I approached Dave, who was sitting on the edge of the diving board at the far end of the pool and hit him with the news. "Did you hear those whistlers right over there? About fifteen, twenty minutes ago?" I asked excitedly. "No. I was in the house. Why?" he responded. "Because they were ours! Bobby and Marco found our stash and swiped it," I followed.

"How did they find it?" Dave questioned. "I don't know, but I'm pretty sure it was during the street hockey game. And that's why they didn't want to play the second half," I answered. We both took a second to simmer over the news.

"So, what are we going to do?" Dave then asked. "I don't know yet. I let Bobby think that Dad might already know, but he doesn't. We just need to think about it. We should tell Mario and John, anyway," I added. "Johnny's right over there, in his garden," Dave said, as he gestured to the Padovani's backyard. "Okay, let's go tell Johnny and he can update Mario," I suggested.

Dave and I walked over to the chain link fence, at the back of Nano's garden, that separated our yard from the Padovani's. "Hey! Hey!" I shouted to John, who was kneeling with his back to us as he tended to some pepper plants. John swung his head around to us and I signaled him to come over to the fence. We delivered the grim details to John and asked him to pass along the news to his brother.

Just as John turned from us and headed for the back slider of his house, I heard Mom call out for me and Dave. "Michael! David!" she shouted, as she waved for us to go see her. "What the f?" I said under my breath. As we started towards Mom, I suggested to Dave, "We can talk more about it tonight. When we're alone in the tent. We just need to figure a way to get them back."

XV - Fagiano Dicino Alla Piscina
(Pheasant by the Pool)

Mom was waiting for me and Dave on the upper patio deck. "Your father could use some help. We're both running around trying to get ready for the cookout. Can you boys go into the garage and grab the bag of charcoal? It's sitting on the shelf under Nano's work bench," she explained. "Sure, Ma," we answered. Dave and I opened the fence gate and left for the garage.

"Where do you think he has the fireworks?" Dave asked, as we walked towards the garage. "I don't know. But we need to try and figure that out," I said.

Just then, as we were turning the corner of the walkway and into the garage, we ran smack into Bobby, who was coming out of the garage. "You little liar!" he exclaimed. Trying to not look startled, I answered him with my own question, "What are you talking about?"

"Dad didn't want to talk to me," he shot back. "Well, maybe he did. And he just couldn't because the other dads were around or maybe it was the aunts," I reasoned. "Where are our fireworks?" Dave jumped in. Bob glared over at Dave for an uneasy three or four seconds, and then looked back over at me.

"He wasn't looking for me. And he doesn't know about the fireworks. Does he?" Bob asserted. "He knows whatever we want him to know. Who knows, maybe he does, maybe he doesn't. Or maybe, we're just waiting to tell him on the morning of the Fourth, so you'll be grounded and miss out on every-thing." I said, bluffing on the fly.

Now Bob's uncomfortable three or four second glare was aimed at me. He then brushed past the two of us, making sure his right arm made solid contact with my left shoulder, and left for the backyard. Dave and I then made our way into the garage to fetch the bag of charcoal, as we had been directed. We walked to the back of the garage towards Nano's work bench.

"Do you think we should really tell Dad?" Dave asked. "No, I don't think we can. But we can make him think that we will," I replied. "Yeah. And he's going to worry about that thing you said. That was a good one," Dave added. "Let's hope so," I answered. We then arrived at the shelf of Nano's workbench that was holding the extra-large bag of Kingsford charcoal. It was an enormous bag. "You're fuckin' kidding me!" I cursed.

Dave and I struggled to lug the extra-large bag of Kingsford's Original beyond the gate and into the backyard. We stumbled up the couple steps of the patio deck and delivered the goods to Dad, who was already armed with lighter fluid in his right hand. "Thanks guys. Pretty heavy, huh?" Dad said. "Yeah, I'll say," I answered.

Just then, we heard a commotion from the patio table by the pool, where Nano and Uncle Phillip were sitting with the aunts. Nano and Uncle Phillip rose abruptly from their chairs and began pointing to the branches of an oak tree, that sat at the foot of Mom's rock garden about ten feet away from the tent. Dad grabbed the bag of charcoal from us, "Why don't you go see what all the fuss is about," he said. Dave and I rushed over to the table and chairs by the pool.

"What is it?", I asked. "It's a quail up in the tree," Uncle Phillip said. We all squinted through the sun to try and see what he was talking about. "A what?" I asked. "It's a quail, a bird," Nano answered tersely. "A bird? So, what?" I responded. "Oh brother," Aunt Gray chimed in. "It's a damn bird. They're going to want to eat it, for Christ sakes," she added. "You be quiet, Grace," Uncle Phillip replied. Suddenly, I knew this was serious.

"Michael, go get us that net over there on the fence," Uncle

Phillip directed, as he pointed to the pool skimming net that was hanging from two hooks on the chain link fence. I darted to the other side of the pool and grabbed the long pole and net from its resting place on the hooks and returned it to Uncle Phillip, as instructed.

"Good boy," Uncle Phillip said to me, patting me on the head, as he began to lengthen the pole by twisting the fastener at one end and drawing the section of the pole from within. Nano grabbed one end, with his cigar still firmly tucked to one side of his mouth, and the two brothers carried the net towards the oak tree.

At the foot of the tree, the two brothers, who were both a towering five foot, four inches, raised the net into the tree branches above. Revealing the extent of the "prize" in the tree above them, the brothers quickly shifted into Italian. As if the fowl might be onto their plan, if they kept their exchange in English.

They clumsily moved the pole around the mid-sized oak, twice getting the skimming net hung up in the branches. They resembled two clowns at a circus who would intentionally fumble their task at hand. However, there was nothing intentional about their bungling around. They looked like two remarkably undersized pole vaulters attempting to use the same launching rod at one time. Their clumsy efforts gained attention, as my aunts were now standing by my side and staring upward.

I fully expected that the trio had arrived on the scene to throw barbs at the duo, but, to my surprise and shock, they began to coach and encourage them as the pair continued their attempt to "fish" the bird out of the tree. It was mostly Italian gibberish to me, but I could tell from the tone and their demonstrative hand gestures that they were actually rooting against the bird. Amazingly, the quail just sat there unconcerned, as if it knew their attempts were futile. This went on for a good couple of minutes, but without a bird in hand. I could tell that frustration was beginning to set-in by the volume of the Italian being spoken and the more forceful hand signals coming from my aunts.

Dad, having already lit the coals in the grill, walked over for a closer look, "Will you please?" he said, with a slight grin on his face. "We almost have it," Uncle Phillip said, as he took one hand off the pole to signal up at the tree.

"Stupido! Don't let go of the pole, mannaggia," Nano shouted at him. Just as Uncle Phillip regained his grip on the pole, while cursing under his breath, the quail lifted off and flew away. It was as if the bird had grown tired of watching the Keystone Cops-like efforts to capture it. As the bird departed the scene, spirits amongst the first-generation crew fell instantly, and some familiar Italian curse words immediately followed.

"You were never going to catch that bird," Dad informed them. "What are you talking about? We almost had it," Nano shouted in response. "Still, if you had, it wouldn't even feed one of you," Dad observed.

"Michael, take the net for them," Dad instructed. And, just as I was taking hold of the net and, as we all turned from the foot of the tree, we heard a thunderous "Bang!" It was so loud. Simultaneously, everyone turned and looked behind us, searching for the source of the explosion. The only thing I could think of was that someone had set off an M-80 firework. The M-80 was pretty much the most powerful firecracker around and would detonate in a huge explosion. But it wasn't a firework at all.

Aunt May, having witnessed it all, pointed to the back of the house. It was a bird, a huge bird. And it had flown right into the side of our house. "There were two of them, flying together," she explained excitedly. "They were just flying along together and then Bam! One flew right into the side of the house. And the other one just flew over. And it kept going. Just like that, bam! Into the side of the house. Mother of God, can you believe it?" she rambled on.

"What is it?" I asked. Just then, Mom flew out the back door of the house and onto the deck, "What the hell was that?" she asked, with worry in her voice. "It's nothing. A bird flew into the side of the house," Dad answered. "Nothing? The whole house shook," Mom replied. "Looks like a pheasant," Dad announced.

We all rushed over to take a closer look. "Yeah, it's a pheasant, all right. They're not known to have great eyesight. It must have gotten distracted by something," Dad reasoned. It wasn't a bloody seen, but it was disgusting to me, nonetheless. The bird was sprawled out on the patio deck, its body contorted in an unnatural way.

As I stood over the bird's body, I was squeamish about the whole encounter. But what looked like a crime scene to me, looked like a windfall to my elder family members. Without hesitation, the crew jumped into action.

In their eyes, one pheasant was apparently as good as a half dozen quails. Within seconds, they had set a plan to de-feather and process the bird. The only thing undecided was what sides would they serve with their pheasant. Nano took the lead and leaned over to pick up the bird by its broken neck. He proudly posed with the bird and presented it with his arms outstretched to the group. Although it was a grisly end for the pheasant, I couldn't help noticing just how beautiful the bird's feathers and bright colors were.

XVI - Affari di Famiglia
(Family Matters)

Dad had hotdogs, burgers and sausages going on the grill. As he worked away on the grill, the aunts were working over the poor pheasant at a folding table that we had set up for them. Aunts Polly and Gray did most of the work, as Aunt May watched wearily off to the side.

It was pretty amazing to see. It looked as if both Polly and Gray had once worked at a butcher shop, the way they handled the bird so skillfully. In almost no time, they had those beautiful feathers off the bird and were ready to process it completely. Nano and Uncle Phillip watched over them anxiously, as if they could somehow do it better. I squeamishly decided not to watch, opting instead to look away. To me, it was an unlucky bird rather than tomorrow night's meal.

As the two amateur butchers finished the deed, they placed the trimmed cuts into a large bowl and covered the top with Reynolds Wrap aluminum foil. They then walked it into the kitchen to refrigerate it overnight. Nano and Uncle Phillip then stepped forward to clean and disinfect the area, placing any remaining bits of the carcass into a dark, green heavy-duty trash bag. And just like that, the backyard poultry hunt came to a successful end. Just not for the poor pheasant.

Mom and Dad had all the food for the cookout set out on a folding table. Thankfully, it wasn't the same table used earlier to clean and butcher the pheasant. It was a pretty impressive spread, with the assortment of meats that Dad had nuked on the grill and a full selection of sides that Mom and the aunts had prepared.

One of the sides, which was a staple of Mom's and one that I really didn't care for, was a platter of Deviled Eggs. But like on many family occasions, they were on the menu and ready for the taking. I was a hard pass but did notice that they seemed to be a favorite of most of the adults.

Many of the side dishes came directly from Nano's garden. The side dishes included sauteed zucchini slices, tomato and basil salad, a string bean salad, fried eggplant, as well as my favorite, fried zucchini blossoms. Like with most of our cook-outs, the adults were seated poolside and under an umbrella that shaded them from the sun. All of us kids were seated at the picnic table on the upper patio, which was a good forty feet away from the adults' table.

It was a less than cordial meal, as Dave and I were still fuming over our missing fireworks. Pam and Steve seemed blissfully unaware as they chowed on their hot dogs. But Bob had a clear, almost arrogant, aura about him as he bit into his second burger. You could just tell that he was pleased with himself for not only pulling off the heist, but for denying us of our spoils. It was infuriating. I decided, why not poke the bear?

"You know, you're never going to get away with this." Bob just smiled and then took another bite into his burger. "You won't," I added. "And what are you going to do?" Bob shot back. "Whatever it takes. I don't care if it's a day from now, or a week, a month or even years, but if you don't give them back to us, I'm going to get even. You just watch," I threatened him.

"Oh, what are you going to do? I'm so scared," he answered, mockingly. "Just give them back Bobby," Dave chimed in. "Pfft!" Bob scoffed back. "Why would I do that?" he asked. "Because they're ours," Dave responded. "Well not any more they're not. What's the saying, finders, keepers?" Bob countered.

At that point, I got up from the table and looked him straight in the eye. "I'm just telling you, whatever it takes, I'll do to get you back. So, chew on that with your second burger," I warned.

As I walked away from the table, I could hear Pam and

Steve emphasize my threat with a collective, "Ooh … aah," but then laughed it off together and, by doing so, sort of stole my intended thunder.

Unfortunately, my closing exchange with Bobby at the picnic table was the only fireworks uncovered for the rest of the day. However, the adults had apparently made some after dinner plans while they were sitting together by the pool.

Mom seemed unusually excited and was buzzing around to clean up after the cookout. The aunts were all chipping in and had another assembly line going in the kitchen. Everyone had used paper products to eat outside, so most of the work was to wrap-up and store any leftovers. With all the games going on in the afternoon, we had gotten a late start to dinner; at least for us. It was now nearly eight PM, as the kitchen hummed along with activity.

Dad bolted through the back door with his grilling utensils in hand, "Lou, this is the last of it," he said, as he handed the over-sized fork and spatula to my mom. "I'll go grab the film and projector," he went on, as he headed out of the kitchen for the hallway leading to the staircase.

"What's going on? What are we doing?" I asked Mom. "We thought it would be nice to watch some home movies outside," Mom answered. "Really?" I followed. "Yes, we're going to watch our wedding video. I don't think you kids have ever seen that. Have you?" she asked. "No, I don't think so, anyway. How are we going to watch it outside?" I followed. "We're going to try and watch it by using a sheet that I'll hang from the clothesline as a screen," she replied. "A sheet? I don't think that's going to work, Mom," I suggested. "Sure, it will. You'll see," she answered.

My brothers and I were tasked with setting up folding chairs on the backyard lawn. We had a half dozen in place up front, all facing Mom's clothesline. We had another half dozen patio chairs set up behind them to account for everyone. We left an open column in the middle of the chairs and set up the card table at the back to hold Dad's film projector.

Dad had already set the projector on the table and was running an extension cord from the back of the projector to the outdoor outlet that was located just above the foundation of the house. It was now just after dusk and the whole crew was assembling in the seating area. Mom was working diligently to lay two white bed sheets side by side on her clothesline. She put the finishing touches to her homemade movie screen by affixing clothes pins to the corners of the two sheets, holding them firmly in place.

There was no wind at all, so it suddenly seemed possible that we might pull off this plan. Mom then made one last stop, just before kicking off the show. She quickly opened a bottle of white wine that she had placed on the picnic table and poured it into eight small juice glasses that she had waiting on a tray.

As Dad made the final adjustments, feeding the thirty-five millimeter film from the back reel through the projector and onto an empty reel that sat at the front of the projector, Mom handed out the glasses of wine to the adults who were seated and anxiously waiting for the show.

"Okay, for you kids, this is from Mom and Dad's wedding. The scenes getting ready at the house and at the church are all in Somerville and everything at the reception is actually from right here in Stoneham, at the Plaza," Dad informed us all.

The projector kicked on and, son of a gun, there it was, showing clear as day on the two bed sheets. The film was surprisingly shot in color but without any sound. The first scenes were taken at Mom's house, which, very conveniently, was directly across the street from the church. All the aunts sounded out with a bunch of "oohs" and "aahs" as we saw Mom in her wedding dress, posing on the floor of her living room.

"What are you doing on the floor?" Pam asked. "That's just how they had me pose," Mom answered. We then saw the brides-maids place their bouquets around the edge of Mom's wedding dress and position them just so for the camera. Mom and Dad had been married for nearly thirteen years and it was kind of weird to see them back before any of us were around.

"There's your mother, Louise", Aunt Polly noted. "Yes, … aww," Mom sighed. "You know, I never noticed until now, but she doesn't look well here. You can tell she was sick," Mom continued, with a touch of sadness in her voice.

My grandmother, my mom's mom, had passed away just a couple years after my parents were married and I unfortunately didn't remember her, as I was only a couple of months old at the time.

The scene then shifted across the street to the church. The camera focused on five guys standing at the top of the steps leading into the church. They were standing in a straight line, on one step after another and all wearing tuxedos. I couldn't pick my dad out of the bunch, not because the cameraman was filming from a great distance but because it was hard to recognize Dad.

If four guys on the screen hadn't simultaneously started patting one guy on his back, I wouldn't have been able to pick Dad out of the lineup. It wasn't necessarily because he looked so much younger, but more because he looked so much more … ethnic, I guess.

His hair was slicked back a bit and his olive-colored skin looked even darker on film. He looked like a real "Guido." Like right-off the boat Italian. "Oh Bobby, look at you. How handsome!" Aunt Gray chimed in. "What happened to you?" she teased.

"Me? Look at you. You're at least a foot taller in this film. And that doesn't count the six inches that your bouffant has grown since then," Dad teased her back. "Oh, you stop it. You're bad, Bobby," she quipped back with a smile.

The film fast forwarded from pre-ceremony outside the church to post-ceremony with both family sides crowding the steps of the church. It was really cool, but also a bit odd, to see everyone, their thirteen years younger version, being shown on the two bedsheets in my backyard today.

After just a couple of minutes of film shot outside the church, which included the scene showing Mom and Dad getting into their limousine, the action shifted to the reception. The first shot at the reception hall showed Mom and her wedding party posing for pictures and then similar shots with Dad and his groomsmen. This was followed by bride and groom family shots.

There was an unmistakable and collective exhale among the adults as the projector rolled and showed Mom and Dad alongside Nano and Nana. This was followed by a hush across the backyard, with the only audible sound coming from the sput-tering projector reels. My attention turned from the film to my family seated together on our back lawn.

I could see my aunts begin to choke up and then noticed Nano take off his glasses to wipe away a tear. Dad was sitting next to Mom, and I saw her put her arm across his shoulders, as he pulled a handkerchief from his pocket to dab at his eyes and nose. I felt an instant pit in my stomach as my eyes returned to the film. I couldn't determine if the feeling I was experiencing was due to my own raw emotions of having seen Nana on film or if it was more in response to seeing the pain and grief on the faces of my family. Nonetheless, it was a sad moment in an oth-erwise happy and memorable family occasion.

The mood soon returned to an upbeat feeling, as the film shifted to scenes of dancing and toasting of the couple at the reception. This was followed by a scene of the newlyweds, now having changed into more casual attire, getting ready to depart for their honeymoon with a big send-off from both sides of the family.

The last scenes of the film were some of the best and showed Mom and Dad honeymooning on the island of Bermuda. As usual, Dad was hamming it up for the camera, doing his best "before and after" muscle poses on the pink sandy beaches. The highlight, and fitting finale, had Mom and Dad trading off film-ing responsibilities, showing each other riding mopeds, complete with riding helmets, at various picturesque spots on the island.

As the final stretch of the film made its way through the pro-jector, everyone, led by the aunts, began to clap with approval. Pam and Steve quickly jumped up in front of the make-shift film screen and danced in the light of the projector. Mom, looking very pleased with the screening, stood, and announced that we'd be having coffee and desserts inside. Aunt Gray took the oppor-tunity for a final shot at Dad, "Bobby, maybe just coffee for you. If you want to get that boyish physique back," she said with a smirk and snicker. Dad just shook his head and laughed it off, as we all headed towards the kitchen.

XVII - Il Più Cari Amici
(Closest Friends)

The Padovani brothers showed up just in time for dessert. The adults were having their coffee, pastry and after dinner drinks in the living room, while we stuffed ourselves on treats at the kitchen table. We were heading out back to camp out in the tent again right after we finished dessert. We were anxious to regroup and consider our next moves, if there were any, to retrieve our fireworks.

Once we finished the last few cookies, we gathered our things and were ready to head outside. Mario, Johnny, and Steve left through the back door, while Dave and I planned to go the long way and pick up a few more Dr. Peppers. "Mom?" I called out. "We're heading outside for the night," I informed her. "Okay. No fooling around out there, Michael. And get your rest. Aren't you going to say good night to everyone?" she followed.

Dave and I took a single step into the dining room. "Good night, everyone," we said together. "Good night," the room echoed back. "Your grandfather and I might be out back a bit later, after we finish our coffee," Uncle Phillip informed us. "Okay, I guess we'll head out now," I responded.

Dave and I took a step back and headed for the basement door. We quickly made our way down the stairs, hoping not to be beckoned to return for some reason. We made our withdrawal from Nano's vast supply of soda and took off for the backyard through the garage. Dave and I entered the tent, each of us carrying a few cans of Dr Pepper. The guys already had the Red Sox game on, but the mood in the tent was a far cry from what it had been the previous night.

Last night, we had all this pent-up energy and excitement building as we made our plans to trek over to the Coyne's to buy our fireworks. Tonight was a different story, as we were now left with the dim prospects of trying to retrieve any of our goods. The adventure of the day, the risks we took and our big score as a result, still gave us a lot to talk about though.

"I can't believe we did that today," Mario said with real surprise. "What if they found out? What if we got caught?" he went on. "That was crazy. Just crazy! I don't know how you kept your shit together! I was sweating it. Just standing in the back, I couldn't help but just stand there and sweat," Mario added. "I know, right? It just happened. We didn't plan for it, it just happened. And Johnny drove the get-away bike," I stated.

Everyone looked over to John with a smile on our faces, he looked back at us with his own sheepish grin. "But easy come, easy go, for us anyway. I don't know how we let that happen. Should have hidden it better," I shared. "You think there is anything we can do to get it back?" Dave asked. "I don't know. I can't think of anything," I answered after a short pause.

"What if you tell your dad that Bobby stole it?" Mario chimed in. "That's the problem, it's basically the perfect crime. How do we tell on him without getting in trouble ourselves? Even if my dad forced him to hand it over, he'll never then just hand them back to us. There must be some other way," I reasoned. "Where do you think he has them?" Dave then asked. "I don't know. My bet is somewhere at the Palermo's. Probably somewhere hidden in Marco's room," I answered.

"Maybe we could get Matteo to help us out and look for them," Mario offered. "Yeah, I thought of that. But I don't think Matteo is going to risk fucking with Marco. Let's be honest, that would be suicide," I asserted. We all shook our heads in agreement, knowing that was a true statement. "But everyone keep thinking.

Maybe there's a way. We just have to figure it out," I encouraged.

As we settled in for the night, we tuned in to the day's baseball broadcast, as the Red Sox had just taken the lead over the Brewers. The club hadn't shown much promise this season but there's something about listening to a summer night's ballgame on the radio, especially in a tent with a bunch of guys.

Then, without warning, the cover over the tent's entrance flung open and Uncle Phillip, with a loud "Roar," poked his head into the tent. I'm not ashamed to say that we all jumped a bit out of our skin, or at least jumped out of our sleeping bags. Uncle Phillip had a huge smile on his face, pleased and proud of the scare that he had put into us. He then backed out of the tent and was replaced by Nano standing in the tent's opening.

"What's going on in here?" Nano shouted with a huge grin on his face. We instantly erupted in laughter. Nano backed out of the tent and then a third head popped into the tent, "What's going on in here?" we heard again. This time it was Mario and Johnny's grandfather, Ray Padovani, the senior. We responded with another wave of roaring laughter. Steve was actually cackling which just further fueled all of us.

Nano returned into the tent and ordered us to get to sleep. "What are you doing out there?" I shouted to him. "We're having a glass, or two, of Mr. Padovani's homemade Limoncello," he answered.

Ray Padovani, Ray senior, like Nano and Uncle Phillip, was from the seaside town of Gaeta, located about sixty miles north of Naples, Italy. Although all three of them grew up in the same town in Italy, they were only acquaintances back then during their early lives.

In a fairly miraculous coincidence, and almost thirty-five years later, Nano and Ray senior moved into homes with their sons' families that stood back-to-back in a suburb north of Boston and more than four thousand miles away from their hometown back in Italy. Although they weren't close friends as kids or as young adults in Italy, they were the closest of friends now, and their grandkids were best of friends.

We reclined in our sleeping bags and listened to both the baseball game on the radio and the happy chatter outside. From time to time, we could hear the clinking of glasses as, no doubt, another dose of Ray senior's limoncello was shared by the three friends. There were also a few moments of sharply raised voices, quickly followed by laughs and a couple curse words in Italian.

I had asked Mario to interpret for us what was being said during those outbursts. Mario, and his brother and sister, were all fluent, given their good fortune of not having been separated by a floor or apartment in their home, as we had been. Most of the chatter that he interpreted for us, seemed to revolve around complaints about not getting respect from us grandkids, soccer scores or the good old days in general. As the banter slowly died down, we each drifted off for the night.

Sabato 3 Luglio, 1976
(Saturday, July 3, 1976)

XVIII - Il Bambino Petardo
(The Firecracker Kid)

Just as planned, I was up early the next morning to retrieve the papers and get another early start to my paper route on Saturday. I just really wanted to be done with it. And besides, we had another pretty busy day ahead of us. Dave and I had been enlisted to travel to Nahant with Dad, Nano, and Uncle Phillip. We were apparently heading there to pick up some supplies for tomorrow's clambake.

As for my route, the Saturday papers were always the smallest and therefore the lightest of the week, but even more so on this day as it was the day before a holiday. This helped me make quick work of things and, in almost no time, I hit the last house on my route and pedaled for home.

As I biked the last hundred yards or so, I saw a small figure at the corner by the Palermo's, directly across the street from the empty lot. I peered forward trying to make out just who it was. I could tell, as I squinted intently, that it was a kid, but I wasn't sure who. As I got about fifty feet away, I realized that it was the Palermo's cousin, Joey. I didn't know Joey's last name; I just knew he was their cousin and would visit once a year over the summer.

Joey, who was a few years younger than me, was a pretty hyper kid and was infatuated with firecrackers. We actually gave him the nickname, "The Firecracker Kid," because he was so over-the-top and crazed about firecrackers. I think he was a kid with ADD or something, so we didn't give him a lot of crap about it. But he couldn't shut up about firecrackers and pretty much hounded everyone looking to get his hands on some.

I don't know, maybe it was just that we'd only see him around the Fourth of July, but he definitely earned that nickname. I rode over to him to see what he was up to.

"Hey Joey, you here for the holiday?" I asked. Sure enough, he had what looked like a firecracker in his hand and he was waving it around as if it were a toy plane. He barely acknowledged me, as he made a buzzing noise with an occasional explosion sound, as he slowly flailed the firework in his right hand. I looked closely at what he was holding and could see that it was actually the business end of a bottle rocket, which had already detonated.

The color on the rocket's wrapper caught my attention, as it was the same insignia on the rockets that we had brought home from the Coyne's a day earlier. I quickly became more interested in what Joey was doing, "Hey, where'd you get that, Joey?" I asked. He continued playing, without any response.

"Hey!" I shouted. "I asked where'd you get that," I repeated, raising my voice. He responded simply by pointing to the empty lot across the street. "Was that Marco's?" I questioned him further. "Yeah, it was, I guess," he answered. "Did you see him light it?" I pressed.

He looked up at me and shook his head, no. "He has a lot of them and said that I could watch him set them off later. But only if I don't touch them before then," he answered, happily.

"Oh yeah, that's cool. Did he tell you not to touch them because you saw them in the house?" I asked. He shook his head, again indicating, no. "So, you haven't seen the fireworks then," I went on. "Well, I did. But then he took them out of the house," Joey explained. "Oh, that makes sense," I said, trying to put him at ease.

"Where did he take them, after he left the house?" I probed. Joey paused for a second and, for the first time, looked up at me from the curb that he was sitting on, "Over there," he answered, as he pointed to the woods behind the Palermo's back yard. "The woods?" I shot back eagerly.

Once again, Joey answered with just a shake of his head, but this time it was a nod. And I had my answer. I should have put it together on my own, but it had just escaped my mind amidst my fury over the ordeal.

A few weeks earlier, I had spotted Marco, Bobby, and Ricky dragging wooden pallets into the woods that Ricky's dad, Mr. Ferraro, had brought home from his scrap metal yard. The three of them had made at least a couple of trips from the Ferraro's garage and into the woods behind the Palermo's. I assumed they would be breaking up the pallets and burning them in the woods, but maybe it was more than that. One thing was for sure, I would need to investigate it immediately.

I took one last glance down at Joey, and ended our talk with, "Yeah, I figured," and then sped away to put my bike in the garage.

XIX - Recupero
(Retrieval)

Just as I rode back into my driveway, Mario came into view from the walkway leading from my back yard. "Where are you going?" I asked. "I was going to head home for a while. I need to mow the lawn sometime this morning," he replied. "Listen, I think I know where the fireworks are," I put it out there.

"What? Where? How do you know?" he questioned. I gestured by nodding my head towards the Palermo's. "Joey, 'The Firecracker Kid' … he was playing with a bottle rocket when I got back from my route. And I asked him where he got it," I answered. "And he told you where they are?" Mario continued. "No, not exactly. He told me that Marco had them and that he had brought them somewhere into the woods," I said. Mario pressed, "So, what does that mean? Where in the woods?"

"I'm not sure, but I think it has something to do with the pallets I saw those guys carrying a couple weeks ago," I responded. "So, you don't know where they are?" he asked pointedly. "No, but they could only be in a general area. So, let's go look," I said assertively. "Now?" he asked. "Yes, right now. Let's go! It won't take that long. You can mow your lawn as soon as we get back," I finished. "All right, whatever. Let's go look," he conceded.

We rushed from the garage and headed for the woods. Since it was still just before 8:30 a.m., I figured that we had an hour or so to search the area behind the Palermo's, before Bobby, Marco, and Ricky even got out of bed. To be on the safe side, we headed into the woods from the back of the Oliveri's house, which led to the junior high school athletic fields. If anyone were to see us, they'd just assume that we were heading up to one of the fields.

We crossed from the Oliveri's yard and onto a path in the woods. Once we got about thirty or forty feet onto the path, we came to a fork in the trail. The footpath to the right led to the fields up at the school, so we went left. We followed the pathway behind the Schaefer's house, which took us deeper into the woods but closer to the Palermo's. The ability to see the street and homes on Fieldstone dimmed with each step we took, as the trail ran away from the neighborhood and closer to Buckman's Pond. After another fifty steps or so, we stopped and crouched down to see where we were in relation to the Palermo's.

"Can you see anything?" I whispered to Mario. "Not sure," he answered. "Wait here," I directed, as I crept forward into the brush. Although the tree limbs and brush continued to obstruct my view, I could make out the distinctive red, brick tone of the siding on the Palermo's home. I knew that we were in the right vicinity.

I backpedaled ten feet or so to return where I had left Mario. "Okay, we're right behind the Palermo's now," I told him. "Let's look around here and see if we can spot anything," I suggested.

"What are we looking for?" Mario then asked. "Not sure. Just any signs that they were in here somewhere," I shot back.

So, we began to slowly survey the area. The underbrush off the pathway in this area was fairly thick, but, as we plodded ahead on the trail, we came to a small clearing. There was a distinct change in the wooded area off to the right of the path where elm and oak trees had been replaced with an area of tall, bamboo-like ratans.

It's funny, I had been all through these woods more than a hundred times, but I had never noticed this thicket of odd plants. "Have you ever seen this before?" I asked Mario, pointing to the bamboo plants. "No, I've never noticed this before. It's weird," he answered.

These bamboo, reed-like saplings were everywhere and had

overtaken the surrounding region of the woods. The stalks were completely out of place. It was a type of plant that, until now, I would have only expected to possibly find in a jungle or somewhere tropical. But definitely somewhere other than here.

We headed a bit further down the path and came to a stretch that had obviously been trampled over. The bamboo plants, bent in half, were a clear sign that someone had been here recently. We took a quick glance at each other and then cautiously stepped off the path and stepped into the thicker brush. After only a few steps, the area opened into a clear set of pathways that led deeper into the bamboo. A system of trails had been carved into the wicker plants, creating a maze of routes in and around the wooded area.

"How did they do this?" Mario asked. "It's just bamboo. They must have used a baseball bat or hockey stick to chop at it," I reasoned.

We followed what seemed to be the primary pathway as it led us further away from the Palermo's and Fieldstone Drive and closer to the pond. After another thirty feet or so, the wooded area opened up further into a clearing that housed a small fort-like structure. "What the hell is that?" I asked. "Looks like a fort," Mario answered.

The expanse of the cleared area was impressive and had all its bamboo folded over on top of itself, kind of like one of those crop circle things you saw on TV. The fort, which sat in the middle of the cleared area, had been constructed and assembled with the wooden pallets that I had seen the three punks carrying a few weeks earlier. We approached the front of the structure slowly and cautiously.

"Do you think anyone's in there?" Mario asked with a concerned voice. "I don't know. Probably not, it's too early," I answered.

The fort was probably eight feet by ten feet and was constructed by using the pallets for both its flooring and walls. They had hammered pieces of plywood to the pallets to entirely close-in the structure, except for the door which was made from a repurposed screen door panel. It was super cool and, if I wasn't so pissed off, I would have appreciated the ingenuity that went into it.

We surveyed the area, making sure that no one was in the fort or in the vicinity. When I was sure that the coast was clear, I gave Mario the all-clear sign and we snooped our way up to the front of the fort and pulled the door open.

"I'll go in first. You keep an eye out here," I told him. He nodded yes, as I knelt down and peered inside. It was vacant, of people anyway. I took a deep breath and scooched inside the structure. I immediately realized that they had swiped Mom and Dad's spare carpeting, left over from last year's family room project, to line the floor. Although the lighting wasn't great, they had cut linear slots into three of the four walls which let in a fair amount of light.

I crept further inside and found a couple more Hood milk crates, that had obviously been pilfered from the back of Friendly's, serving as coffee tables. Even more notable and impressive, they had three repurposed car seats serving as recliners that I could only assume had also come from Mr. Ferraro's scrap yard. Though, without question, the most noteworthy item, or in this case items, was the massive stack of Playboy magazines.

"Holy shit," I said aloud. The place was littered with them! It was the motherload of stockpiles. They must have had a full decade's worth of issues. It was like I had entered some kind of Playboy Fort Knox!

Although my first instinct was to grab a seat and peruse through a few magazines, I knew I had to get out of there quickly. I slid deeper inside and found an old, beat-up, green metal Coleman cooler sitting in the corner. I took a quick look over my shoulder to ensure that Mario was still on the lookout. Once satisfied that we were still alone, I opened the lid of the cooler. JACKPOT!

I immediately recognized the plastic bag that we had brought to the Coyne's a day earlier. I lifted the bag out of the container and looked inside, "Yes!" I exclaimed out loud. "Yes! Fuckers," I said in a hushed voice.

"Did you say something? What is it?" Mario asked from the doorway. "I've got it," I answered. Mario crept into the fort to see what I had found. "You got it?" he asked excitedly. "Yes. All of it," I answered.

Just then, Mario noticed the stack of Playboys. "Holy shit! What is this?" he asked. I whipped around and hastily slid back towards the door. "It's their stash of Playboys," I replied. As I slipped past the stockpile, I grabbed a magazine for our troubles, and slipped it into the bag with the fireworks. "Let's go, let's get out of here," I directed. "You gonna take that?" he asked. "Yeah, why not? They took something of ours, so seems right," I answered. We both turned towards the door and hastily exited the Playboy fortress.

We decided to take an even longer route home, to avoid any chance of being spotted with the plastic bag in tow. We made our way out of the bamboo maze and turned onto the trail that led back towards the Oliveri's back yard. When we hit the fork in the path, I made a quick detour off the trail and took a few steps into the underbrush.

"Where are you going?" Mario asked. "We need to hide the Playboy out here. And look," I said, pointing into the underbrush. "That old piece of metal. We can use that," I continued.

I rushed forward to the old piece of scrap metal that was on the ground lying at the foot of a tree. I pulled the Playboy out of the plastic bag and stashed it under the piece of rusted metal. I quickly surveyed the area and spotted a small boulder, "Mario, can you grab me that rock over there", I said pointing to the stone. He picked it up and brought it to me. I took it from him and laid it on top of the scrap metal, in hopes of protecting the magazine from the elements.

"Do you think that will work?" he asked. "It's better than nothing," I said, as I repositioned the stone, so it set squarely on the rusted metal.

We then hustled back to the trail and turned left towards the fields at the high school. Once we reached the school grounds, we walked along the fence line, staying just off the school property, and kept on the path until we reached the far side of the Collazo's back yard. We decided to cross from there and make our way through the Collazo's yard and onto Fieldstone.

This was now the most dangerous part of the journey, as we would have to cross in front of the Ferraro's house to get back to my house and the safety of my garage. We slowly emerged from behind some shrubs that outlined an electrical box in front of the Collazo's and took a good look around. It was still pretty early, probably not even 9:30 a.m., so there was very little going on.

I could see Herb Schaefer on his riding mower making passes on his lawn. Other than that, there was no one in sight. So, we decided to walk casually back to my house, keeping the plastic bag in my right hand, in an effort to obstruct anyone's view from the Ferraro's home. The distance we had to travel couldn't have been more than sixty or seventy yards, but it seemed to take forever.

I scanned to my left to see if we had caught anyone's attention at the Ferraro's … nothing. I looked further to my left to see if there was anyone in front of my house or inside the garage … clear. Lastly, I gazed forward and to my right at the Palermo's house to see if there were any signs of life … nothing again! We got to my driveway and thought it was now safe to take off into the garage.

We sprinted inside and immediately scrambled to find a hiding place. "What are you going to do with them?" Mario asked. "We need to find a good hiding place. Some place that Bobby won't think to look and somewhere that no one will just stumble across them," I said.

I deliberated over it for a second and then it came to me. I rushed from the garage and into the basement. Once inside, I made sure no one was in the room and then, after confirming that I was alone, I flung the door open to Nano's wine cellar. I quickly dropped to my knees and pulled out some large pans from under the shelving that held his barrels of wine off the basement floor.

"In here? Do you think that's a good idea?" Mario questioned me. "Yeah, Nano is only in here to refill bottles. He doesn't touch the rest of this stuff until the fall," I responded.

Nano only used these particular pans to process his wine, but since that was a once-a-year endeavor, this would be a perfect hiding spot for our stash. I pushed the plastic bag deep under the shelving, making sure it was directly under one of his giant oak barrels, so that no one could see it, and then pushed the pans back under the shelving and in front of the bag.

"Can you see anything?" I asked Mario. "No, that's good,"

he answered. We were still in a bit of shock that we were able to find and recover our fireworks. We were pumped! "Let's get out of here and let Dave and Johnny know," I said excitedly.

We closed the door to Nano's wine cellar and sped out of the basement to let the guys know that they were ours again.

Mario and I rushed into the back yard, looking for Dave and Johnny. We found them sitting at the picnic table on the upper patio, eating breakfast.

"Hey, guess what?" I asked them. "What?" Dave replied. I looked around to make sure no one else was in the back yard,

"We just found them and got them back!" I exclaimed. "No way!" Dave responded. "Yep, Mario and I just brought them back," I continued. "Where'd you find them?" Dave wanted to know. "Those guys have a fort in the woods behind the Palermo's. They had them hidden there, I answered. "Yeah, and that's not all that they have hidden there," Mario offered. "Oh yeah, what else?" Dave asked.

Mario and I took a quick look at one another and smiled. "They have a shitload of Playboys," I reported. Dave and Johnny perked up with this news. "Yeah, like a Guinness Book of Records number of Playboys," I added.

We all chuckled at this thought. "Anyway, we swiped one and hid it somewhere in the woods. We can check it out later; a while after they find out that the fireworks are missing and the shit hits the fan," I reasoned.

This seemed like a good plan to all. With that, Mario and I grabbed a seat, pleased with our morning's work, and decided to have some breakfast.

XX - Il Viaggio al Mare
(The Trip to the Sea)

After eating breakfast outside, Mario headed home with Johnny, so that he could finally get to mowing his lawn. I headed inside and joined Pam and Steve in the family room. They were playing the board game "Sorry," as they were sprawled out on the carpet floor.

I switched on the TV and turned the dial to see what was on. It was Saturday morning, so there were plenty of cartoons on the tube. As I flipped channels, I came across the Wimbledon Tennis Championships and decided to check it out. I was shocked to learn, and thought it was pretty cool, that they actually played tennis on grass. I never knew that was a thing and it definitely caught my attention. I was also surprised to see a guy, who looked a lot like what I had thought Jesus looked like, was winning the tournament.

My "alone" time, however, was short-lived as Dad walked in less than five minutes later and whistled to get my attention. I immediately and instinctively swung my head around to answer his call.

"You ready, buddy?" he asked. "Yep, I'm ready," I answered. "Okay, head down to the basement and help your brother and grandfather load a few things into the back of the wagon," he said. With that, I got up from the couch, turned off the TV and headed for the basement.

When I got to the basement, Dave had already loaded just about everything we needed into the back of the car. We had two good-sized coolers, a crabbing net, and a few Hefty trash bags. Dave and I climbed into the far-back of the station wagon and Dad closed the door behind us. He and Nano took their seats in the front row, while Uncle Phillip plopped down in the back seat.

Uncle Phillip then turned to me and Dave and asked, "You boys ready for our trip to Nahant?" We answered, "Yes," together. "You know, your grandfather really got his start in this country in Nahant," Uncle Phillip informed us. "Really, he did?" I asked. "That's right. He didn't tell you?" Uncle Phillip questioned. "No, I don't think so. I don't remember him telling us," I replied. "Of course, I told you! But you don't listen. That's the problem!" Nano shouted from the front seat.

"Mike! What are you doing? We're talking about it now. Now's your chance to tell them everything. They're listening," Uncle Phillip shot back.

"They don't want to know. They just want to sit and watch the television," Nano responded, softening his tone. "Fine, I'll tell them then," Uncle Phillip answered, as Dad pulled out of the driveway, and we got on our way.

"You see boys when your grandfather first came to this country it was a different time. He didn't come here because he wanted to. He did because he needed to, to help our family. Anyway, he came to the U.S. in a way that was considered illegal, which really just means without permission.

So, if you came here without permission, it was hard to find work or even a place to stay, somewhere to live. So, you needed to rely on friends or family who were already here, people who lived here with the approval or permission of the Government. And your grandfather was lucky enough to have distant relatives here, in the Boston area, right in Nahant where we're going now.

You see, we had a cousin living here in Nahant and he and his whole family were willing to help him. Ray, who we're going to see today, is one of those cousins. And Ray's whole family gave your grandfather a place to live and somewhere to work and a way to make a living by fishing on his boat. And, then your grandfather would send some of that money home to the rest of our family, still in Italy.

"And, you know what happened?" Uncle Phillip then asked us. "No, what?" I asked, my interest now piqued.

"After a couple years, the Government announced a program that allowed people, like your grandfather, who came here without permission to come into the country legally, in the eyes of the Government, and, in the end, even become a US citizen. Just like your grandfather did," Uncle Phillip finished.

"Yeah, after he spent six months in Canada first," Dad chimed in. "What!?" I asked, surprised by Dad's statement. "That's right, he had to spend six months in Canada," Dad responded.

Uncle Phillip chuckled quickly, "That's right. I almost forgot about that," he added. "Well, I didn't forget. I was there for a full winter. So cold! And the snow!" Nano jumped in. Uncle Phillip turned to me and Dave and, with a smile on his face, said, "He hates the cold."

"I can't believe you were in Canada," I said to Nano. "Why Canada?" I asked. "Canada and the US had a treaty in place. Which meant, to come into the country legally, or with the Government's permission, he needed to cross the border from Canada," Dad answered the question.

"So, you see, this is sort of a homecoming today for your grandfather. Back to where it all started for him, and also how he would meet your grandmother just a couple years later," Uncle Phillip added.

"Wow, that's kind of cool, Nano," I said. "You see Mike, they listened. And now they know," Uncle Phillip asserted. "We'll see. We'll see, if they remember," Nano responded.

I had been to Nahant before, usually once or twice a summer when Mom and Dad would take us to the beach. We would actually go to Short Beach, which was a little more private, and also known to many as Coast Guard Beach.

The ride to Nahant took about thirty minutes. Unfortunately, there wasn't a very direct route to Nahant, not from Stoneham anyway. So, Dad navigated the back roads through Wakefield, Saugus and Lynn to get to Nahant. Dad was sort of a guru when it came to directions and specifically the less traveled roads.

There were very few towns or cities in Massachusetts where Dad wasn't familiar with the local roadways. He not only knew how to get from points A to B, but could also cite the street names and local landmarks of any otherwise obscure area in the Commonwealth. It was a real, and unparalleled, talent of his.

We made our way through some sketchy areas of Lynn and drove through what looked like the downtown area. As we drove away from the City's Center, we crossed a causeway and entered a more open, airy space. It was kind of odd how fast the scenery changed from a well-defined urban zone to more of a beach and marina sort of landscape.

We approached a very large rotary, as the ocean came into view through the windshield of the Vista Cruiser. I could see the large parking lot and long retaining wall ahead of us, which lined the full expanse of Lynn Beach. Out the right side of the car, you could see a marina with some waterfront restaurants that bordered Lynn Harbor.

We pulled into the big roundabout and quickly turned right onto the long boulevard that led straight to Nahant. You could see the clear signs of Lynn's industrial area to our right, across the large body of water that led to Broad Sound. Out the immediate left side of the car, a series of cement barriers served as a median and separated the traffic from in and out of Nahant. And further beyond that, was the long stretch of Lynn Beach and the open ocean.

It was a really hot day. It was still before noon, but it was already hot. The kind of hot where you could see the heat coming off the pavement in front of you. And the boulevard was a long, straight stretch of road and the waves of heat were lifting off the pavement as far as you could see. At the end of the boulevard, there was another, yet far smaller, turnaround that allowed those traveling in the left lane to reverse direction and those driving in the right lane to continue straight and enter the town of Nahant, on what now became a single-laned road.

XXI - Vista della Costiera
(Coastal View)

Once in Nahant, the area we were driving through became more familiar to me. As we drove, I immediately recognized the chalk-white, wooden building, which was the Coast Guard Station, that was located on the edge of Short Beach. The large structure had a distinctive tower, which resembled a church steeple, and gave the building a unique look and character.

We drove past Short Beach and crossed into what, I guess, was Nahant proper. We stayed on Nahant Road, which was one of the few primary roads in Town. As we wound our way through the many turns of the road, the area became more residential, and the street narrowed considerably. Dad made a turn onto what looked like a private road and slowed the car as he pointed towards the passenger side window,

"There … behind these homes. You can actually see the Boston skyline," he said. We all peered out the windows, trying to get a glimpse of the city through the back yards of the waterfront homes on our right.

"Where are we?" I asked. "We're as far as we can go on Nahant," Dad answered. "We're a little early to meet Ray, so I thought we'd make a quick stop and take you to see Baileys Hill," he continued. We then approached a sharp turn in the road and Dad pulled to the side, parking the car on a narrow strip of grass on the side of the road.

"Okay, we're here. Let's get out and have a look," Dad said. Dave and I climbed over the back seat and followed Uncle Phillip out of the car. "What is this place?" Dave asked. "This is Baileys Hill. It's a park and historical area," Dad answered. "Bobby, I haven't been here in years," Uncle Phillip added, with an approving smile on his face. "Let's head up the path and check it out," Dad suggested.

We started our way on the trail and walked up the large hill jutting from the landscape. Although it appeared pretty steep, the hill had a well-defined footpath that was easy to walk. Within a few minutes, we hit the summit of the hill where an incredible view came into focus.

It was amazing, just awesome! It was a bright, clear day and we could see for miles. The vastness and expanse of the ocean was simply massive. To our right, and off in the distance, we could see Boston Harbor and the city's skyline on the horizon. The five of us stood there for a moment and took in the view, and then Dad explained what we were looking at.

"So, off to the right is the city, the harbor and waterfront area and right behind that is Boston's downtown and financial district, where you see all those skyscrapers," he said, as he pointed to his right. "And that area extending out just in front of the city, that's Winthrop. And behind it, is Logan Airport … look, right there," he said, again pointing to his right. "Here comes a plane now, coming in for a landing. Do you see it, you two?" he asked me and Dave. "Yeah, I see. That's wicked cool," I answered.

We all took in the view for another moment, and watched the large, rolling waves approach the cliff's rocky edge. "What's that over there?" I asked, as I pointed to a huge cement bunker-like structure that was built into the side of the cliff. "That's a concrete military battery. It was used to house two large artillery guns during World War II," Dad answered. "What for?" I followed. "Because this area, all of Nahant really, with the height of the hills and its location to Boston, was the perfect place to defend Boston Harbor," Dad replied.

"Can you believe that boys? When your father was just about your age, we had to put these big guns here into the hill to defend the city, in case the Germans attacked. Can you believe what it was like to grow up back then?" Uncle Phillip asked us. "No, that's crazy," I answered.

I took another look at the huge encasement built into the hillside and wondered what it must have been like to need these massive guns in this small town. As I contemplated that question, I noticed Nano still staring off into the distance.

"Hey Nano, where did you live when you were here in Nahant?" I asked. "I lived way over there," he answered, pointing to his left. "You can't see it from here, but it's the section we first passed when we entered Nahant. It's actually called Little Nahant," he replied. "You know, I still think this area reminds me of back home in Gaeta," Uncle Phillip asserted. "Don't you think, Mike?"

Nano didn't respond but took another look around. "What do you say, Michele?" he asked. Nano paused for a few seconds. "Yes, the seashore. But no, not the water. The water off of Gaeta is much more blue. Here, it's dark and gray," he answered, as he took one more glance at the view from Baileys Hill.

XXII - Il Gigante del Mare
(Giant of the Sea)

Once down the hill and back to street level, we piled into the station wagon. "Let's get over to Town Wharf and meet up with Ray. He should be back in by now," Dad said. We drove through Nahant's small neighborhood roads, weaving in and around a handful of one-way streets, until the road opened up again to a beachfront area, separated by a retaining wall. We turned onto Willow Road and traveled a stretch.

The rocky shoreline and calm waters bordered the roadway as we traveled alongside the seashore. "This is Tudor Beach. And the water further out there is Dorothy Cove and Nahant Harbor," Dad relayed to us, as he pointed towards the water. "Where are we going now, Dad?" Dave asked. "Just a bit further," he answered.

We drove another minute or two and then turned right, onto Wharf Street. As we made the turn, we could see many boats, buoys, and vacant moorings just offshore to our right. The street, still lined with homes on our left, approached a small marina in front of us, which was complete with a ramp and a landing used to launch boats from the roadway. At the street's end, the road emptied into another parking area with a large wooden wharf extending out into the water from the rear of the parking lot.

On top of the wharf was an old, weathered wood building that looked like it had stood there since the beginning of time. And at the far end of the wharf, a couple of wooden ladder

                                    Forza!

staircases extended down from the pier to a dock, where a few commercial fishing boats were tied up nearby. Dad drove to the far lot, closest to the wharf, and parked the car in a spot facing the landing.

"Let's go find Ray", Dad said as he put the car in park. "Whoa, this place is cool," Dave said, as we all scrambled out of the car. "Yeah, it's a beautiful spot, for sure," Dad agreed.

As Uncle Phillip held the back door open for me and Dave to climb from the rear of the station wagon, he took a deep breath and added, "Can you smell that? That's beautiful, fresh, sea air. Can you boys smell that?"

Dave and I took a quick second to take a deep breath, just as our uncle had. "Yes," we both agreed. "There's nothing like it," Uncle Phillip continued. "It's the best part about living near the ocean," Nano chimed in, agreeing with his younger brother. "Let's head inside, Ray's probably there already," Dad said.

We walked from the car and headed to the old wooden structure sitting on the wharf. A couple seagulls, perched atop wharf posts, were surveying the marina for their next meal, suddenly took flight and screeched loudly as they flew away, seemingly disturbed by our approaching footsteps. It was an incredibly picturesque view, like straight from a movie scene, I thought to myself.

Dave and I asked Dad if we could wait outside, as the adults went into the wharf building to check on things. He took no issue with that, as long as "we stayed out of trouble". So, Dave and I stayed outside on the wharf and watched the waves crash up against an outcropping of large rocks that outlined the open-water side of the wharf.

Beyond the ledge that was jutting out from the ocean, floated an array of watercraft that were tied up to moorings about a hundred yards offshore. Dave and I took turns trying to throw small rocks just beyond the rock shelf that protected the pier from the otherwise unabated waves. We raised the stakes, double or nothing, on the imaginary bets that we wagered with each other to see who could throw a rock the furthest.

Just as I set a new mark in our competition, we caught a glimpse of an old, wooden lobster boat steaming towards us and the wharf. The boat was moving at a good clip, and you could tell that whoever was steering the vessel had great familiarity with the waterway approaching the wharf. Just then, I noticed Dad, Nano, and Uncle Phillip appear from the back of the wharf. They then cautiously walked down the ladders that extended from the wharf's edge to the dock, which rested about a foot or two above water level. It became clear, at that point, that they were headed to meet their cousin Ray, who must be on the lobster boat that was fast approaching the wharf.

The lobster boat edged up slowly to the dock, just as Dad, Nano, and Uncle Phillip arrived to greet it. Dave and I hustled up the pier and towards the staircase that led to the dock. This caught Dad's eye and he quickly turned and gave us the halt sign, so we waited and watched from the wharf. I could see Nano and Uncle Phillip waving eagerly, as a rope was tossed from the boat and straight into Dad's hands. Dad pulled the rope in tight and then wrapped it around a dock cleat.

I saw a figure at the back of the boat that leaned over and did the same, fully securing the boat to the dock. Just then another figure emerged from the cabin and stepped over the boat's rail and onto the dock. It was a giant of a man, wearing an old ball cap and dressed in full fishing bibs and complete with a pair of rubber boots.

This hulking figure made a direct line to Nano and Uncle Phillip and wrapped his huge wingspan around both of them. This must be Ray, who, until now, I had pictured as a similarly sized man, somewhere between five foot and five and a half feet tall. But, as it turned out, Ray was at least a foot or more taller than both of them and, from a distance, they looked like two kids greeting their father at the dock after a long day of fishing.

"That guy's huge!" Dave offered. "Yeah, I know. Nothing like I pictured," I replied. I then watched Ray put his arm around my dad and pull him in for a hug. Nano and Uncle Phillip looked on, smiles all around. And then the four men turned and started towards the staircase, heading right for me and Dave.

We met Dad and the crew at the top of the staircase leading from the dock below. Dad immediately introduced us to the lobster boat captain. "Boys, I want you to meet a special relative and friend of the family, and an especially close relative to Nano and

Uncle Phillip. This is Ray Palumbo," Dad said, as he pointed to the enormous lobsterman.

"Uncle Ray," the captain insisted, as he extended his huge hand looking for a handshake in return. I reached out with my right hand and saw it disappear into the goliath's palm, as he grasped and shook it gently. "That's a good grip you have," he said. I knew this was a nice, but empty, compliment as I simply couldn't get a grip on any part of his massive hand.

"You're huge!" Dave chimed in, without much couth. Ray laughed out loud, a booming laugh that matched his size, "Yeah, I've heard that before," Ray responded. Ray then reached out and shook Dave's hand, just as he had mine. Dave's hand was completely enveloped by Ray's.

"So, what have your grandfather and uncle told you two about me?" Ray asked. "Just that you are cousins. And, that Nano had lived with you a long time ago," I answered. Ray put one of his hands on Dave's back and the other on mine and steered us forward towards a door leading into the wharf building.

"That's all true. We're actually third cousins, I believe. And they've been very good friends back to me," Ray added, as the six of us head into the old, wooden boathouse.

Once inside, Dad and Ray stepped aside to talk alone in a small room. The rest of us waited in the open area as a couple of workers carried in a large, grey container with rope handles from each end. They placed the bulky vessel down on the floor, near where we were standing. Just then, Dad and Ray returned from the office and approached the four of us. Ray was holding a tray in his hand with a small basket on top,

"You know, I was up on Cape Cod Bay early this morning and picked these up for you all," Ray said, as he extended his arm holding the tray out for all of us to see. "Quahogs!" Uncle Phillip exclaimed.

The basket on the tray that Ray was holding held a handful of large clams. Beside the basket, a small bottle of lemon juice rested on its side and a wooden handled knife with a flattish blade sat next to it.

"You get these this morning, Ray? Uncle Phillip asked. "Yep, just this morning. I have a friend who clams right near some traps I keep up there and I bartered with him this morning," Ray answered.

Ray then took one of the clams in his huge hand, grabbed the short knife and, in one motion and a flick of his wrist, popped the top part of the shell off the clam. The clam, now exposed, was large, yellowish and jelly-like.

"Who wants the first one?" Ray asked. "I'll take it, Uncle Phillip replied. "Do you want some lemon juice, Phil?" Ray asked, as he held the small bottle in his hand. "No, I like it just like this," Uncle Phillip responded. Ray shook his head, approvingly. "Mike, how about you?", Ray then asked Nano. "Sure, I'll have one too," Nano replied.

Just then, Uncle Phillip raised the large half-shell clam to his mouth and, with one giant slurp, sucked the entire clam into his mouth and pretty much swallowed it whole. This was quickly followed by an even louder slurping noise to my right, which had come from Nano as he glugged down his clam. This was actually a pretty horrifying sight. I wasn't sure what was worse, the sound, the sight, or the thought of them eating the slimy raw clams right out of the shell.

Dad and Ray then joined in, at least using the lemon juice as a condiment of sorts and downed a clam each. Ray happily shucked a couple more clams for Nano and Uncle Phillip, who repeated their noisy feeding frenzy. Ray then took a look at me and Dave and asked, "You boys want to try one?" "No, that's all right," I answered. "Looks disgusting!" Dave added. Ray just chuckled softly and took a glance over at Dad, almost suggesting that he had somehow failed in raising us properly.

"They don't know what they're missing," Uncle Phillip chimed in. "Well, are you boys ready to take a look at the lobsters?" Ray then asked, with a big grin on his face. "They're in here?" Dave asked. "They sure are," Ray replied.

Ray then bent over and lifted the lid to the plastic crate, "Forty lobsters, all two pounds or more," he said, proudly. Ray then reached over and pulled a lobster from the top of the pile, waiving it slowly at eye level in front of Dave and me.

"You ever seen one of these, still alive, up close?" he asked us. Dave and I took a good look at the lobster, which still looked pretty big, even in Ray's mammoth hand. "No. But we've seen crabs up real close," I answered. "Crabs? Probably on the Cape, huh?" he asked, in return. Dave and I shook our heads indicating, yes.

"Bet those crabs didn't have claws on'em like this," he asserted, giving another wave of the crustacean in front of us. "Nope. But we did see one bite Uncle Phillip's finger pretty good last year," I said. This was met with instant laughter, Ray's roaring laugh being the loudest.

"I think I heard about that story", Ray said, as he looked over to Uncle Phillip. "Michael, we keep those stories for the family only," Uncle Phillip chimed in. "What? Phil, you trying to hurt me? If anyone is part of your family, it's me!",Ray exclaimed. Uncle Phillip shrugged his shoulders and then nodded in agreement. "You're right, Ray. You're right. You are family," Uncle Phillip conceded.

"So, are we going to see you tomorrow, Ray?" Dad asked. "Yes, I'll be there. I'm looking forward to it! Mike, will you have your wine ready for me?" Ray responded. "Yes, of course, of course," Nano answered. I really hadn't heard many requests for Nano's wine, but there's always a first.

"Now Bobby, remember to keep these cold, right up until you're ready to cook them. I've lined each layer with seaweed, this should help keep them fresh. And right before you cook them, pull the elastic bands from their claws. I'll give you two pairs of our pliers to help, but be careful when you do," Ray instructed, as he handed Dad two pair of what looked to be special pliers. "Got it. And thanks again, Ray. This is great and really appreciated," Dad responded. "Happy to. Now, let me get my guys to help you carry this out," Ray finished.

Ray stepped away for a quick moment and returned with the two workers who had brought the crate to us earlier, "My two guys here will carry this out to your car for you. See you tomorrow," Ray said. "See you tomorrow, Uncle Ray", I said. I got one last tap on my back from Ray, and we headed out for the car with our lobsters in tow.

XXIII - Quaranta Passi
(Forty Steps)

"One more quick stop before we head home," Dad stated, as we got back into the car. With the large container of lobsters in the back of the wagon, along with the empty coolers that we brought, Dave and I were now sitting in the back seat with Uncle Phillip.

"Where are we going now, Dad?" Dave asked. "Just down the street a bit. We're going to make a quick pit stop at a small beach that I know," Dad answered. This seemed a bit odd to me, as we had just loaded the lobsters into the back of the car, but I didn't question it further. We must have driven less than a mile in total before we reached our destination.

Dad pulled into a small parking lot that overlooked a remote cove with a secluded, rocky beach below. "Okay, this is Forty Steps Beach. Anybody have a guess why it's called Forty Steps Beach?" Dad asked. "Is it because it only takes forty steps to get from one end to the other?" I offered. "Close, but that's not it. Any guess, David?" Dad continued. "No, I can't think of any-thing," Dave responded.

"Okay, I'll tell you then. You see that staircase behind us and to the left?" Dad asked, as we all turned our heads to find the stairway that he was pointing out. "Well, that's the only way down to the beach. And guess how many steps there are in the staircase," Dad continued. "Forty!" I answered, enthusiastically.

"You got it," Dad said, pointing at me.

"That's a lot better guess than only forty steps from one end of the beach to the other, Michael. It would have to be three or four hundred steps, I bet, to get from one end to the other," Uncle Phillip added, with a smile. "Well, it looks small from here, I reasoned. "That's because we're up high," Dad replied.

Dave and I climbed out of the car and met Dad at the back of the Vista Cruiser. "What are we going to do here?",I asked. "You'll see," Dad quickly answered.

Dad then opened the tailgate of the wagon and pulled out the two coolers that we had brought from home. He quickly lined both coolers with the large trash bags that we had brought with us. Just then, Uncle Phillip and Nano met us at the rear of the car.

"Bobby, your father, and I will wait for you up here. Too many steps and, this way, we'll keep an eye on the lobsters," Uncle Phillip announced. "That's fine, Uncle Phillip. Let's go, boys. I'll carry this one, you two can carry that one together. Just go slow and be careful on the steps," Dad instructed us, as he grabbed hold of the larger Coleman cooler and the crabbing net, before heading to the staircase.

Dave and I each grabbed hold of a handle on the ends of the cooler and lifted it away from the car's tailgate and followed Dad to the forty-step staircase. Dave and I lagged well behind Dad, as we made our way down the steep staircase. Dad shouted out to us, once or twice, reminding us to be careful. Once we got down to water level, we could see that the beach was entirely vacant, other than the three of us.

There was little to no sand on this beach, but was rather lined with thousands, maybe millions, of small, rounded stones that had been smoothened over, undoubtedly by the ocean water rushing over it all. Interwoven with the smooth stones, were what looked to be an equal number of empty seashells of various sizes and colors.

Dave and I lugged the cooler over to where Dad was standing, at the very edge of the water. There were tiny, rolling waves slowly unfolding onto the beach, limited by the rocky shoreline that protected the cove from the open water. Dave and I plopped the cooler down beside Dad, who was now untying his off-white

Converse sneakers, as he sat on the cooler that he had carried down to the beach.

"What are you doing, Dad?" I asked. "I'm getting ready to get what we came here for, boys. Now, do like I'm doing, take off your shoes and socks," Dad instructed us.

Dave and I sat and shared an edge of the cooler that we had hauled to the beach together. We quickly shed our shoes and socks and were ready for our next instructions.

"Okay, we're here to grab some fresh seaweed. We're going to need it for the clambake tomorrow. So, I want you guys to help me gather some right at the water's edge and we'll put it into the coolers that we brought with us. You guys can use the crabbing net to gather it up. "Now, spread out a bit and let's get some fresh seaweed," Dad said, cluing us into his plan.

"Seaweed!? We're going to eat seaweed?" Dave asked. "No, not to eat. But it will help with steaming all the food in the clambake pit and give everything that fresh smell and taste from the ocean," Dad answered.

With that, Dad waded straight in, with the water getting to about halfway between his calves and knees. Dave and I quickly followed and took a couple steps into the water. "Whoa! This is wicked cold!",I shouted. Dad chuckled a bit and said, "Yeah, not warm like the water from the Sound that you guys' swim in, on the Cape. This is the open ocean," Dad explained. "So, cold!" I complained.

"Come on! The faster you get in and get this done with me, the faster it'll be over, and we can head home to the warm pool water in your back yard," Dad teased.

We started to gather clops of seaweed, using the crab net. The seaweed here wasn't like what we were used to seeing on the Cape. This was thicker and a darker green. There were large clumps of it, with long, snake-like tentacles that made it look like the plant was alive underwater. I could see small, bubble-like pods that were mixed in with the tentacles.

As we walked a few feet off the shoreline, I was struck by just how clear the water was here. I could see clear down to my toes without any murkiness clouding my view. As we gathered quantities of sea plants, we made intermittent trips to the coolers to offload our catch. After about fifteen minutes, we had gained enough seaweed to satisfy Dad. Both coolers were near to overflowing with green, and a few brown, bunches of seaweed. Dad finished the job by topping off both coolers with a bit of beach water.

"Let's get our shoes back on and get going. The cooler's going to be much heavier on the way up than it was on the way down, so you might have to take a couple rest breaks on the steps," Dad cautioned us. We got our shoes back on and began the trek back to the car. Dad wasn't kidding, the cooler now weighed as much as me and Dave, so we had to take it slow as we climbed back up the staircase.

As we struggled to make our way up the steps, I kidded Dave that I was at least glad that the beach wasn't called Eighty Steps Beach. Dave and I were pretty spent by the time we reached the top step of the staircase. Thankfully, Uncle Phillip and Nano met us there and carried the cooler the rest of the way back to the car. Once there, Dad had repositioned the lobster crate slightly, so that he could now wedge the two coolers into the back and up against the tailgate, to limit any movement and water spillage.

"How was the water?" Nano asked, with a big smile. "It was cold," I said, emphatically. Nano and Uncle Phillip got a chuckle from this. "Yeah, I bet it was," Uncle Phillip chimed in. "Let's get going. Your mother packed us all sandwiches, so we can eat as we drive home," Dad advised us. "Good, I'm starving," I said. "Me too," Dave added.

We all returned to our seats in the car and got started on the return trip home. As I sat there in the back seat, I got a sudden sense of accomplishment; that we had gotten a lot done together and saw some cool things in the process.

XXIV - Intrappolato
(Trapped)

It was super hot out by the time we got back to our house in the mid-afternoon. Nano and Uncle Phillip left the car and headed straight for the backyard. Mr. Schaefer, who had been outside of his house when we pulled into our driveway, came over to check in with us.

"How'd it go, Bob? Did you get everything?" he asked, as we got out of the car. "All good, Herb. You want to have a look?" Dad replied. "Sure, let's see what you got," Herb answered.

Dad pulled the large crate forward and opened the lid. He grabbed the first lobster in his reach and lifted it towards Herb for his review. "Wow, that's a big guy. Are they all that big?" Herb wondered. "Yes, they're all two to two and a half pounds," Dad answered. "Are you going to have one, Herb?" I asked.

Mr. Schaefer was the only adult on the street that insisted everyone address him by his first name, which we all did. "Me? No. I don't eat lobster. But Ellen is having one, I believe," he said. "Yes, I have her down for a lobster," Dad confirmed.

"You should see what Cos brought back from the market in Chelsea," Herb went on. "He had six large coolers filled with hamburgers, hot dogs and sausages. And you should see the corn. My god, it's like he had a whole field's worth of corn stacked into the back of his Cadillac. It was quite a site. We could feed an army with what he brought back," Herb stated.

"Good, we're going to need it!" Dad exclaimed. "And all the

ladies are in their kitchens baking. Ellen's been baking cakes and brownies all day. We're all going to be so fat," Herb continued, chuckling. "Going to be!? I think we're all there already," Dad replied.

As the two of them continued chatting it up, I got that odd feeling and sense that I was being watched. I looked up above our two garage doors and into the large bay window that over-looked our driveway from our family room. There, I made out a figure staring down at us. It was my brother, Bob. It was a terrifying site, like the scene in a horror film when the innocent unexpecting victims suddenly spot the haunting image of the deranged killer who was, until then, unknowingly stalking them.

Bob looked down at us, really just at me, and made a slow, deliberate motion, clenching his right fist and then pounding it into his left palm. He repeated this menacing signal a couple more times, before I leaned over and whispered to Dave, "I guess Bobby knows what we found." Dave took a quick look up at the window and then back over to me. "Yeah, looks that way. What are we going to do?" he asked. "Well, he looks pretty mad. I say we stay away from him until he cools down. Why don't we go over to see Mario and Johnny, and get away from here?" I suggested.

Before we made our escape, Dad first put us to work and had us bring the smaller cooler and gear from the beach into the basement. He then took it from there and began to stockpile the lobsters and seaweed into the basement fridge. Once we were released from our tasks, Dave and I made a quick exit for the safety of the Padovani's.

Dave and I hustled over to the Padovani's, aiming to avoid a dust-up with Bobby. We scurried down the Padovani's driveway and rushed into their backyard to find Mario and Johnny. As we opened the fence gate and stepped into their backyard, we could hear a commotion coming from their extensive garden. We paused for a second and peered toward the perfectly manicured and cultivated rows of vegetables. As we gazed to the rear of the yard, we abruptly heard loud and raucous laughter followed by excited shouting in Italian.

"Is that them?" Dave asked. "I think so. But I don't think

they're alone. Let's go check it out," I answered. We took off for the front of the garden, which was separated from the backyard lawn by a homemade picket fence. Once at the gate, I could hear Mario's voice coming from behind the garden shed, that sat at the rear of the garden. He was speaking to someone in Italian but melding his words with intermittent bursts of laughter.

"Mario. Hey, Mario!" I called out to him. I heard a few more short blurbs in Italian and then Mario appeared from behind the garden shed. "Hey," he greeted me and Dave, with a huge smile on his face. "What's going on back there?" I asked, as Johnny now also emerged from the back of the shed, sporting an equally large grin on his face. "It's my grandfather. An animal was getting at his plants, so he built and set a trap back there. And he caught it!" he declared. "He did? What is it?" I asked. "It's a woodchuck. You know, a gopher. And now he wants to eat it!" Mario said, barely getting the words out, as he couldn't help but snort as he said it.

"He wants to eat it?" Dave chimed in. "Yeah, first he wants to shoot it with his shot gun and then cook and eat it!" Johnny piped in, matching his older brother's howl. "Seriously?" I asked.

Both brothers nodded their heads, yes, and continued to cackle. Just then, the Padovani grandfather, Ray Senior, came out from behind the garden shed, holding a makeshift trap that had been constructed using an old, mesh waste barrel and some chicken wire. We could clearly see the animal enclosed in the homemade device, as the senior Padovani proudly held up his catch for all to see. He greeted us with his huge smile, a tooth or two missing, and in his very broken English.

"Michele and Davide! You see what I have? I got him, the little bastard," he exclaimed. "What is it?" I asked him. "Hedgehog!" he barked. Mario cackled out loud, "It's not a hedgehog, it's a gopher," he exclaimed. Ray Senior just shrugged this off.

"And what are you going to do with it?" I asked. "I'm going to eat him," he answered sharply. This set us all off, as the four of us erupted instantly into raucous laughter. "You can't eat it," Mario asserted. "Why not?" Ray Senior insisted. "We don't even know for sure what it is," Mario answered, still snickering.

This caused Ray Senior to take a long gaze down at the creature he had captured in his trap. After a second or two pause, he looked back up at us and declared, "No. I eat it." This produced a fresh round of laughter and amusement, even Ray Senior flashed another smile.

We continued our banter with the elder Padovani, as Mario and Johnny's dad, Ray Junior, returned home from work and joined us at the front of the garden.

"Michael and David! How are you?" he greeted us warmly. "Hi, Mr. Padovani," we answered. "What's going on here?" he then asked, glaring at his father and the contraption that he had fashioned together. His tone, and language of choice, then changed dramatically, as he questioned his father sternly in Italian.

The two exchanged words, all in Italian, with the volume rising with each interchange. The two men made demonstrative hand gestures at one another as they continued to make their sentiments known. After one last, loud point made by Ray Junior, Ray Senior placed his self-made, over-sized mouse trap on the garden pathway and walked back to and into the garden shed. Ray Junior then turned to us, and with a night and day change in his tone, restarted his conversation with us, as if none of the preceding two-minute squabble in Italian had ever happened.

"So, are you boys excited about the party tomorrow," Ray asked. "Yeah, for sure," we all answered in unison. "And Mike, what do you think?" he then turned and asked me directly.

This last look to me by Mr. Padovani, to sort of confirm what was just said, was actually a common occurrence. I don't know if it was because I was the oldest in our little social group of four, or something else, but I was pretty much thought of as the ringleader and Mr. Padovani always treated me as such. One thing I knew for sure was that Mr. Padovani was one of the nicest people I had ever met or known. He seemed to be in a perpetually good mood, notwithstanding the fiery exchange of words that had unfolded with his father over the trapped gopher just a few moments earlier.

But he looked to me for my thoughts, and I was more than happy to share them with him, "Yeah, I can't wait. The Fourth is pretty much my favorite holiday of the year. Well except for

Christmas," I answered. "Good, good. It should be a great day," he agreed. "What are you going to do with the gopher?" I asked, as the curiosity got the better of me. "Oh, him? Well, we're not going to eat it, that much I can tell you. I'll take him deep into the woods on the other side of the street and let him go. He won't bother Nonno's plants from there," he said. "Oh yeah, that makes sense," I replied. "Did he tell you that he was planning to shoot him with his shotgun first?" Mario asked his dad. Ray Junior cracked a slight smile and said, "Yeah, I heard that was part of his plan".

After Mr. Padovani left the garden with the trap, and with the gopher as his captive, Dave and I had the chance to talk alone with Mario and Johnny.

"So, the good news is that we have our fireworks back and they're safe and sound in a good hiding spot. The bad news is that Bobby already knows, or is at least pretty sure, that we found and swiped them back," I said. "How do you know that he knows?" Mario asked. "Well, when Dave and I got back from the trip to Nahant, we were unloading stuff from the back of the car and I looked up in the window and saw Bob staring down at us," I explained.

"So, how does that mean he knows we took them back?" Mario pressed. "Because, when he was looking down at us from the window, he was making this threatening gesture at us," I described. "What kind of gesture?" Mario went on. "He was pounding his fist into his fucking hand, if you need to know. Meaning, he was going to pound us once he got us alone," I reasoned. "Oh yeah, then, he knows," Mario conceded. "Yeah, he knows. Or he at least knows that they're gone and he's just assuming that it was us," I added. "So, if he's not sure, aren't we kind of in the clear?" Mario rationalized. "Not really. If he just assumes it was us, then he'll just kick our butts anyway", I answered.

It was clear to me that, even though we had reclaimed what was rightfully ours, there was no way that Bob would allow us to have or use our own fireworks, not without creating a huge problem for us, and very likely a nasty and painful problem.

"We could just keep them in our hiding spot until the end of summer, I guess. And then light them off a little before we go back to school?" I offered. "Wait the whole summer? No way," Dave replied. "Well, what's your plan?" I argued. "I don't know," Dave replied. "No, you don't. But you know it'll be my ass, and my head, that Bobby comes for first," I responded.

Dave just shrugged this off, seemingly suggesting that the risk to my ass and head was a risk worth taking. "Will he be away at all? Before the end of the summer?" Mario asked. "Away? Away where?" I shot back. "I don't know. Will he be going somewhere? Sleep over at a friend's or go to camp or something?" Mario clarified his question. "All of his friends are in this neighborhood. And when the fuck have any of us ever gone to camp?" I responded, abruptly. "I don't know. I was just saying," Mario trailed off.

"No. We need a real plan. Someway, where we get to use the fireworks, but where we also don't have to worry about Bobby," I stated concisely. "We should just all chip in and send him away somewhere on vacation," Johnny offered, jokingly. "That's actually a better idea than Mario's fucking camp idea," I exclaimed.

Mario just seemed to shrug off the grenade I tossed at him. "What if we offered to split the fireworks with Bobby. Maybe that way he'd just leave us alone. I mean, we got more than half of them for nothing anyway," Mario proposed. "Are you insane? I'm not giving Bob shit. We risked our ass to get those fireworks, then he friggin' steals them from us? No way I'm giving anything to him. Besides, I don't think he even cares about the fireworks. He only cares about keeping us from having them because that's what he does. That's his thing. He's only happy if he can be a huge dick, that's it! So, unless we give all of them to him, we're screwed," I exclaimed.

We paused here for a second, all considering the realities of the situation and trying to think of a way out of it. I looked around at the three of them, hoping to see a glimmer of some idea ready to pop. But there was nothing. It seemed hopeless. And then, it hit me. A crazy idea, but one that might give us what we wanted; the opportunity to enjoy our fireworks, while also being free from any hassle coming from Bob.

"I've got an idea," I shared. "Yeah, what is it?" Dave asked. "Well, let me ask you guys this first, how important is it that we light off the fireworks ourselves or is it okay if we're just there when they're lit?" I put to the three of them. "It doesn't matter to me," Dave replied, quickly. "Me either," Mario and Johnny both agreed.

"Okay good, then just hear me out. What if I give the fire-works to my dad? Tell him that I found them in the basement?" I suggested. "What good will that do?" Dave asked. "Think about it. If I 'turned them in' to Dad, what is he going to do with them? I'll tell you. First, he's going to assume that they're Bobby's, not ours. After all, why would I hand them over to him, if they were mine, right? So, then he has them, the day before the Fourth of July. He thinks they're Bob's, and he teaches Bobby a lesson and lights them off himself tomorrow on the Fourth. We could even suggest it, that he lights'em off tomorrow," I insisted.

"I don't know. It might work," Dave agreed, hesitantly. "It will work. It has to. Besides, it's all we got," I concluded. "Yeah, I guess so. It's worth a shot," Mario conceded. "But won't Bob just pound on you later?" Dave questioned. "I don't know, maybe. But it'll be harder for him to do it because he'll already be in Dad's doghouse. So, he's kind of screwed if he does. And I can maybe play it up with Dad when I hand over the fireworks," I reasoned.

Everybody kind of took in the plan and thought it over for a moment, "So, are we good? Is this what we're doing?" I followed. "I'm good," Dave replied. "Us too," the two Padovani's agreed. "Okay, but we all agree, right here, this is our story. And nobody says a word different, if asked … nothing. You swear?" I demanded. I took a look into each of their eyes and waited for their word in return. And, following a nod from each of them, I knew we had our plan.

XXV - Inganno
(Deception)

Dave and I got home shortly before dinner time. My goal was to stay out in the open, and away from Bob, to avoid any clashes. This meant staying close to Mom or Dad or Nano and my aunts and uncle. This seemed doable, given dinner wasn't that far off, and would allow me some time to pick a spot to put our plan into action.

We walked into the house through the front door and headed straight for the kitchen. Mom was there at the stove boiling water in her biggest pot to make enough pasta for everyone. She was battling Aunt Polly and Aunt Gray for space in and around the oven. My two great aunts were fast at work searching Mom's cabinets for certain seasonings and spices. As I stepped into the kitchen, I was immediately hit with a strong, pungent odor.

"What is that smell?" I cried. "It's the pheasant cooking. Isn't it nice?" Mom replied. The smell was overpowering and just wafted around the kitchen, like a cloud of stench hovering over and across the stove. "No. It's disgusting!" I declared. "Oh Michael, don't be so closed minded. You have to try it. It'll be delicious. There's nothing like it. Eating fresh, right from the wild. None of that store bought garbage that you people have been eating your whole lives. This is living!" Aunt Gray argued. "No thanks," I responded. "You can try it. And you might be surprised and actually like it," Mom stated.

"Did Dad come inside yet?" I asked, changing the subject. "No, he's out back with Nano and Uncle Phillip. Now, don't go too far. We'll be eating in less than twenty minutes," Mom answered. I took a quick glance around the kitchen, trying to make out any signs that Bob was in the area. I quickly determined that the coast was clear, and I made my way out the back door to find and check in with Dad.

I found Dad, Nano, and Uncle Phillip sitting on lawn chairs on what was normally our pitcher's mound for wiffle ball games in the back yard. Nano had his go-to, a fresh mint leave, in his left hand and was making an occasional wave with it under his nose. Uncle Phillip was the first to greet me.

"Michael! What did you think of our visit to Nahant today?" he asked. "I liked it. I thought it was really cool and I had fun," I said. "Good. Good. I'm glad you liked it. And that you got to meet Ray. And to learn something about where your grandfather first lived in this country," he added. "Yeah, me too," I agreed. "Did you see they're cooking the pheasant inside?" Dad then asked. "Yeah. I smelled it right away. It stinks," I said.

This got a fast chuckle from the three of them. "Yes, it has a strong smell," Nano began. "He said stinks, Mike!" Uncle Phillip interrupted, with a smile on his face. "Yes, stinks. But the taste, woo. Unbelievable!" Nano countered. "Are you going to try some, Michael?" Uncle Phillip asked. "I don't know. I haven't decided yet," I replied. "Oh, you have to! Just give it a try. You won't be sorry," Uncle Phillip encouraged.

"Is it almost ready, then?" Dad asked. "Mom said about twenty minutes," I responded. "Okay, good. I've got one thing for you to do before dinner, Michael," Dad said. "What is it?" I followed. "Just head downstairs and bring up two 7-Up bottles for dinner. The big bottles," Dad directed.

Bingo! Dad just gave me a reason, actually a task, that required me to go to the basement. Not that I couldn't have just walked down there on my own, but, now that I've been sent on an errand there, it'll be more plausible when I hatch the plan and I turn in the illicit goods.

Although I knew this would help me, I suddenly got a sinking feeling in the pit of my stomach. I didn't feel great about telling this white lie to ultimately deceive Dad and carry out this scheme. But what choice did I have!? Or did we have? We had made such huge efforts and taken enormous risks to get the fireworks in the first place. We rode our bikes to the edge of town, we took the extreme measure of swiping some of the fireworks so that we wouldn't get ripped off, we found the stash where Bobby and Marco hid them and then took the risk to swipe them back. Inside, I knew it was justified. But I still felt crappy that, in order to remove Bobby from the equation, I would have to hoodwink Dad as part of our ploy. It didn't feel great, but I was all in, and there was just no way that I was going to let Bob win.

I walked around the front of the house, through the garage and into the basement. I did a quick check, walking to the staircase leading up to the hallway upstairs, and made sure that I was alone. Once I could confirm that I was alone, I opened the make-shift door to Nano's wine cellar and quietly slipped inside. I quickly headed for the planks in the far corner that were supporting the large wooden scotch barrel. That barrel, holding Nano's latest vintage, also perfectly hid our fireworks stockpile from plain sight.

I dropped to my knees and carefully began to remove the porcelain pans that further concealed our hideaway spot. As I rushed to recover our goods, I could actually feel my breath quicken and my heartbeat accelerate. My hands were even a bit shaky, as I tried to quietly handle the ceramic pans, and I could feel the sweat building on my brow.

"This isn't even the hard part, how am I going to pull this off?" I thought to myself. I hesitated for a second or two, took a deep breath and regained my composure. I reached under the shelving and grabbed the plastic bag holding our fireworks. I took a fast glance inside the bag, doing a quick inventory in my head, and then slid the pans back into place under the shelves. I slowly slithered out of the wine cellar, after first peeking my head out the door to make sure no one had since joined me in the basement.

Once out, I looked for a credible place where I may have stumbled across 'Bob's fireworks.' I knew it would need to be someplace close to where the 7-Up bottles were kept, as I was

sent there by Dad to retrieve two bottles. I looked over to the
heap of cases and bottles of soda sitting on the basement floor and
scanned the space for a credible spot and story.

As I glanced over the area, the large cedar dresser behind
the pile of soda caught my eye. I rushed over to it and pulled
open one of the doors. It was perfect! The old bureau hadn't been
touched in years. It was largely used to store Dad's old uniforms,
hats, coats, and boots from his Army days. Seeing that it sat
directly behind the soda, where I had been sent on my errand,
it was easily plausible that Bob had stashed the fireworks here
and, in his rush, had failed to fully close the dresser door. In fact,
it was even possible that the door had failed to close entirely as
the plastic bag holding the fireworks was caught in between the
doors.

And that is what caught my attention when I was there to
get the soda, I thought to myself. This story was very believable,
and suddenly, I felt better about my chances. With that, I grabbed
two bottles of 7-Up and, with one in each hand, I wrapped the
end of the plastic bag around my right wrist and sped out for the
backyard to sell my story.

I walked into the backyard, struggling to juggle everything
in my hands. Once on the patio, I placed the soda bottles on
a small table at the foot of the deck. I took a deep breath and
looked around to see who else was in the backyard. It was still
just Dad, Nano, and Uncle Phillip, so I decided to act quickly
before anyone else might appear on the scene.

I hastily approached them, as they continued chatting together. Nano was loudly telling one of his stories when I reached the
trio, "Hey Dad, can I talk to you a second?" I asked. Dad took
a quick glance at me, his facial demeanor turning more sober.
"Okay, what is it?" he said, as he stood and took a look at the
plastic bag that I was grasping in my right hand. I took a fleeting glance at my grandfather and uncle and then back at Dad.
"Umm, can we talk over here?" I asked.

Dad walked with me a few steps away, so that we were
alone, "What is it, Michael? Is there a problem?" he asked. I began to get that feeling again, as my heart raced, I took a deep breath
and, with the plastic bag held tight in my grasp, I extended my

right hand towards him. "What's this?" he asked. I pushed my hand towards him again, "Look. I found this in the basement," I answered.

Dad took a long look into my eyes, seemingly almost peering right through me and then took a quick glance into the bag. "Where'd you find these?" he asked. "They were in the wooden dresser, right behind where we keep the soda. Part of the bag was sticking out of one of the doors, so I took a look to see what it was," I answered. "And you think these are Bobby's?" he questioned. "I don't know whose they are," I replied.

Dad took a second to let things soak in, and then gave me his instructions, "I want you to go get your brother, Bob. And I want you both to meet me in the basement." And after a brief pause, he followed, "And Michael, no funny business," he instructed me.

I immediately left for the deck stairs, heading for the back door leading into the house. Once inside, I headed straight for the family room, assuming Bobby was there controlling the late day television programming. My suspicion was confirmed, as I found Bob there, plopped on the couch in front of the TV. "Bobby, Dad wants to see us in the basement," I informed him. Bob swung his head around and stared me down. "What for?" he demanded, as he scowled at me. "I don't know. He just told me to come get you and for us to meet him in the basement," I informed him, lying through my teeth.

I could tell that Bob had some immediate doubts about the message I was delivering. He slowly rose from the couch, giving me the stink eye the whole time and made his proclamation, "Well, whatever it is, it's not going to save you from getting what's coming," he said, threateningly.

"What is that supposed to mean?" I replied, acting surprised. "You know what it means. And, you know what it's about," he continued. I suddenly felt a bit better about what was about to happen. Now, I actually couldn't wait to get downstairs, so that I could frame my older, sometimes menacing, brother.

Bobby and I walked down the stairs, single file, and into the basement. Dad was already there, standing near the mound of soda, which was located directly in front of the dresser that I had earlier claimed housed the fireworks. Dad waved us over to him,

"Come over here," he directed, sternly. Bob and I picked up our pace after hearing Dad's tone.

"Now, I don't know what's going on between you two, but it's going to stop now. I'm not going to let this constant fighting continue and ruin the holiday for all of us. Do you understand me?" he asked, rhetorically.

Bob and I nodded yes, both our shoulders slumping noticeably. Dad took a long look at both of us, measuring our body language for a true read if the message had been received. Apparently, he was satisfied enough to move on to the primary topic, "Good," he answered, following a dramatic pause. "Now Bobby, what can you tell me about this," he asked, as he raised the plastic bag, stuffed with fireworks, that he had waiting behind two bottles of Dr. Pepper.

I immediately felt a rush of heat overcome my entire body. Bob did himself no favors, by quickly swinging his head and irately peering at me. "Well, they're mine now. And I don't want to hear a single word or see any gestures from either of you. Is that clear?" Dad ordered. "But the fireworks …," Bob interjected. "I said, not a single word. And, if there's another issue from either of you, then both of you can sit in the house together tomorrow and miss the block party. So, just knock it off and let's enjoy the holiday. It only comes around every two hundred years, for Christ sakes! Now get out of here, go," Dad finished.

With that, Bob and I turned and headed back for the stairs, neither of us uttering a word. As I walked up the stairs, I thought to myself, "Jackpot." I got what basically amounts to a reprieve from Bob for at least a good week or two, I also would likely avoid any of Marco's wrath given the outcome, I also got one quality Playboy magazine stashed safely in the woods, and I had a decent chance of being around for the eventual fireworks display. Not a bad result, I reasoned with a slight grin on my face.

XXVI - Cena di Pasta e Fagiano
(Pasta and Pheasant Dinner)

I walked into the kitchen, following the exchange with Dad and Bobby in the basement, and was met with a rush of frenzied activity. Small Italian women, and men, moved in and around my average sized mother, trying to get dinner together. There was an industrial sized pot, the kind that you might find in the kitchen of a Knights of Columbus or local fire house, bubbling up a cauldron of bow tie pasta. Of course, that's what it was to me and my siblings, but, to my aunts and uncles, it was better known as Farfalle.

The pot was boiling on over-drive, occasionally spilling over onto the stovetop and landing with a distinct hissing sound. Mom kept her eye on the steaming pasta as Aunt Gray tended to an only slightly smaller pot of her famous meat sauce. Typically, any form of tomato sauce in my house was a pretty dicey situation. My mom, who was full-blooded Irish, always made a valiant effort, but her sauce typically tasted like jar sauce, and it was just missing something.

The other sauce usually found in our kitchen was made by Nano's hands and was an entirely different story. Now, you'd think, having been born in Italy, that he might know his way around the kitchen and that his sauce, in particular, would be something special. Well, it was special all right, but not in a good way. Nano had a taste for the exotic and his sauce certainly reflected that perspective.

His method was to throw almost anything that he could get his hands on, or come across, into his sauce. This might be something he picked up while shopping the Italian markets or butcher shops in the North End of Boston or just something he either grew, or even stumbled across, in our backyard. It was a frightening proposition for the unsophisticated palate of a ten-year old kid, who just wanted a bowl of macaroni, sorry … pasta, with a simple marinara sauce.

So, needless to say, I was pretty excited to see Aunt Gray on sauce detail. As I watched her do her magic at the stove, I couldn't help noticing Aunt Polly fighting off Uncle Phillip and Nano, as she scrambled to finish cooking the pheasant. Although Aunt Polly seemed to have things in order, alternating between basting the bird and stirring a sheet tray full of sliced onions, potatoes, and carrots, she was also warding off the two brothers, who seemed to think they knew how to do it best.

But this was a fight that Aunt Polly was clearly going to win and, after a few hand gestures from the pair of impatient onlookers, she successfully shooed them away. Only Aunt May stayed out of the fray, and patiently sat at the kitchen table, with her right cheek resting in her right palm, her customary idling position.

As I took this all in, Mom called over to me. "Michael, go tell your brothers and sister that we're about to eat. And go wash up," she ordered. "Okay Mom," I answered. "And you and one of your brothers, go get four folding chairs and set them up at the dining room table, please," she added.

Of course, the damn folding chairs, I thought to myself. Why couldn't we just leave them out around the table? It's not like we didn't know that we had company. They were staying with us for four "fucking" days, but nope. Putting the folding chairs away after every meal was apparently a must, and fetching the chairs each meal was a regular duty assigned to me. Thank God I wasn't trusted enough to handle the extra leaf to the dining room table, as that thing had to come out and go back in with each meal as well. But on this night, I'd deal with it, as I couldn't wait to dive into the bowtie pasta with Aunt Gray's special sauce.

It was a tight squeeze at the dining room table, but the twelve of us tucked in close, so that we could all eat at the same table. Earlier, Mom had squashed the idea of the kids eating at the "kids table" in the kitchen. That was fine by me, as I thought I could still use the air-cover, from Bob's wrath, that the full family might give me. Just to be safe, I also chose a folding chair far from where Bobby was sitting, and one that was close to Dad's seat.

The cooked pheasant had been proudly placed on a platter at the center of the table by Aunt Polly. She had already scooped the roasted vegetables into a large, ceramic bowl which sat beside the platter holding the wild bird. I felt a little squeamish looking at the pheasant, knowing that just a day earlier it was simply trying to fly over our house and probably headed for the woods just across the street. At least the overpowering odor that had filled the kitchen earlier in the day seemed to have frittered away.

As I gazed over the bird and wondered about its unlucky fate, Mom and the aunts brought the pasta and meat sauce to the table. As I leaned forward to get a good look at the sauce, no longer mourning the pheasant's loss, Uncle Phillip sat beside me. "Are you going to try the pheasant, Michael?" he asked me. I paused for a second, "Um, I don't know. I really wasn't planning on it," I said. "Come on, where's your sense of adventure?" he followed. "I don't know. I guess it's just not here with the pheasant," I responded.

Uncle Phillip chuckled and then hit me with, "I want you to try it for me. Because I know you will like it or, at a minimum, that you will be happy with yourself for trying something new. Will you do this for me?" he pressed. This was a tough one. I had no interest in trying the pheasant. It actually made me feel sick, just thinking about it. But, in the end, there was just no way that I could say no to Uncle Phillip.

I paused another second, desperately searching for a reasonable, last second excuse, but I had nothing. So, I turned to Uncle Phillip and said, "Sure. I'll try a small piece, I guess." "Atta boy, Michael. I knew you would. And I really think you're gonna like it. There's nothing like a wild bird freshly killed," he assured me. I almost puked hearing it put this way.

But I quickly got refocused onto Aunt Gray's sauce, and figured eating a small piece of pheasant would be well worth the price to pay. Mom and Aunt Gray quickly began to dish out portions of pasta and hand them down the line of the table. Nano, impatient as ever, walked over to the platter where the roasted pheasant rested and, in a single motion with his right hand, grabbed and twisted one of the drumsticks off the bird.

"Mike!" Aunt Polly shouted. "What? What?" Nano answered. "What are you an animal? For crying out loud!" she exclaimed. "I thought I've seen it all. But this is a new low. Even for you, Mike," Aunt Gray chimed in. "What are you teaching these kids? For Christ sakes!" Dad added.

Nano just shrugged it off and, with the drumstick still in his hand, walked back to his chair at the head of the table. Uncle Phillip chuckled softly and then elbowed me to my side to get my attention. As I looked over to him, he gestured with a nod of his head back toward my grandfather. "Look at him eat," he said. "He doesn't care. He doesn't give a shit. He just wants his pheasant," he said, with a huge smile on his face, as if he was proud of his brother digging in like a caveman.

"Can you try not to eat like a slob, so we can all enjoy our dinner?" Dad pleaded with Nano. The two exchanged a quick glance just as a bowl of pasta was plopped on the placemat in front of me. I wasted no time and dug right in, likely resembling Nano in some small way, as I attacked the bowtie pasta in front of me.

"Don't you want some parmesan cheese, maybe a piece of bread with your pasta?" Uncle Phillip asked me. "Okay, sure. I'll have both, please," I answered. "Well, if you like cheese, Michael, get ready for this. Aunt Polly and I made a special trip to Boston to pick this up. This is 'Parmigiano Reggiano,' the best parmesan cheese in the world," Uncle Phillip insisted. "Really?" I asked. "Absolutely. There's nothing like it. This is the King of Cheeses," Uncle Phillip added.

"What makes it so special?" I followed. "Well, you see, it's made from cow's milk from a couple of very special provinces in Italy. And the cows are only fed certain kinds of grasses and hay, which makes for a better, more pure cheese. And when the cheese is made, it's aged at least twelve months. Can you believe that? A whole year, at least, before it is ready to be eaten. You know, they've been making this cheese, almost using the same process, for close to a thousand years," he exclaimed. "Really, a thousand years?" I asked. "That's right. It's very special. And you know what? It goes great with your Aunt Gray's sauce. Here, let me grate some for you on your pasta," he offered.

With that, Uncle Phillip pulled my bowl of Farfalle closer to him and began to slowly grate the cheese onto my pasta. He slowly, and gently, swiped the block of cheese against the box-shaped grater, as he made sure to cover all the pasta in a thorough layer of ground cheese. After he made the last pass against the grater, Uncle Phillip placed the Parmigiano Reggiano back on the table and then with a forceful "thud" he slammed the palm of his hand against the cheese grater. I immediately thought to myself, "Hey, that's exactly how Nano finishes when he grates cheese," and then Uncle Phillip made a second, hefty "swat" of the palm of his left hand against the metal cheese grater.

I couldn't fathom how these finishing blows to the cheese grater weren't incredibly painful. But, nonetheless, it was a mutual practice and ritual shared by my grandfather and great uncle. "That should be good, Michael. Now, enjoy! Buon appetito!" said Uncle Phillip.

I, again, dug right in and hastily began to feast on my pasta. This brought a smile to Uncle Phillip's face as he happily declared that I was a real Italian. "It's good. Isn't it?" he asked. I, not wanting to delay any further, just looked up and nodded, "Yes".

Everyone's focus then shifted to their own plates and the table chatter was replaced with the clinks and clanks of silverware knocking against Mom's dinner plates.

I was nearly done with my second bowl of pasta when it suddenly was time to pay the piper. As I took aim with my fork at the last bowtie shaped piece of pasta, Uncle Phillip slid a small slice of pheasant meat onto my plate.

"Are you ready, Michael?" he asked. "Ah, sure. I guess," I answered. "Good. It's a small piece. Just give it a try," he continued, using his knife, extending from his right hand, to gesture towards the sliver of pheasant meat resting on my plate.

I took a quick glance over to Dad, and, with a nod of his head, he pretty much suggested that I now had no choice. So, in one swift motion, I lifted the piece of pheasant meat and ate it. I chomped down hard on the wild bird meat and chewed quickly.

As I raced to complete the deed, I realized that the room had gone dead quiet. I looked up and around the table, as I finally swallowed the pheasant and noticed that all eyes were fixed on me. Everyone had stopped eating and paused to see if I would eat the pheasant and, if so, what I thought of it.

"What do you think, Michael? Do you like it?" Uncle Phillip pressed. "It's okay," I answered. "What does it taste like?" Dave joined in. "I don't know. Maybe a little like chicken. But not really," I responded. I couldn't quite put my finger on how to describe the taste, but I thought to myself that it tasted a bit "earthy" or almost bitter. I reasoned that it's not bad, but it's also not good.

"Well, I'm proud of you for trying it, Michael," Uncle Phillip piped in, as he put his arm around me. "It's an acquired taste, huh?" he added, which got a chuckle from all the adults. "Why don't we clear the table and get ready for dessert?" Mom offered.

And with that, all the women at the table sprang into action and began clearing the plates. The rest of us stayed in our seats and I noticed Dad shoot me another look. He nodded at me again, but this time with a small, approving smile that made me feel like the entire ordeal was worth it.

Desserts were plentiful and again included a mix of Italian pastries and assorted cookies. Mom brought the adults coffee in her finest Porcelain China coffee cups. The cups were adorned with bright floral patterns, served atop delicate saucers with matching floral designs and complete with ornate miniature saucer spoons. The kind of tableware that only came out on special occasions. There was a noticeable buzz at the table, seemingly capturing everyone's excitement and anticipation for the big holiday block party tomorrow. I couldn't wait!

There was just something special about this holiday, especially with the majority of the neighborhood coming together to celebrate. We've had parties and get togethers in various neighbors' backyards, but we had never had a planned and coordinated block party where the street was closed-off to traffic and with so many families participating and chipping in together. This was special, and it was a perfectly fitting match for the historical and momentous occasion of the country's bicentennial celebration.

The cookie plate was passed around the table, and I made a couple choice selections. I grabbed one cookie that was shaped like a shell with a bright red cherry in the center and another one that was oval shaped with one half that had been dipped in chocolate. Everyone settled in and seemed content with the dessert assortment.

As I started into my second cookie, the shell shaped one, Dad hit us with some news, "Can I have everyone's attention, please?" We all paused with our sweets and looked at Dad, seated at one end of the table. "In honor of the big holiday, and for our extended family who is staying with us this weekend, and on what looks to be a beautiful summer evening, we'll be having a quick fireworks presentation out front. Just as soon as it gets dark. A precursor of sorts before tomorrow night's show. And … and, we have Bobby …, and Michael I guess, to thank for it!" he announced.

This news was well received at the table, except for Mom, who didn't like fireworks and shot a look over at Dad, indicating as much, following his announcement. I immediately looked to Dave, to see if he acknowledged that all we had schemed had worked exactly to plan.

But, before I could get Dave's attention, I made direct eye contact with Bobby. He was glaring right at me, with a wide smile on his face, satisfied that he had caused the ultimate and final forfeiture of our fireworks. My reaction, in return, surprised, even shocked, him as I answered back with an even bigger, wider grin.

In the end, why would I care who would actually light the fireworks? I just wanted to be able to witness and enjoy them. And after the whole ordeal that started with our ill-gotten-gains from the heist, to being subject to theft ourselves, to finding the stash, swiping them back, hiding our loot and then framing Bob for possession – this seemed like an acceptable result and a pretty good end to the entire affair. So yes, my beaming smirk back at Bob was a victory lap of sorts. And any sign that I was content with this announcement quickly caused Bob's smile to fade.

XXVII - L'Atto di Apertura
(The Opening Act)

It was a beautiful summer night, perfect for a fireworks display. The sun was just dipping below the horizon and, seemingly on demand, the streetlights sprang into action. The whole family was seated on lawn chairs in our front yard and anxiously awaited the show. Mr. and Mrs. Palermo also took to lawn chairs and sat directly across the street from us on their stone walkway.

Apparently, Mom had called the neighbors to let them know of our plans, and make sure that they wouldn't be startled by the blasts of the fireworks. The Schaefer's were also out in their front yard, ready to take in the spectacle. Of course, Mario and John Padovani had arrived on the scene. Dave and I quickly brought them up to speed on how things went down over dinner, which ended with Dad announcing the fireworks show.

Dad, who was dressed in a pair of his familiar Bermuda shorts, was fast at work organizing the pyrotechnics. He had a row of fireworks laid out on top of the stonewall that separated our front yard into two tiers. As he got ready to begin the show, Mr. Palermo, crossed the street holding a glass jug in his left hand and climbed onto our front lawn. I wandered over to get a look at what he had in his hand.

"Good evening, first generation Italians!" he shouted, in his typical bigger-than-life voice. "What do you have in your hand there, Cos?" Uncle Phillip asked. "Why this? Just a little homemade grappa that I thought I'd offer to you real Italians over here, as we celebrate America's birthday. Can I interest anyone in a taste?" he offered.

Without hesitation, the whole crew happily accepted his offer. Mom quickly got up and ran inside to grab some cordial glasses. "You made this, Cos?" Uncle Phillip followed. "I did. Me and my kid brother, Tony. We made it last fall. We got the leftover skins, pulp, and seeds from my Uncle Zeppie. He has quite a winemaking operation over there in Medford. Of course, nothing like what Mike makes here," he answered, as he gestured toward Nano, as a sign of respect.

"I have my wine right here Cos, if you'd like a glass?", Nano quickly shot back, as he pointed to his own glass jug resting beside the right leg of his lawn chair. "How can I say no, Mike?" Cos quickly answered.

As Nano began to pour his wine into Cos's glass, Uncle Phillip chimed in. "If you really want to see some fireworks, just drop a match into that jug and then stand back," he joked, with a wry smile on his face. This got a good laugh from the adults seated together, with all of them shaking their heads in agreement. Just then, Mom returned from the house, with a tray holding small, three-ounce, decorative cordial glasses.

As Mom handed out the mini-glasses to the crew, I circled-back to the Padovani brothers and Dave, who were still standing near our front wall, patiently waiting for the fireworks show.

"What's going on over here?" I asked. "Mario and John brought some punks for us," Dave answered, as Mario extended his right hand to show me. "Cool, where'd you get them?" I asked. "I had them left over from last fourth of July", Mario responded. "Awesome, let's light them up," I suggested.

I grabbed the Bic lighter that Dad had set aside on the wall's edge and swiftly lit four punks: one for each of us. We each took one and held the corner of the punk's wooden stem in our mouths. This, of course, did nothing but bring the distinct odor of the burning ember closer to our faces. But we thought it was cool and it helped us pass the time before the fireworks show kicked off.

As the four of us leaned against the front wall with our punks in hand, I spotted Marco Palermo emerge from his front door. He made a straight line for us, noticeably swinging his cast-wrapped left arm as he strode toward us. I took the punk from the corner of my mouth and held it by my right side. I could see that Marco had made quick work of his cast, now covered in handwritten notes etched in dark, black marker.

My eyes were immediately drawn to a Lynyrd Skynyrd logo that was written graffiti style in the center of his cast. Just beneath the Lynyrd Skynyrd logo, "Free Bird" was penned in prominent, red marker. It was a really cool cast and just added to Marco's tough-guy persona. As he reached us, he looked me straight in the eye.

"So, I understand you were in my place, out back in the woods behind my house," he said, accusingly. This was followed by a long pause. "Good for you," he said, to my surprise. "That took guts," he continued.

"But now, let me make this very clear for you. I find out that you go in there again … uninvited … and I'll thump your skull. You got it?" he directed to me. I looked right back at him and answered, "Yeah, I got it." "Good. Now you can't say that you weren't warned," he finished.

He took one good look over at me and then to Dave and the Padovani brothers. "What do you guys have, punks?" he asked. We all just nodded, yes. "Do you know those things are made from camel shit?" he asked. "You guys are all holding camel shit up to your faces", he asserted. "Camel shit?", I asked. "Yeah, camel shit," he answered. "I think these are just made from sawdust or something," I replied.

"Nope. It's made from camel shit. And you guys are putting camel shit right up to your faces," he insisted. He took one last long look at the four of us, shook his head, and then left headed back to his front door. We weren't sure what to make of it, but we were just happy that he had come and gone without any more than a threat to "thump my skull," if I were to make my way back into his fortress in the woods.

Just as Marco made his quick exit from the scene, Mr. Schaefer rushed across the street and approached Dad, "Hi Bob!

I thought I'd come over and lend you a hand. If you want some help?" he offered.

Mr. Schaefer, Herb, was essentially the biggest kid in the neighborhood. He was a great guy and was often seen organizing, and participating in, pick-up games of half-court basketball or touch football games. He was a real kid at heart and, just like us, he loved fireworks.

"I've got a long-reach lighter, if you need it, Bob?" Herb offered. "Sure, Herb, I could use a hand. I'm no expert with fireworks, so, if you can help me from hurting myself, or anyone else for that matter, I'd appreciate it," Dad answered. "No trouble at all. Let's see what we've got here," Herb continued, as he looked over the array of fireworks strewn across the front wall.

"Okay, you've got a lot to choose from here. Why don't we start with these? It's not quite dark yet, but these will work well now before we lose all the light," Herb added, as he pointed towards a stack of Jumping Jacks. I immediately thought that Herb knew what he was talking about. Jumping Jacks are firecracker sized fireworks that, unlike a traditional firecracker that would explode with a bang shortly after being lit, would hop and spin wildly in a colorful display of bright green and yellow sparks. Jumping Jacks would also make a distinct "whizzing" sound as they danced and spun within an inch or two of the ground, which certainly raised their cool factor. And, as Herb suggested, dusk was a great time to light them off.

Dad and Herb started the show with the Jumping Jacks. The two of them would alternate setting a firework down on the street, lighting the wick and then running like hell for cover. It was a bit funny to see the two of them light the fuse and then run away with some panic in their step. Nonetheless, the Jumping Jacks were a big hit with the crowd, getting lots of oohs and aahs as the fireworks shot out bright sparks as they spun wildly in the street. The older crowd, all but Nano, who remained a skeptic, even clapped to show their appreciation.

Once the applause ended, Mr. Palermo yelled out to Mrs. Palermo, who had decided to watch from her own front yard, "Lillian, is our homeowner's policy paid up to date?" This got a good laugh from the crowd, as Mrs. Palermo just waved him off from her perch across the street, the firecracker kid sitting closely by her side.

As the banter continued on my front patio, I glanced over and caught a glimpse of Dad and Herb wedging a Roman candle between two soft-ball sized rocks. They were taking care to ensure that the firework was aimed harmlessly towards the vacant open lot next door. I immediately wondered if this was a good idea. In a flash, Herb lit the fuse of the Roman Candle and sprinted away. The first couple of colorful fireballs, or stars as they were known, shot out from the Roman Candle and, as planned, fell safely to the ground at the open lot. The crowd assembled was thrilled and applauded with each star shot from the candle.

And then, what had seemed so predictable to me, happened. Just after the third burst that propelled another bright green star, the candle wedged between the two rocks dislodged and fell on its side. The candle's mouth was now pointing directly at the front of my house, and my family gathered on the patio.

In a flash, the next burst from the candle shot a star right over the heads of the group assembled out front. This was instantly met with collective shrieks and squeals from the senior members of my family. Immediately following the next burst, again cruising over the crowd, and bouncing off the front of our house, Dad sprang into action and grabbed the Roman Candle sitting on the sidewalk. He held it outstretched in his right hand and pointed it toward the vacant lot, for what turned out to be the final burst from the firework tube.

Once it was clear that the final shot had been expended, the crowd, now an angry mob, began to yell and shout at the two fireworks operators. Nearly all of what was being shouted was in Italian, which I couldn't understand. But I did know, from prior exchanges with Nano, that the shouts and cries from the patio were not words of praise. As the buzz died down, a familiar voice barked out loudly in English, "Lil, forget the homeowners. Is my life insurance paid up?" Mr. Palermo yelled to his wife, still sitting safely on her own front patio.

As she did in response to his first joke about insurance, she reacted simply by waving him off. Meanwhile, Dad didn't say much to try to defend himself. How could he? He just laughed and shrugged it off, apologizing to all who were nearly scorched by the flaming stars that had been propelled towards them.

As the jeers began to fade away, Nano forcefully chimed in. Once again, this was in Italian and directed at Dad, "Il tubo! Il tubo! Prendi il tubo! È nel garage. Quello che usiamo con il torchio," he exclaimed, using both hands to gesture and emphasize his point. Of course, this meant nothing to me, but Dad seemed to understand.

Following Nano's insistence, Dad quickly made his way into our garage. He emerged just a few seconds later, holding a roughly two-foot metal pipe above his head for all to see. This was apparently what Nano, from his post on the front patio, had instructed Dad to retrieve. The pipe was a make-shift tool that Nano had commissioned during our wine making process last fall. He used it as a fulcrum of sorts to add leverage in the crushed-grape squeezing phase of our wine making.

To accomplish this, we slipped the pipe over the press's attached handle, allowing for greater force to be applied with the same, or even less, effort. The pipe, and enclosed handle, was turned counterclockwise to compress on the wooden blocks beneath it and squeeze or press more of the fermented crushed grapes into a dark purple liquid extract. That extract, after further storing and fermenting, would become Nano's vintage for that upcoming year.

Herb greeted Dad as he returned with the pipe in hand. "Great idea, Bob. Here, we can stick that right into the turf," he said, pointing to the grass median strip between the curb and sidewalk.

Dad and Herb swiftly excavated a small hole and sank one end of the pipe into the ground. Dad then sped back to the garage and re-emerged with one of the Hood milkcrates that Marco had so catastrophically tried to jump over on his bike just a couple days ago. He then placed the crate under the front of the pipe, using it as a support, to buttress the metal cylinder skyward at an angle slightly less than ninety degrees.

This set-up seemed far more reliable and safer, clearing the way for the fireworks show to resume. Without delay, Dad and Herb began to arm their contraption for launch. They selected and loaded a skyrocket into the pipe, one from the roughly half-dozen types of skyrockets that we had amassed. Herb carefully bent the rocket's fuse and draped it over the lip of the pipe, leaving the skyrocket poised for ignition and launch.

Dad wasted no time, stepping forward with the long lighter in his hand and setting it afire. The rocket's wick lit and sizzled, as the pair retreated from the launch site. Once the sparkle from the fuse reached the lip of the pipe, the firework abruptly disappeared into the mouth of the pipe.

After a pro-longed second of waiting and anticipation, the silence was pierced by a bellowing "whooshing" sound and immediately followed by a bright object shooting from the open-end of the pipe. The rocket rapidly soared above the glowing streetlight and into the now black sky. Once it reached what looked like a hundred feet in the air, the rocket exploded with a loud bang and a burst of yellow and white sparkles that glimmered and crackled as they slowly drifted downward. It was a good one! And the crowd appreciated it, breaking into immediate and approving applause.

Without hesitation, the ground crew was right back at it loading the next skyrocket. This pattern was repeated over and again. Each launch ending successfully with a blast, followed by a bright display of gleaming and flickering colors, and then by applause. It was truly a great night and show. And it was enjoyed by everyone: family, friends, and neighbors! What a great way to end our day, also giving our crew in the tent something to gloat about, as we anxiously awaited tomorrow's big celebration for the Fourth.

Domenica 4 Luglio, 1976
(Sunday, July 4, 1976)

XVIX - La Corsa è Iniziata
(The Race is On)

It was a restless night in the tent. I don't think in total that the five of us got a combined dozen hours of sleep. We just couldn't. The anticipation for our clambake and the block party was just too overpowering.

I was so fidgety I just got up and decided to knock off my paper route early. It was the last day of the week in my rotation with Bobby and I was looking forward to handing it back off to him for the next seven days. Usually, Sundays were the worst day of the week for a paper boy. The papers were typically three times the size of any other day, due to the bulky comics and ads sections that dominated the Sunday Boston Globes.

But today was unique, the Sunday Globe on a holiday was a different animal. It was a very slimmed down version to the traditional and cumbersome Sunday edition. As I turned from the walkway leading from the backyard to the driveway, I was overjoyed to find a tiny wad of bundled papers sitting at the edge of the driveway. "Jackpot!" I said aloud to myself.

I grabbed the bundle, only needing one hand, and carried it to the garage. The papers were razor thin, basically the magnitude of a good-sized circular. I made quick work of folding the papers and loaded them into the basket at the front of my bike. Although weary from a nearly sleepless night, I hurriedly sped off down the street, looking to make record time in delivering the Sunday paper.

And it was a record. I made the full circuit in just over 20 minutes, opting for vicinity tosses rather than the typical door stoop drop-off. I made my return home crossing back onto Fieldstone Drive right at 8:00 a.m. As I approached the final right turn on the oval, I spotted what appeared to be nearly every dad in the neighborhood.

They were gathered, all sporting shockingly colorful Bermuda shorts, and huddled around the clambake pit located just beside the Palermo's driveway. I pedaled my way straight to the Palermo's and spotted a couple more dads standing waist deep in the recently excavated pit. There was quite a bit of chatter accompanied by some animated gestures and loud outbursts.

As I coasted into the driveway, and to no big surprise to me, I caught a glimpse of Dad firmly planted in the middle of the pit. From what I could gather, the spirited debate was over how to best set up the firewood for the bake. It was literally a, "How many Italians does it take to light a fire?" moment, and the dads on scene were enjoying every second of it.

As I came to a stop at the foot of their gathering, I was warmly welcomed, "Michael! How are you? Happy fourth!" the dads said together. "Thanks. Happy fourth. What are you guys doing?" I asked. "We're just having a little fun before the party. And your father is just having a little fun back at us, being a know-it-all. That's all," Mr. Palermo answered, loudly.

As Mr. Palermo's words seemingly hung in the air, all heads turned towards the street as the distinctive rumble from a backhoe tractor approached the Palermo's driveway. As the engine noise drew closer, I caught a glimpse of Mr. Oliveri seated high at the controls of his construction machine. As he sped our way, I noticed his bucket, that was half raised and cupped forward, was loaded with a huge pile of cut firewood.

He raced the tractor from Fieldstone Drive and onto the short private road, Karen Drive, that fed directly into the Palermo's driveway. The dads immediately sprang into action and Mr. Oliveri quickly found that he had a handful of foremen who all rushed to provide conflicting instructions to the backhoe operator. Wisely, Mr. Oliveri simply ignored the swarm of hand gestures and shouts directed towards him and brought the load of kindling forward and then expertly delivered it across the clam bake pit to rest perfectly against the Palermo's wooden fence.

The dads on the ground, after giving a thumbs up to Mr. Oliveri, hurriedly got to work and began to stack the wood in uniform fashion. The wood delivery seemed to ratchet up the excitement amongst the dads about the day's celebration ahead, as they all chipped in to stack the logs.

Just as the backhoe made its exit from the scene, Mr. Schaefer arrived, whipping around the street corner, and swinging into the crowded driveway, riding his classic green and yellow colored John Deere riding mower. His mower was the very top of the line, highest quality and it was truly Mr. Schaefer's pride and joy.

The Schaefer's had a beautifully kept and very large lawn. The backyard lawn was an immaculate field of green grass. And it was large, probably one hundred fifty feet wide and at least as deep as it was wide. And from early spring to mid-fall, Mr. Schaefer, sitting atop of his riding mower, was a regular Sunday morning fixture in the neighborhood. He pulled up close to me and the dads, proudly sporting his pair of aviator sunglasses, shut down his mower and addressed the assembled group.

"Morning fellas, Happy Fourth," he greeted them. "Happy Fourth," they responded together. "What's with the mower, Herbie?" Mr. Palermo asked. "I thought I'd bring it over and do a quick pass in your backyard Cos, before the party gets started," Mr. Schaefer answered.

"Well thanks, Herbie. That's awfully nice of you," Mr. Palermo responded. "Happy to help," Herb said. "Say, that's some mower you got there, Herb," Mr. Limone offered. "Yeah thanks, Jimmy. It's a good machine. Far nicer than the last one I had," Herb answered.

"You've got a riding mower too, don't you Jimmy?" Mr. Palermo questioned. "Well yeah, I do. But nothing like what Herb has here. Mine is almost twenty years old and probably only has a quarter of the horsepower of what Herb's has," he replied. "You know what would be fun?" Herb quickly asked, clearly excited. "What's that?" Mr. Limone responded. "Why don't we kick off the festivities today with a lawn mower race around the block? Me and you Jim, right at the stroke of noon," Herb finished.

"Oh, I don't know. That wouldn't be all that much of a race, Herb. I mean, I just told you that my mower is almost twenty years older than yours and has one quarter the engine," Mr. Limone reasoned. "Come on, Jimmy. It'll be fun! And the kids will love it. Don't you want the kids to have a memorable day today?" Herb argued. "Come on, Jimmy. Sounds like fun. And Herb's right. It'll be great fun for the kids!" Dad chimed in.

"Okay, okay … I'll do it!" Mr. Limone conceded. "But I want odds! And no gloating after the fact, Herb!" Mr. Limone went on. "No, no, I promise, Jimmy. I'll be a modest and gracious winner. Just make sure you show up at noon. We'll start right from in front of Bob's house," Herb said, with a huge grin on his face and pointing back towards the front of my house.

"Let me make a quick run over Cos's lawn out back and then gas up for the race," he finished, as he hit the start button and brought his John Deere machine back to life.

As the dads returned to the job at hand in the pit and Mr. Schaefer rode off to the Palermo's backyard, I made a quick exit for my house to relay the news of the big race coming at high noon.

I zipped up the front steps and sped into the house. I hustled past my mom and great aunts, all hard at work doing who knows what in the kitchen. Uncle Phillip and Nano were seated at the kitchen table sipping on their espressos. They barely noticed me as I whipped past them, headed for the back yard. They were intently listening in to their local AM Italian news station on the radio. I had no idea what was being said, but given the speed, volume, and tempo of the speaker, you could tell someone was upset with someone somewhere.

As I got to the door leading to the back yard, I could hear Nano and Uncle Phillip scoff loudly together. Obviously, they held a dissenting opinion from the speaker's point of view. I took a step outside and saw the gang sitting at the picnic table on the patio, eating their breakfast. I rushed over to them, half out of breath, and hit them with the news.

"You guys will never guess what's going on," I said, as all heads turned to me. "What?" Dave answered. "Let me guess, Bobby re-stole whatever fireworks were still left," Mario chimed in, wisely.

"No," I said, equally flippant. "Mr. Limone and Mr. Schaefer are going to race their riding mowers around the block at noon," I informed the group. "What? Why?" Dave followed. "Yeah, Mr. Schaefer's going to kill him," Mario added.

"I know. That mower he has is like something NASA made," I agreed. "Plus, Mr. Limone's mower is like forty years old," Mario went on. "I bet Mr. Schaefer will lap him!" Dave exclaimed.

We all laughed at the thought of Herb making a full revolution around the block and whipping past Mr. Limone. I immediately pictured Herb, sitting high on his mower, swinging around Mr. Limone, and leaving him behind in a cloud of grass shavings. "Yeah, not much of a contest. But it'll be funny to see," I said, with a smile.

After I downed a Thomas' English muffin in the back yard, I headed back over to the Palermo's, this time with Dave, Mario, and John. There was still a group of dads huddled around the clam bake pit. Half of them had now gone shirtless as they congregated around the hole. I quickly spotted Dad, still from the chest up anyway, as he continued his work from inside the pit.

We strode up to the dads, who were loudly enjoying themselves. Mr. Palermo was the first to greet us. "Hey boys, you ready to see us light this sucker?" he asked, with clear excitement in his voice. "You bet," we answered collectively, with wide grins on our faces.

"Okay, Bobby let's torch this thing," Mr. Palermo directed, as he handed a container of Kingsford lighter fluid to Dad. Dad wasted no time and swiftly drenched the pile of firewood and kindling in the pit with Kingsford's finest. After he nearly emptied the whole container of charcoal fluid onto the stack of wood, Dad reached out with his right hand and two other dads quickly grasped his arm and pulled him up and out from the crater.

Not a second after Dad was back at street level, Mr. Palermo lit a long matchstick and dropped it into the center of the wood stack. And with a gush of air whooshing upwards, the fire lit in spectacular fashion. There was an immediate cheer from the dads, proud and excited they had successfully gotten things underway.

I took a brief glance at all the dads' faces standing around the pit, which was now holding a roaring fire, and found nothing but pure delight and smiles. It really was something, their collective and palpable excitement. Just then, Mr. Palermo barked out his next chorus of instructions.

"Okay, boys. Now, nobody get too close. We can't have anyone get hurt. The wives would kill us," he joked, getting a laugh from the gang of dads. "What happens next?" I blurted out. "Well, we let this fire burn hot, for a good few hours. We keep adding wood, as needed, and get this pit super-hot. You see, we don't cook with the fire going. We use the fire and the coals to get the stones at the bottom scorching hot. When ready, we then shovel out any remaining bits of wood, lower in the food that'll either be bundled or in big pots, cover the pit with that canvas tarp over there and let the hot stones do their job," Mr. Palermo answered, definitively. "Oh, cool," I answered.

"Why don't you boys go do something. This is going to burn for a few hours, like Mr. Palermo said," Dad added. We all just shrugged our shoulders but continued to look on at the blazing fire.

"Well, that's it for me for now," Mr. Limone chimed in. "I apparently have to go get ready for my lawnmower race with Herb. Which leaves me just a little over an hour to get my pit crew working on my ride," he finished, with a wide grin on his face.

"Okay, Jimmy. Good luck," Mr. Palermo answered. "Can we come with you to check it out?" I asked, eagerly. "Sure, why not. You boys with my Louis can be part of my pit crew." Mr. Limone replied. "Awesome," I answered, looking over to Dave and the Padovani brothers. "Let's go and get after it," Mr. Limone encouraged. We turned and began to make our way down the street to the Limone's house.

As we exited the Palermo's property and reached the street, I looked back over my shoulder towards the Palermo's driveway and could still see the flames rising out from the clam bake pit. It was an evocative and unforgettable scene.

XXX - Il Regolatore Pneumatico
(The Pneumatic Governor)

We got to the Limone's house and walked right into the garage. Off in the far-right corner sat Mr. Limone's riding mover. It was a twenty-year-old, I'd call it vintage, Snapper riding mower. It looked like the original paint was probably red, but it was tough to say as it was covered with a film of grease and dirt. It certainly looked like it had lived a hard life and it was also only about half the size of Herb's premium John Deere mower.

This was going to be a slaughter, but still Mr. Limone glowingly pointed out his dilapidated, old machine. "There she is, boys!" he said proudly, pointing to the heap of junk in the corner of the garage. "Wow, that looks old," Dave observed out loud. "Old!?" he shot back. "She's more reliable than old. But yes, this will be a tall task today, for sure," he continued, after a short pause. "Let me get Louis out here and he can give us a hand to fill'er up and get her ready," he said, as he walked to the door leading from the garage and into the lower level of their split-floor style home.

As Mr. Limone set off to get Lou, the four of us took a few steps closer to look over the Snapper mower. "Wow, this thing is old," I said. "You're not kidding," Mario replied. "I'm not even sure it'll make it all the way around the block," I added, as the four us chuckled at the thought of having to push the mower back to the garage in shame.

Mr. Limone re-emerged into the garage, now with Lou following right behind him. "Okay, boys. I've got Louis with me and we're going to get this thing going and then we'll shock the world!" Mr. Limone declared, optimistically.

"What's up fellas!?" Lou greeted us, slapping us all five as he stepped into the middle of the garage. "So, what's this I hear, we've got a race today?" Lou continued. "That's right. Your Dad's going to race Herb on his riding mower," I answered, pointing towards the Limone's tired, old Snapper machine.

"On that piece of crap?" Lou answered with a question of his own. The four of us immediately burst out with laughter in response to Lou's candid statement of the obvious. "Louis, shhh, she can hear you," Mr. Limone shot back. "Dad, she's so old, I doubt she can hear anything at her age," Lou quipped. Even Mr. Limone had to join us in chuckling at Lou's quick response.

"C'mon, let's get her out of there and into the open," Mr. Limone continued. "Yeah, I guess we really ought to practice pushing her," Lou added. "That's enough, Louis," Mr. Limone answered, as we all laughed just a little bit louder.

We very carefully pushed the mower out of the garage and into the Limone's driveway. Getting the Snapper mower into the sunlight did little to enhance its image. There were no two ways about it, it was an old and, on its very best day, "modest" machine. Lou picked up on his verbal assault. "Man, this looks even worse in the light!" he exclaimed with a wry smile. "Seriously, Dad. This thing is a jalopy! No, no. That's actually an insult to jalopies," he went on, with all of us chuckling.

"Is that right?" Mr. Limone replied, with his go-to catch-phrase. "Yes, that is right. You see, this is what the youth today would refer to as a "shit box," Lou continued. "Louis, watch your language!" Mr. Limone answered, with a smile of his own.

"Now, this is what my generation would call an American-made classic. Reliable, strong, and durable. No parts made in Japan on this baby!" Mr. Limone declared, as he softly tapped the steering wheel with his clinched fist.

"Well, you still got no chance," Lou asserted. "We'll see," Mr. Limone responded, with surprising confidence. Just then, as we were all looking over the small-statured riding mower, a car pulled up alongside the curb directly in front of the Limone's house. We all glanced over, as the front passenger door of the metallic blue Cutlass Supreme slowly opened. A woman, holding a ceramic bowl in her hands, rose from the passenger seat. Just as she got to her feet, a man, the car's driver, raced around the front of the vehicle to assist the young woman.

Mr. Limone squinted his eyes to peer over at the couple and then greeted them loudly. "Nancy, you made it!" he announced. "Hello, Uncle Jimmy. Happy fourth!" she replied back. Mr. Limone sped over to her and the young man accompanying her. "I'm so glad that you were able to come," Mr. Limone said, as he kissed her on her cheek.

"Well, thank you for inviting us. We're so excited to be spending such a big holiday with you all," she continued. "And who is this?" Mr. Limone asked, as he shifted his attention. "This is my boyfriend, Derek," she replied. "Boyfriend, is that right? "Mr. Limone answered, again with his go-to phrase. "Yes, thanks for having us today," Derek added, as he extended his hand to Mr. Limone.

"Well, thank you too Derek. It's great to meet you and happy to have you here with us," Mr. Limone responded, as the two men shook hands. "Is that Louis over there?" Nancy asked, as the five of us were still standing beside the riding mower. "Hi cousin Nancy," Lou responded, as she gave him a big hug. "I can't believe how big you've gotten," she declared. "Yeah, they feed me pretty well here," Lou answered, jokingly.

"How are you boys doing?" Derek asked, as he approached us all. We all just answered with a simple, "Hey." "What do we have here?" Derek then asked. "Oh, this is my riding mower," Mr. Limone chimed in. "Yeah, he's going to get slaughtered in a race around the block in about twenty minutes," Lou answered, with a big grin.

"Yeah well, we're gonna gas her up and see if we can make a few modifications that might give us a fighting chance," Mr. Limone answered. "Well, Derek can give you a hand Uncle Jimmy. He's a mechanic," Nancy declared. "A mechanic, is that right?" Mr. Limone followed, again with his go-to. "That's right. I've been a mechanic for just over a dozen years. I think I can maybe help you out, find some extra horsepower for ya," Derek offered.

"Really!? You think you could do something with this piece of shit?" Lou asked. "Oh my god, Louis. You are too funny," Nancy chimed in. Derek briefly paused in his inspection of the engine, looked up at Lou and chuckled. "Yeah, I think there's a way," Derek answered. "Then you must be some mechanic, all right," Lou followed.

Nancy made one more, quick glance over at Lou and then to her uncle, Mr. Limone. "Okay, I guess I'll leave you boys to it. Uncle Jimmy, are Aunt Dolly and Lisa inside?" she asked, as she smiled and scoffed softly once more.

"Ah yes, honey. They should be right inside, probably getting things ready in the kitchen," Mr. Limone answered. "Great, I'll go say hello and bring this inside," she said, gesturing to the porcelain bowl in her hands as she headed towards the Limone's front door.

The all-male pit crew returned its attention to the Snapper mower, all eyes following Derek's every move. "So, you really think you could do something with this?" Mr. Limone asked Derek. "I sure do. Nothing fancy or intricate. But you see this right here?" Derek asked aloud. We all leaned in to get a look at what Derek was pointing to. He was pointing to a small, boomerang-like structure on the left side of the engine. There was a spring of some sort connecting the boomerang to some other part of the engine.

"Okay, yeah. I see it," Mr. Limone answered. "Okay, good. This is your governor. And what the governor does is it regulates the speed and overall acceleration of your motor. And with a fairly simple adjustment to the spring here, actually shortening it up, will leave your throttle wide open," Derek finished. "And that'll give her more speed?" Mr. Limone asked.

"Exactly. The only thing is, it'll only have one speed. Fast," Derek explained. "Well, fast is what we want in a race, isn't it!? "Mr. Limone replied. "I'd say so," Derek answered. "Okay, let's go for it then!" Mr. Limone shouted excitedly.

"Ten-four. Let me grab a few tools from my car and we'll get right to it," Derek declared. "Perfect," Mr. Limone agreed. "If this works, it'll be a miracle," Lou offered. "Oh, it'll work.

You just wait," Derek finished, as he sped off to retrieve his tool kit.

Derek got right to work, as we all watched on intently. He expertly wielded his tools, displaying the precision of a surgeon with a scalpel. He made quick work of his task, announcing after no more than five minutes that the machine was ready for a test drive.

"That ought to do," Derek declared. "Really, that quick?" Mr. Limone asked. "Yep, it's really a simple thing. Like I said, it's just shortening up the governor spring to the carburetor," Derek replied, definitively. "Well, why don't you give it a test ride, Dad?" Lou encouraged. "You think it's ready for that, Derek?" Mr. Limone followed. "Sure is. Climb on and let's see what she can do," Derek urged. "Okay, then. Stand back everyone. Now, watch me peel out and burn some rubber!" Mr. Limone said, excitedly.

We all took a couple steps back, as Mr. Limone mounted his ride. "All right, here goes," he said, as he pressed his foot on the mower's brake and gave the key, located just under the steering wheel, a turn. The engine immediately jumped to life, revving like any common lawn mower.

"Geez, sounds good," Mr. Limone shouted slightly. "Doesn't sound any different than usual," Lou piped in. "No, but it'll ride different," Derek shouted back. "I'll give it a try," Mr. Limone announced, his voice still elevated. "You can put her right into fifth gear to get going," Derek instructed.

Mr. Limone shook his head, acknowledging receipt of Derek's directions. He then re-positioned his foot on the brake and, with his right hand, grabbed the shift and adjusted the gear from neutral into fifth. He gave us all one last look and nodded as he shouted, "Here goes!"

And, in the blink of an eye, Mr. Limone took off in a flash. It was incredible! The force of the mower's immediate acceleration caused Mr. Limone's head to jerk backwards almost violently. In an instant, the mower, carrying a startled Mr. Limone, sped out of the driveway and onto the street. We stood there, in shock, as the decrepit, old mower was now zooming away from us at high speed.

"Are you fucking kidding me!?" Lou shouted. Hearing this, Derek turned back towards us, the five of us standing there stunned by what we were seeing, and with a wide smile on his face just said, "Told ya."

At this point, Mr. Limone seemed to have wrestled back control of the mower and was making his way back towards us. He steered the souped-up old mower from Citation Drive back onto Fieldstone. He had the widest grin on his face, kind of like a kid at an amusement park. He took a quick glance to his left, then to his right, and then raced back across the street and into the Limone driveway.

He again grabbed the shifter and maneuvered the stick back into neutral as he came to an abrupt stop. We were all just amazed at the transition and the now blinding speed of his mowing machine. Mr. Limone, still sporting his beaming grin, shouted to us over the mower's idling engine, "Now that was fun! My god. I can't believe how fast she is. That's amazing," he continued.

"Yeah, I knew that would do the trick," Derek responded. "Do you think she can keep up that speed for a full lap around the block?" Mr. Limone asked. "Oh yeah, no question. No problem at all," Derek assured him. "Herb's going to flip out. He's not going to know what hit him, man!" Mr. Limone exclaimed.

"Is there any way his mower could go that fast?" Louis asked, as he chimed in. "Not unless he does the same thing I just did," Derek answered. "That's insane," Lou added, wearing a grin that matched his father's from a few moments earlier.

"Now, can we get over to the start line at the mower's usual speed? You know, turtle speed?" Mr. Limone asked. "Sure thing, I can adjust the give on the spring and then readjust it back just before the race gets going," Derek answered.

"Beautiful, beautiful. This way, Herb's not going to know what hit him until the starter's pistol sounds," Mr. Limone shouted, excitedly. "He's gonna totally shit his pants!" Lou added. "Lou-is! Watch your mouth!" Mr. Limone answered. We all burst out laughing, knowing that Lou was absolutely right. And just as the laughing died down, Mr. Limone added one last comment. "He is going to shit his pants, though."

XXXI - Via Ai Motori!
(Start Your Engines!)

We sprinted back to my house to jump on our bikes ahead of the big race. We cackled the entire way back, as we anticipated the pure shock that was about to unfold, given the newfound speed that Mr. Limone's old jalopy had now secured through Derek's wizardry.

When we reached the front of my house, we found a row of lawn chairs lined up at the very end of our driveway. Seated there were my three great aunts and Mom. They were chatting with Mrs. Palermo and Schaefer, who were seated directly across the street from them in their own lawn chairs. Standing immediately behind my aunts and Mom, was a mountain of a man who was talking with Uncle Phillip and Nano. I immediately recognized him as my very recently discovered Uncle Ray.

There was no mistaking it, he was so enormous. He just towered over my grandfather and uncle. Uncle Phillip met us at the edge of the driveway, "Boys! Your Uncle Ray is here, just like we said he would be."

"Boys. Happy fourth!" Ray greeted us, with his giant hand extended. I reached out with my right hand, and watched as it disappeared into Ray's huge mitt, just like it had at the wharf a day ago. "Hi, Uncle Ray," I responded, as we shook hands. Dave quickly followed suit and shook hands with the behemoth.

"Ray, these are the Padovani brothers. You know their grandfather Ray Senior and dad Ray," Uncle Phillip said, as he introduced the brothers. "Boys, good to meet you," Ray offered, as Mario and John just stared upwards, in awe at the huge fisherman. "We're here to see the race, Michael," Uncle Phillip stated. "Mannaggia! Can you believe these people? They're crazy! Crazy people!" Nano exclaimed.

"What Mike? What do you care? They're just having some fun. Fun on the Fourth of July," Uncle Phillip responded, with a wry and wide smile. "Fourth of July? What do lawnmowers have to do with the fourth of July? They're crazy … all of them!" Nano exclaimed. "What, you don't think they should have some fun? It's fun, Mike. It's a race. And it's fun," Uncle Phillip shot back, knowing each justification would just set my grandfather further off the deep end. "Then you're crazy too!" Nano answered.

"You know what would make this more fun, Mike? How about a glass of your wine to start the day's festivities?" Ray suggested. "Now you're talking. You see, someone who knows what they're talking about," Nano said, in a huff. "Well, I can't disagree with you if it's going to keep me from having a glass of wine. Can I?" Uncle Phillip asked. "No, that's right. You can't,"Nano answered. "Okay then, okay. I agree. Let's have a glass to celebrate our agreeing to something," Uncle Phillip reasoned.

As the three senior male Italians on the scene departed for the garage on their way to Nano's wine cellar, we followed close behind to retrieve our bikes that were strewn about the garage floor. We each mounted our rides and rolled out of the garage and onto the driveway. Immediately, we stopped abruptly in our tracks. There, sitting in the middle of the street, was a State Police cruiser with its lights flashing.

As we slowly approached the vehicle, the unmistakably large frame, almost Uncle Ray sized, of Mr. Desanto exited the police cruiser. It was an odd image as, unlike previous encounters when we saw Mr. Desanto climbing out from his State issued vehicle, he wasn't wearing his traditional and sharp military-style trooper's uniform. On this occasion, he was wearing a pair of plaid

Bermuda shorts, a floral Cabana shirt with gladiator style sandals on his enormous feet and, to top things off, he was puffing on a big old cigar.

Herb, the expected "sure thing," was already on the scene. He was standing directly behind the police car and was proudly addressing the crowd that had already assembled. Herb was boasting confidently about his superior mower and his chances as the favorite to win the big race.

Mr. Desanto, in his commanding voice, barked out for all to hear, "Let's get this show on the road!" "We're still waiting for Jimmy," Mrs. Palermo replied. We sat on our bikes and quietly listened in as Herb continued with his bluster, when we finally saw Mr. Limone sputtering towards us slowly, proudly piloting his old Snapper riding mower towards us.

He was wearing a bright red little league batting helmet on his head, with an ear-to-ear grin on his face. He was clearly still in "Turtle" mode, cleverly disguising his newfound speed, as he was barely able to keep ahead of Louis and Derek, who were walking close behind him and seemingly gaining ground.

As he rounded the turn, the aunts and moms gave him an encouraging cheer and he responded by emphatically waving his right hand in the air with his right index finger extended, signaling to all that he was Number One.

"Oh, I guess he is going to bother showing up after all," Herb exclaimed. "That's it?" Aunt Gray wondered aloud. "Geeze, that thing has to be as old as we are," she joked. "Let me go get my mower. Get ready to set your eyes on a real state-of-the-art machine," Herb said, conceitedly.

Mr. Limone drove his mower in front of the crowd gathered at what seemed to be the start and finish line. He made a slow, plodding turn in order to reverse direction, so that the racers would head in the downhill direction rather than uphill. He came to an abrupt stop, shifted gears, and then turned the key on his mower to the off position. The crowd at the starting line, which had now swelled to include moms, dads, and kids, welcomed him with a loud cheer.

"You sure you want to risk it and shut off that motor, Jimmy?" Mr. Palermo shouted out for all to hear. "Oh yeah, no worries, Cos. I have my secret weapon here in Derek. He's my personal pit crew for the race," he answered, gesturing with his thumb towards Derek, who responded with a quick smile. "Well, I hope he's a miracle worker!" Mr. Palermo shot back. "Oh, he is. He is," Mr. Limone quickly answered.

Immediately following this exchange, Derek got right to work. He again dove in on the left side of the engine and began to put a small clasp on the spring extending from the governor, to tighten the tension. In ten seconds or less, Derek rose and gave a nod to Mr. Limone, indicating that the job had been done. "Ready and raring to go!" Mr. Limone shouted, still sporting his huge grin.

Just as Mr. Limone made his final checks sitting on top of his ancient mower, Herb emerged from his garage humming aboard his sharply colored green and yellow John Deere mower. He had his sweet ride in gear and its engine just purred, as he sped from his driveway towards the starting line. He received a generous and supportive ovation from the large crowd. And he immediately acknowledged his adoring fans by rising to his feet while still in motion and waving to all feverishly.

Herb certainly looked the part, as he sported his trusty aviator sunglasses while wearing his go-to riding gloves that he often wore while taking his Mercedes convertible out for a spin. He pulled up alongside Mr. Limone, still seated on his trusty Snapper mower, and gave him the once-over, slowly glancing up and down at his competitor and his relic of a machine.

"You ready for this, Jimmy? Or should I really ask, do you have any last words?" Herb asked, mockingly. "Bring it on, Herbie. We're going to shock the world today!" Mr. Limone shot back.

Dad, who had somehow named himself the race's Grand Marshal and rules committee, stepped forward to officiate the start of the race. "Okay, racers ready?" Dad asked from the middle of the street. Both racers gave him a quick nod to signal all systems go.

"The rules are simple, one full lap around the block and the driver who returns here first to the start-finish line wins. No bumping, no short cuts, no pushing or pulling in any way. Nick will be out front in his pace car leading the way. And that's it, like I said, simple rules," Dad announced. "Bob, is taunting allowed?" Herb asked, with a cynical smile. "Allowed? It's encouraged!" Dad responded, with an equally wide grin.

With the race rules announced, Mr. Desanto climbed back into his cruiser while the two racers were positioned side-by-side on their mowers at the start-line. Mr. Desanto slowly began to head down Fieldstone in his repurposed pace car. Dad shouted to get the show on the road. "Okay, racers on your mark, get set … go!" They were off!

Herb, riding his top-of-the-line green machine, smoothly transitioned into gear, and sped forward. Mr. Limone on his antique mower, having bobbled the gear shift, sprung, and recoiled forward and came to an abrupt stop. Herb immediately looked over his shoulder and burst out laughing as he raced ahead. The anxious onlookers let out a collective groan, assuming the worst for Mr. Limone's chances. But that lasted only a brief second, as Mr. Limone regained his composure and once again grabbed the shifter and then put the mower into fifth gear, as Derek had earlier instructed.

This time, the old, red mower took the gear change and, with a slight screech of its wheels, exploded forward. The crowd, without exception, gasped in shock and awe as the diminutive, old machine took off at a staggering speed.

"There she goes!" Lou shouted, with an excited and proud look on his face. Mr. Limone's little red mower looked like it had been shot out of a cannon. In a flash, he closed half the distance that Herb and his mower had on him. I instantly howled out loud and mounted my bike. "Let's go!" I shouted, as I began to pedal off and chase after the mowers.

Dave, Mario, and John quickly joined me in the pursuit. By the time the two mowers reached the turn, Mr. Limone had nearly drawn even with Herb. Like a classic scene from a Saturday morning cartoon, Herb took a quick glance and then followed with an immediate double take at Mr. Limone, who had now pulled even with him. The old, red mower continued to accelerate to Herb's outside right as they made the turn at the bend of the road. Herb's face was classic! It was utter shock and dismay, which only triggered all of us to howl out loud again.

As they came around the turn, Mr. Limone rapidly pulled

ahead, waving goodbye to Herb emphatically as he shot to the lead. I jammed down on my bike brakes, skidding skillfully under a controlled fishtail stop. I was quickly followed by Dave and the Padovani brothers. "Let's head the other way and catch them as they're getting close to the finish line," I shouted.

The four of us remounted our bikes and began pedaling in the opposite direction. As we came around the turn, we could see the crowd still gathered at the finish line in front of my driveway. We shouted out to them trying to report what we had just witnessed but we were giggling so much that I don't believe they could understand a word of it.

I stopped again, this time right in front of Dad, and fought to get the words out. "He's winning," I was able to spit out. "Who's winning?" Dad asked. "Mr. Limone's winning. He's flying … like Speed Racer!" I shouted. "What!? Jimmy's winning? I didn't think he'd even make it around the block," Mrs. Limone added. "We're going to see if they're coming. C'mon guys!" I exclaimed, getting back up on my bike.

With that, the four of us raced to the next lamp post which was located just around the bend from the Ferraro's house. I looked back at the small crowd gathered in front of my house and caught a glimpse of a few anxious fans gesturing excitedly towards us. I swung my head around to see if I could catch a glimpse of the racers, but nothing yet to report.

"Why don't Mario and I head down the street a bit to see if we can see them coming?" Dave offered. "Sounds good to me," I answered. Dave and Mario promptly began pumping their pedals and sped away on their bikes, heading further down Fieldstone. They only got a hundred feet or so before they abruptly circled back and began pedaling even more vigorously, reversing direction, and headed back towards where Johnny and I had been left waiting.

"What are they doing?" I wondered out loud. Johnny just shrugged his shoulders slightly, as we both peered down the street. By the time that Dave and Mario had covered about half the distance of their return trip, I could see that they both were sporting huge grins on their faces. Mario began waving his right arm above his head, holding his bike's handle bars only with his left hand.

"They're coming! They're coming!" Mario shouted. "Who's winning?" I shot back. He immediately began cackling and tried to spit it out and report back to us. "It's Mr. Limone," Dave interrupted, still with a huge smile on his face. "He's way ahead!" Mario finally found his words.

They both screeched again, as they tried to catch their breath. "He's right behind Mr. Desanto's cruiser. You can't even see Herb behind him, he's so far ahead," Dave added. "Let's go tell the others!" I shouted, excitedly.

The four of us got back on top of our bikes and began to pedal intensely back towards the crowd gathered in front of my house. As we pedaled toward them, I could see several heads leaning forward from their beach chairs trying to get a glimpse of us hurrying back towards them. We whisked back down the street with blurring speed. We couldn't wait to report the news back to the excited crowd.

As we propelled our cycles closer to the finish line, I could see the dads stand and begin to approach us eagerly. I even witnessed Nano rise from his chair and peer toward us. I got to the line first and, with great precision, came to a screeching skidding stop right on top of the start-finish line. I immediately received a few oohs and aahs from the moms seated on the sidelines.

"What is it, boys? Who's winning?" Mr. Palermo shouted excitedly. I paused a half second, trying to catch my breath and to contain myself from laughing wildly. "It's Mr. Limone!" I reported loudly. "He's way out in front! You can barely see Herb behind him in the distance," I exclaimed.

"Really? Jimmy's in the lead?" Mrs. Limone wondered out loud. "Good lord, I really didn't think he'd finish the race. Derek, what did you do to that old eye-sore?" she continued. Derek shrugged his shoulders modestly, feigning his surprise.

"Here they come!" Dad shouted. Everyone, except the great aunts, stood and looked anxiously down the street towards the Ferraro's house. Mr. Desanto gave a blast from his siren and then pulled to the side and into the Oliveri's driveway, clearing the way. Mr. Limone was zipping down the street towards us. He raised his right arm above his head and shook his fist enthusiastically towards the crowd. He had a big and proud smile on his face as he sped towards the finish line.

As he grew closer to the crowd gathered, he began to flex his muscles, shifting his pose to show his flexed right bicep. He even took his left hand off the steering wheel for a brief moment to help prop up his otherwise pliant arm, then kissed his bicep as he crossed the finish line to a loud and welcoming crowd. It was quite a moment and Mr. Limone ate up every second of it.

He brought his vintage mower to a stop just in front of the Palermo's house as he continued to receive his well-deserved congratulations and accolades. "I did it! I did it, Dolly! I shook up the world! I am the greatest! I am the greatest!" he shouted to Mrs. Limone, channeling his best impersonation of the true champ, Muhammad Ali.

As Mr. Limone's celebration continued, Herb had just reached the Ferraro's house. He looked completely dejected as he covered the remaining one hundred feet atop his once un-beatable John Deere mower. He crossed the finish line with no fanfare. Only Mrs. Schaefer approached to greet him as he came to a full stop. "We were waiting for you," she said to him with an honest smile. "Yes, and for some time, I take it," he answered, as he glared over towards Team Limone.

"Oh, let Jimmy have the day. There's always next year," she responded with a full and sincere smile. Then, with the buzz of excitement still hovering over the scene, a loud and harsh screeching whistle pierced through the air. It was Mrs. Palermo, who had learned how to whistle like a dock worker from her youth spent in and around the North End of Boston. An immediate, and obedient, hush fell over the crowd.

"Listen everybody, listen to me," she barked out loudly, in her customary gravelly voice. "Listen," she paused for a brief moment. "We're ready to start our block party," she announced. This was immediately followed by a loud cheer from the group.

"Listen, listen …," she shouted, somehow raising her voice even a notch higher. "I want all yous kids to go home and get into your bathing suits and come over to my backyard to swim. And for you ladies, you can bring what you have for appetizers over with you. Cos has a table set-up in the shade on the patio and we'll get started from there. You can all get into your suits too. It's going to be a hot day and the pool's not just for the kids. All right, let's go, let's go … chop chop, as they say," she shouted, as she turned and began to walk towards her front door.

With Mrs. Palermo's announcement complete, the group on the scene immediately dispersed and dutifully set out to follow her instructions.

XXXII - Ora di Festeggiare!
(Party Time!)

There was a distinct buzz of excitement at my house and a rush of activity to get ready for the party. My siblings and I all hurried to our rooms to get into our bathing suits. Mom and the great aunts were hustling around the kitchen, loading pre-baked appetizers into countless Tupperware containers and onto serving platters. Dad was already across the street, no doubt stoking the coals in the clambake pit and checking on the burn. Nano, Uncle Phillip, and newly found Uncle Ray were getting primed in the backyard.

I could hear the trio outside the second-floor bathroom window that faced our backyard, which was wide open amidst our family's constant battle to cool a house without air conditioning. I could hear the three men toast one another with "Salute!" which was quickly followed by the distinct clinking sound of glasses being tapped together and lastly followed by a loud exhale, "Ahh!"

The party had already begun for them. Despite this distraction, I was able to quickly change into my bathing suit. To save the time, I simply threw the shorts I had been wearing into the cabinet under the bathroom sink. I swiftly bolted out of the bathroom, aiming to head directly for the Palermo's backyard and, more specifically, their new, lavish inground swimming pool.

"Michael, take an appetizer plate over with you!" Mom shouted to me, as I raced down the staircase and straight for the front door. "I can't, I have to help Dad ...," I drifted off, as I sprang out the door and headed for the Palermo's. I could hear Mom shout after me, but it was too late. I had enough momentum and speed behind me to be considered gone and in the clear.

I sprinted intently to the Palermo's backyard. As I rushed down across my front lawn, I saw Mr. Desanto setting up one of those orange police horses on the spot in front of my house that moments earlier had served as the big race's start-finish line. I stopped in my tracks to ask what he was doing,

"What's that for?" I questioned. "Oh, hey Michael, this is to block off the street so that cars won't come around and interfere with our block party," he answered. "Is that legal?" I pressed. He chuckled briefly, "Well, yes, it is, if you file for a permit with the town which we did, and they approved. So, yes, we're legal and by the book," he added. "Oh, cool. I guess I'm gonna head over to the pool now," I replied. "I'll see you over there. I just need to set another one of these up over by my house and we'll be good to go," he concluded. Once again, I sped off towards the Palermo's backyard and pool.

As I arrived at the Palermo's driveway, I crossed paths with Dad and a couple of the other dads, as expected, keeping watch over the fire pit. Dad was dialed in. He was poking and probing at the logs in the blazing fire with an old hockey stick, trying to incite the fire from a slow burn to a raging blaze. A couple of the other dads watched on with great interest, puffing on foul smelling cigars while sporting a cold can of Schlitz beer in their free hands.

"You're the first one here, Mikey!" Mr. Palermo declared. "I am?" I asked, while trying to hide my excitement with his news. "Well, you're the first one of the kids anyway," he answered. "There may be a mother or two back there, but you'll want to avoid them at all costs. Otherwise, they'll have you running around doing things for them. My advice to you is run straight for the pool and jump in. Don't look around. Don't make eye contact. Just get into that pool," he continued, with a smile on his face.

I looked around at the other dads, looking for some sign of agreement or consensus but they all just kind of shook their heads and smirked. Finally, Dad looked right over to me and gave me the green light. "Go ahead. Someone has to be the first in," he said. I flashed a big grin back at the dads and made my way straight for the pool, just as Mr. Palermo had encouraged.

I zipped through the gate to the Palermo's backyard and raced right for their fifty-foot, resort-like inground swimming pool. The Palermo's had put the pool in a summer ago and everything about it was first rate: from the pool's stylish design, its swanky tile wrapping its borders, the classic look of the diving board which extended over the deep-end and pitched ever-so slightly at an upward angle and lastly to its opulent mosaic tiled bottom which proudly displayed a large "P" at the very deepest part of the pool.

It was every kid's dream and, along with my family's pool, was where you'd find a dozen or so neighborhood kids cooling ourselves at any time during the summer. I crossed over the Palermo's lawn, sprinting towards the sparkling blue water. As I got to the lawn's edge with the pool decking, I slipped off my classic "Spirit of '76" tank top while in mid-stride, dropping it onto a lounge chair poolside.

A second later, I reached the pool's edge and, with speed behind me, leapt far and high off the coping's edge, immediately shaping into a classic cannonball. I hit the cool, blue water with a massive thud, sending a surging wave clear across the deep end. I quickly sank to the pool's bottom, then forcefully pushed off from the smooth, white-plastered floor.

As I shot back upward, I firmly twisted my body so that I would face the pool's shallow end. I re-surfaced abruptly, thrashing my head sharply from left to right and whisking away any water from my hair and clearing my vision. It was a classic "emerging from water" motion that you'd likely see at any pool, beach, lake, or summertime Mountain Dew TV commercial.

As my vision above-water came back into focus, I was stunned to see an army of people striding hastily into the Palermo's backyard. Before I could get a word out, there were three kids in mid-flight diving, flopping, and can-opening into the pool. Moms, dads, and kids kept filing into the spacious backyard, each carrying either a plate, piece of Tupperware, or some pool toy in hand.

In just mere seconds, the long, rectangular pool, which I had only moments earlier occupied alone, was now nearly at full capacity. As I scanned the pool quickly looking for any of my siblings, someone surfaced from underwater directly in front of me wearing a standard, light-blue swim mask. It was Matteo Palermo and, while still wearing his swim mask and with a muffled voice, he greeted me, "Hey, Happy Fourth!" "Hey. Same to you," I replied. "Today's gonna be insane," he went on. "Yeah, can't believe it's finally here," I answered.

"And the fireworks tonight are gonna be sick!" he exclaimed. "Oh yeah, who's got fireworks?" I questioned. "My dad does. He has a shit ton," he declared. "Did he get them from the Coyne's?" I followed. "No, he went into the North End and bought them from some guy on a street corner. Anyway, he bought a boat load and it's going to be ridiculous. It's a hot one, huh? I think we're gonna be in here pretty much all day," Matteo continued. "That's fine by me," I quickly answered. "It's going to be a ridiculous day anyway … pool, games, food, fireworks," he continued. "Yeah, should be a lot of fun. Just wait until everyone gets here!" I exclaimed.

As Matteo and I were swapping previews of the day's events, and as another body was launching overhead with the obligatory scream of "Cannonball!" we heard rowdy shouting from above. We both swung our heads towards the uproar coming from the back of the Palermo's house. There, we spotted Matteo's brother, Marco, heading down the back deck staircase of the house. He was shouting towards my brother Bobby and Ricky Ferraro, who were just arriving at the party.

Marco rushed down the backstairs towards the duo, intentionally continuing to make a scene. Marco, who was shirtless as usual, was sporting his colorfully adorned cast on his left arm – the trophy from his spectacularly failed bike jump a few days earlier. My brother Bob was wearing his favorite "Mr. Gasser" t-shirt, which featured a bright, cherry red hot-rod with an absurdly oversized engine. Bob completed his look with his go-to cut-off jean shorts that fell to just above his knees.

Ricky, standing directly behind Bob and whooping it up towards Marco, proudly wore his Pabst Blue Ribbon bucket hat. He had won the hat by playing the bean bag toss game at the carnival. The carnival had passed through town a couple weeks ago and this trio of friends had stalked the grounds there relentlessly. Ricky's hat was actually very cool, and he wore it as if he knew it. The three met at the foot of the staircase, and I immediately thought that I'd have to keep a wary eye on them, given the literal "fireworks" that had gone down over the prior couple days. But, with that in mind, I took one deep breadth and basked in the reality that the day and party were now fully underway.

It was just after one in the afternoon and the party was in full swing. There had to be at least seventy-five to a hundred people there, between kids, parents, and grandparents. There must be thirty kids in the pool, I thought to myself. The younger kids were loitering in the safer waters of the shallow end, staying close to the pool steps. I was hanging in the deep end, now actually outside of the pool and in line for the diving board.

We were diving in front of Herb, who was seated in a chair poolside. Herb wasn't a swimmer and was deeply terrified of the water. In lieu of the pool, Herb often chose to serve as an impartial judge, scoring each diver after catapulting from the board. Lou Limone was next to go and was whooping it up in line, "Come on now, Herb. You gonna judge me fair after that race with my dad?" he shouted. "Of course, I'll be fair Louis. After all, you, your father, and Derek were fair with me earlier, weren't you?" Herb responded. "Well, you can't break any rules in a race without rules," Lou shouted back. "Good point, Louis. Let's see what you've got," Herb answered.

With that, Lou gave a nod of his head to Herb and took off up the incline of the board. He strode forward and, using all his weight, jumped up and drove down onto the board's edge. The board, as designed, sprung Lou up and outward from its edge. Lou immediately commenced contorting his body, attempting to fully rotate in a ball and a full flip. But something was off, and Lou began to flail badly mid-way around. He barely made a half rotation as his back and butt thunderously slapped harshly into the water. This resulted in a resounding and collective "Ow!" from those of us standing in line.

As Lou's head surfaced back above water, you could immediately see the pain expressed on his face. He gave a quick look to Herb and, with a huge grin on his face, Herb scored Lou's attempt. "Well, I'll give you credit for the high degree of difficulty and the pain you've endured, but that's about it … I give you a 6.5," Herb announced.

This was met with widespread boos, and laughs, from those of us in line. Lou's younger sister Lisa was next to go, and she set out to restore honor to their family name. She, with a look of determination on her face, began her move up the board. Her dive was a simple but graceful traditional dive. She didn't get much air from the board, but she held excellent form and entered the water with barely a splash. Everyone looked over to Herb to hear her score. "Very nice. Great form. No splash at all, 9.5!" Herb announced.

Shouts of, "Whoa! No way!" came from the other waiting divers, as Lisa smiled widely after hearing her score. I was next to go and slowly climbed on top of the board.

My first instinct was to attempt a flip but the image of Lou's terrible fail from just two dives earlier was stuck in my head. I decided to go with the simple, traditional dive in hopes of posting a score like Lisa's. I took a quick glance at Herb to make sure he was ready and then got in motion down the board. I leapt with full force, trying to gather as much spring from the board as possible, and then I was air born!

I initially felt like I was in good form, though the "kick" off the board drove me higher than expected. As I descended toward the water, I struggled to hold the dive as the torque from the board pushed me further forward. I entered the cool water and twisted frontward with my legs coming over the top of me. As I spun underwater, I immediately realized two things, first, my dive was not going to score well, and second, a full bucket's worth of water had just rushed up my nose.

I resurfaced the water, completely dejected. I looked over at Herb as I began to cough and express out the water that I had taken through both nostrils. Herb looked at me and immediately began to laugh, "You okay Michael? You look like you took in about a quarter of the pool water," he quipped.

I choked a bit as I responded but was able to answer, "I'm fine." "Well, I'll give you an A for effort, but the actual result was a D, or a C, if I'm being generous … 6.0," Herb announced. With my below par score in hand, and a head still filled with pool water, I slowly swam off to the shallow end of the pool. It was time to towel off and clear my head.

I grabbed my towel and briskly dried off. I was hungry and it was time to hit some of those appetizers that had been brought in droves by the neighbors. My timing was right as, just as I stepped away from the pool, Ricky, Marco, and my brother Bob loudly reappeared poolside. I did my best not to make eye contact.

As I began to walk away towards the upper patio and the appetizer table, I heard the unmistakable voice of Mrs. Palermo shouting at an eleven on the volume meter.

"Marco Palermo! Do not go in that water with a cast on your arm!" she yelled. "But Mom, it's eighty-five friggin degrees out!" Marco shot back. "You should've thought about that before jumping your damn bike over those milk crates!" she answered, forcefully. "C'mon Ma, it's so hot out today," he replied. "No, no. You're not doing it!" she shouted, as she quickly approached Marco on the pool deck. "But Ma," Marco pleaded. "Nope. Don't 'But Ma' me. You can only go in if you put a bag around that cast," she replied.

"A bag?! What kind of bag? A trash bag?" Marco questioned. "Exactly, a trash bag. And we'll put duct tape around it to keep the water out," she went on. "Are you insane? I'm not putting any trash bag around my arm, Ma!" Marco answered. "Fine. Then you're not going in!" Mrs. Palermo answered with authority. "Seriously, Ma? You want me to put a trash bag on my arm. You want me to be the kid with the trash bag? What are we the white trash of the neighborhood?" he said, not letting it go. "Marco, I'm telling you, you're not going in that pool today with that cast on!" she exclaimed. "Fine!" Marco shouted back, as he stormed off the deck and away from the pool.

"Okay everybody, show's over. Go back to having your fun. Sorry for that," Mrs. Palermo instructed. As the scene with Marco culminated, I resumed toweling off and returned my focus to getting something to eat.

XXXIII - Le Navi a Vela
(The Tall Ships)

I filled my Bicentennial commemorative Dixie plate with an array of hors d'oeuvres and cocktail snacks. Our neighborhood, with so many Italian families, was chock full of great cooks. And those great cooks went above and beyond for the pre-dinner spread at the Palermo's.

As I took my full plate in search of a seat at the patio table, I spotted Mr. Palermo who was fiddling with the rabbit ears of a large RCA television that sat atop an end table. The TV and table rested on the upper patio of the Palermo's backyard and, in front of it, was a row of yellow patio chairs. My three great aunts were seated there along with recently discovered Uncle Ray and the Padovani grandparents.

The two seats immediately in front of the TV were vacant and in front of them stood Nano and my Uncle Phillip. The two brothers were overseeing Mr. Palermo's efforts and were growing impatient with his slow progress in honing into the elusive airwaves. I hesitated for a second, but the curiosity got the better of me, so I approached the group to find out what was going on.

"Hey, what are you doing with the TV outside?" I asked. "We want to see the Tall Ships parade in New York Harbor. You see, the Italian ship that's in the parade today, the Amerigo Vespucci, is the ship that our youngest brother, your great uncle, Pietro served on when he was just a young man," Uncle Phillip answered.

"Really? He was a sailor?" I asked. "Yes, he was. I've told you this before," Nano answered, as he clasped his hands together, gesturing for everyone to see. "No, you never told me that you had a brother who was a sailor," I answered. "I told you. You just don't listen," he shot back. "Well, he's listening now, aren't you, Michael?" Uncle Phillip offered.

I nodded to acknowledge that I was. "Yes, the Amerigo Vespucci is a training vessel for young sailors and our brother, Pietro, served on the Vespucci for just over a year. That's why we're all so interested to see the ship in today's parade," Uncle Phillip explained. "And what happened to your brother Pietro? How come I don't know him?" I asked, innocently.

My uncle glanced over to my grandfather and, after sharing a pained expression on their faces, he answered, "He died during the war … at the end of World War II." "On a ship?" I followed. "Yes, on a ship. He was on the Italian battleship, Roma, when it was sunk by the Germans in 1943," he answered, solemnly.

There was a brief lull and then Uncle Phillip chimed in again, with renewed vigor in his voice, "You know, your grandfather was also a sailor. Did you know that?" Uncle Phillip questioned. "Well, I knew he was before coming to America," I answered, with a tiny bit of doubt in my voice. "I've told you this before," Nano interrupted. "For almost three years!" Uncle Phillip went on, pointing three extended fingers at me.

Now it was my time to interrupt, "You never told me that you were a sailor for three years, Nano!" I shouted. "Mannaggia! Can you believe this? These kids, I tell you," Nano blurted out. "Mike, he's listening, so let's tell him what you did when you were a young man," Uncle Phillip exclaimed. "Go on, Phillip. Tell him! And Mike, you keep your big mouth shut so the boy can hear the story!" Aunt Gray chimed in.

Nano knew not to test Aunt Gray, so he simply looked away and shrugged off his scolding. "Okay, okay. So, your grandfather sailed on a merchant ship, named the "Ettore," as a crew member," Uncle Phillip continued. "The "Ettore"?" I repeated. "That's right. And the Ettore would sail back and forth between Europe and the United States. And do you know one place in the U.S. where your grandfather sailed while on the Ettore?" Uncle

Phillip continued. "No, where?" I questioned back, increasingly intrigued by his story.

"Right where the Tall Ship parade is sailing today, New York Harbor! And that trip in … 1925?" Uncle Phillip went on. "It was 1926," Nano corrected him. "That's right, 1926. In 1926, in New York Harbor, your grandfather did something extraordinary. You could even say, amazing! Do you know what that was? Any guesses?" he asked me.

"No, I don't know. What did he do that was amazing?" I replied. "He jumped ship!" he shouted, emphatically, as he clapped his hands together sharply. "He did?" I asked, not knowing what that meant. "Can you believe it? He made the biggest decision of his life, right there and … he jumped ship. He was only twenty-three years old, and he did it. Can you believe it?" he continued.

I had heard this story before, that my grandfather had "jumped ship" in New York, but I never understood fully what that meant. So, now seemed like the right time to ask. "What does that mean, to 'jump ship'? I don't really know what you're talking about," I countered.

"It means that he decided to leave Italy … for good, forever, and come here to America. Remember, we talked about some of this yesterday in Nahant. Anyway, it was a very big decision, and he had the courage to do it! You know, you wouldn't even be here right now if he didn't do that. And do you know why he did such a thing?" Uncle Phillip questioned. "No, why?" I responded back with a question.

"For family, that's why! You see, your grandfather was the oldest of eleven kids in our family. And at the time, the government in power in Italy was corrupt. They were fascists! And it was no longer a safe place to live so your grandfather, as the oldest, took the first step to leave for America. And once he was here, he had opportunity! And he made something from that opportunity. And he continued to support our family from here. Until more of us could come and do the same. And the harbor where all the ships are sailing today is where it all started. And that's why even your grandfather celebrates "Independence Day" today in America. That's something, huh?" he asked, rhetorically.

With my uncle's words seemingly hanging in the air, I

caught sight of my aunts beaming their approval and even caught an accepting nod from the Padovani grandparents.

"Well, I hate to interrupt this history lesson, but I think I've got the picture now," Mr. Palermo interjected. "That's it, Cos. You did it," Nano blurted out, as everyone peered in a bit closer to see the screen.

"And remember, I explained to you yesterday how your grandfather stayed and worked with Ray's family in Nahant and then he later had to go to Canada and then come into the country legally?" Uncle Phillip finished, pointing towards Uncle Ray.

In response, Uncle Ray raised and tipped a glass towards us. "Ahh, I think I get it now," I answered, things now suddenly adding up for me. I settled in and, with new interest, watched the TV for a few moments with the senior members of my family and of the neighborhood. I glanced over at my grandfather and was struck by his wide-eyed attention to the screen as one enormous, mast ship after another sailed across the TV while we sat together in the middle of the Palermo's backyard.

XXXIV - I Suoni del Fuoco
(The Sounds of Fire)

While watching the tall ship parade, an overwhelming smell began to waft overhead. It didn't necessarily smell bad, but it was strong and very pungent. So much so, that I had to investigate. I took a step away from the TV and, with an exaggerated sniff from my nose, I wondered aloud what it was.

"What's that smell?" I asked. "That must be the clams going into the clam pit," Aunt Gray answered. "You know what it is, it's the seaweed that's going into the pit ... to sit on top of the clams and the lobsters. That's what that smell is," said Uncle Phillip. "Seaweed! Wow, that smells!" I exclaimed.

"Well, you don't cook the seaweed to eat it. You add it under and on top of the food to add moisture, so that the clams and lobsters can steam in the pit rather than just bake. You see, without it, everything would dry out and lose its taste. It's the best way to cook it properly," Uncle Ray offered his expert opinion. "I'm going to go take a look and check it out," I said, as I sprang towards the Palermo's driveway.

I stepped through the Palermo's gate and into their driveway. Dad was on the scene standing on the far side of the pit and holding one end of an old Army canvas tarp. On the fence side of the pit, Mr. Ferraro and Mr. Padovani each held a corner of the tarp tightly and low to ground. Dad spotted me and called me over.

"Michael! Just in time. Come over here and take a look before we seal this up," he directed. I walked over to him, watching my step as I crossed near the pit's corner. "What is it?" I asked. "I want you to see how we set this up, before we cover it," he answered.

I stood by his side and peered into the pit. There I saw a slew of seaweed, stacked a couple of inches deep. Some of the seaweed was already browning and, as I leaned in a touch closer, I could hear hissing as well as a few crackling, and popping sounds. On top, and in the center of the seaweed, there was a huge roasting pan with an array of vegetables. On both sides of the roasting pan, there were several chrome grills where many ears of unhusked corn were placed.

"Wow, that sure is a lot of food. But where are the lobsters and steamers?" I asked. "Well, those will actually cook quickly, so we'll lift the tarp and lower them down in about a half an hour and then cover them with some more seaweed," Dad answered. "Under seaweed?" I shot back.

"That's right. You see, all the wood burned down to just some coals and embers. We scooped out any remaining big pieces with a shovel and then put a thin layer of seaweed over the stones. Then we added the roasting pan with the potatoes, to get those started. After twenty minutes or so, we added the ears of corn in another roasting pan and then another twenty minutes later we'll add the lobsters and steamers, put another layer of seaweed on top and we're in business. Last step is we cover this up tight and let the heat do the rest for another fifteen to twenty minutes," Dad explained.

"That's wicked cool," I responded, as I felt a wave of the heat radiating from the pit. "Okay, let's go guys. Let's cover this up tight," Dad continued. The three men lowered the tarp collectively, making certain that the full pit was covered. Once enclosed, they placed a half dozen cinder blocks around the edge of the tarp to secure it firmly. The last step was to block each side of the pit with four more orange police horses that Mr. Desanto had annexed for the party. And with that, the pit was secure, and the cook was on.

As we stepped back from the penned area, someone hollered

from just outside of the Palermo's fenced yard. "Bobby, you boys have things under control over there?" a voice shouted. "We sure do. How are you doing over there?" Dad shouted back, as he walked toward the voice.

I followed him, curious to see who was doing the shouting. As we reached the fence corner, we came face to face with our neighborhood racing champion, Mr. Limone. He was standing beside an enormous grill that looked like an old oil tank that had been cut in half and repurposed for grilling. He had a large can of Kingston lighter fluid in his hand and was about to take it to the coals.

"Oh good, you're here. Can you give me a hand with this grill top? Cos and Nick already put the coals in, but I want to get the screen off before I douse the coals with the lighter fluid," he stated. Dad grabbed the near end of the grill and the two men lifted in sequence and then leaned the grill screen up against the exterior of the Palermo's fence. "That'll do. Now, let's get some fire starter on these coals," Mr. Limone suggested, as he unplugged the stopper from the Kingston can.

He proceeded to squirt the fluid onto the black coals, drench-ing them thoroughly across the span of the grill. "And … that ought to do it," he declared, as he nearly emptied the entire can of lighting fluid. "Let's get the screen back on before I set it ablaze. Otherwise, it'll be too hot for us to handle it," he reasoned.

In a flash, the grill was back together. Mr. Limone then reached for a cylinder container of long stick matches and pulled out a single match. He gave us a quick look and said, "Well, here goes nothing," as he struck the match against the rough top of the container and lowered the lit match into the grill. The match contacted the coals and, with a near instantaneous "Poof," the fire was lit.

"There she goes!," Mr. Limone exclaimed. "Nice, that took quick," Dad responded. "We'll let this really get going and, in just ten minutes or so, it'll be ready for us to throw on the burgers and dogs," Mr. Limone declared.

Dad and Mr. Limone stood over the massive grill and admired their work as the edge of the coals slowly began to gray. Suddenly, there was a large "Clang" sound that reverberated from the other side of the fence.

"Is that what I think it is?" Mr. Limone asked. His question was met with another booming chime, though this one was more of a "Clink" than a "Clang".

"It is! Should we try to get a game in before eating?" Dad responded. "What about the grill?" Mr. Limone asked. "What if I get Tony or Ray over here to man the grill? You want to play if I can get one of them over here?" Dad responded. "You know I do, partner."

Dad bolted around the fence corner and headed back to the Palermo's driveway. And, less than five seconds later, he returned with Mr. Padovani close behind. "Okay Jimmy, we're all set. Ray was kind enough to say he'd take grill duty," Dad stated. "All right then! Let's go show them how it's done," Mr. Limone quickly replied.

"What is it, Dad? What game?" I asked. "Horseshoes. Mr. Palermo put a pit in recently. We're gonna go play. You want to come watch?" Dad asked. "Yeah, sure. I'll watch," I replied. "Okay then, let's go," Dad exclaimed. "You sure you're all right with manning the grill, Ray?" Mr. Limone asked. "Sure, no problem boys. You're in good hands. I'm a real pro on the grill. I can handle it from here. Just leave it to me!" Mr. Padovani assured them.

We began to make our way back to the Palermo's fenced in yard. I glanced back quickly and watched as Mr. Padovani took immediate and complete control over the massive grill, reaching for a stack of hamburgers and hot dogs that were sitting inside an equally enormous Coleman cooler.

Right as we reached the gate to the Palermo's backyard, I caught a glimpse of Marco Palermo, who was standing at the worktable inside of his family's garage. I slowed my pace to get a better look. I took two steps inside the garage and noticed that he had a small hacksaw in his right hand. He was sawing on something atop the workbench, swinging his right arm intently across the front of his body. I cautiously took another few steps closer to him,

"Hey, what are you doing?" I asked. He abruptly stopped his sawing motion and jerked his head around at me. "What the fuck does it look like I'm doing?" he shot back. "Looks like you're cutting something with that saw," I answered, as I reached the workbench. "Oh, you figured that all out by yourself?" he ridiculed.

Now standing immediately to his right, I looked over and was shocked to find that the target of his hacksaw was his own left arm. Marco was three quarters of the way to freeing his limb from the cast that had wrapped his broken left arm following his massive wipeout from his jump attempt a few days earlier.

"You're taking that off? Why?" I asked warily. "Because I'm fucking sick of it," he blurted back. "Plus, my mom says I can't go in the water with this thing on and it's hotter than hell. So, I'm taking it off," he continued.

I paused for a brief moment. "Ah, got it. That makes sense, I guess," I added. "Of course, it makes sense. That's why I'm doing it," he finished. "Okay, good luck with that. I'm going to go back to the party," I stated. And with that, Marco got back to liberating his left arm from its cast and I headed directly for the horseshoe pit.

I darted into the back yard, following the clink and clank sounds of the horseshoes hitting their mark in the pit. Dad and Mr. Limone were at opposite ends and were teamed-up against what could only be considered the favorites in Mr. Palermo and Mr. Desanto.

I quickly decided that I'd call Dad and Mr. Limone "Team Plaid," as both men sported classic 1970"s plaid Bermuda shorts. Their opponents, two large and loud men, both donned era-appropriate solid colored bathing suits; one in light blue and the other in tan. Both men in swim trunks were also wearing timeless cabana shirts that were unbuttoned from top to bottom.

Further demonstrating their solidarity, Mr. Palermo and Desanto each held a can of Old Milwaukee beer in their left hand, while clutching a lit cigar in their right. They looked the part, for sure, and were bellowing out their own acclaims for all to hear. To myself, I decided to call their team the "Cabana Boys," as it seemed to fit both their wardrobe and joint persona.

I stood to the side with a few other onlookers, anxious to see the action up close. Both teams were taking some practice tosses to get the feel for the weight of the shoes and the distance between the pit boxes. Dad was last to throw and got a "ringer" on his last practice toss.

"That's it, Bobby! And that one counts, right fellas?" Mr. Limone joked. "No way, Jimmy. That's a nice toss Bob, but let's see you do it during live action," Mr. Palermo shot back. Dad just shrugged it off but glanced over to the audience, seeking some belated recognition for his pinpoint toss. But only I signaled back to him with an emphatic thumbs-up.

"Okay Nicky, do you want to throw against Bob or Jimmy?" Mr. Palermo asked his playing partner. "I'll throw from down here, so whoever is brave enough to face me can come on over," he responded, confidently. "Well, that's my side, so I guess that's me, Nick," Dad answered. "Okay Bobby, but I warn you, when the gloves are off, they're off," Mr. Desanto cautioned. "That's okay, I'm happy to take my chances," Dad quickly replied. "Good! I like the attitude. Let's get it started!" Mr. Desanto shouted.

The four players took their position on each side of their respective horseshoe pit, with Mr. Limone and Palermo readying to make their first throws. "Go ahead Jimmy, since I'm on home field, we'll let you throw first," Mr. Palermo suggested. "Okay Cos, awfully nice of you. But be ready to be disappointed from here on in," Mr. Limone answered. This was met with a chuckle from the growing crowd assembled. Even Mr. Palermo let out a small laugh.

Mr. Limone took aim and, with an exaggerated knee bend, lobbed his first shoe towards the far pit. It was a wobbly toss that seemed to lose its altitude at about the halfway point of its journey. The shoe came crashing down about an inch shy of the embedded two by fours that framed the sanded pit area and its target steel stake. Less than a second after the horseshoe's thud sounded from hitting the ground, there was a chorus of loud jeers and snickers from those watching. Mr. Limone tried to explain away his first toss.

"Now, now … that slipped out of my hand. And that's my driving hand and it's a little fatigued after my big race today! Don't worry Bobby, I'll bounce back. Just zeroing in on it!" he claimed. "I hear you, partner. I'm not worried," Dad answered.

Mr. Palermo just shook his head and took a step forward to ready himself on the left side of the pitted area. "Okay, you got this Cos. Show them how it's done!" Mr. Desanto urged his partner.

Mr. Palermo wasted no time and took aim at his target. He took a long slow stride forward and released the horseshoe from his right hand following a pronounced knee bend. The steel shoe flew cleanly through the air, rotating once as it descended to the ground. The horseshoe found its mark, making a distinct "thump" and then "Clang" as it struck the metal target in the center of the pit.

The shoe, which had landed on its open end, rotated forward and then rolled with pace to strike the stake. The force and motion of the horseshoe caused it to flip forward and left it prone, leaning against the pole. Those of us watching let out a collective roar as the horseshoe dangled for a second before coming to rest against the steel rod.

"A leaner!! Nice going, Cos!" Mr. Desanto shouted, excitedly. "What's that worth?" Herb asked from the gallery. "Leaners are two points, a toss within the length of the shoe's mouth from the stake is worth one point and, of course, a ringer is worth three points," Mr. Palermo answered.

The next two tosses found the pit but neither hit the stake. Dad and Mr. Desanto got to work and measured the distance of those two shoes from the stake. "Okay, that's two for us and one for them," Mr. Desanto declared. "What? He got a point out of that last toss?" Mr. Palermo questioned. "He did. Just barely, but he did," Mr. Desanto responded. "How do you like that?" Mr. Limone mocked. "Yeah, yeah. Let's see you do it consistently Jimmy," Mr. Palermo replied.

Mr. Desanto was next to throw. He strode forward and, with an exaggerated follow through, sent the horseshoe hurling towards the pit. He attempted to assist the shoe as it sailed across the yard, arching his body to try and apply some needed body English mid-flight. The horseshoe failed to respond, however, and it fell about a foot outside of the pit, nearly catching the toes of his partner.

Dad was next to go and wasted little time. He peered at the pit and the stake forty feet away, and then took a full stride forward and sent his horseshoe flying. Dad had great form, the best of the bunch, a likely reflection of his experience as a fast-pitch softball pitcher.

His first toss landed directly on top of the stake, emitting a loud "Clang," as the shoe made a full revolution while hugging the steel target. "A ringer! Nice one, Bobby!" Mr. Limone blurted out. The gallery gathered around the playing area let out a loud chorus of hoots and hollers. "Not bad, Bobby. But how's about I drop one right on top of yours?" Mr. Desanto exclaimed.

He took position alongside the pitcher's box, took aim, and began his pitching motion. He repeated his patented and overstated knee bend and then launched his horseshoe towards the far pit. Miraculously, the shoe dove directly over the stake and landed cleanly on top of Dad's horseshoe that had, only a minute earlier, come to rest there.

"Another ringer! Oh my god, can you believe that!? What a toss!" Mr. Palermo screamed over the erupting cheers from the onlookers. "Nice throw, Nick," Dad offered.

I anxiously waited to see Dad's answer to Mr. Desanto's throw. As Dad positioned himself by the pitcher's box, I heard my name shouted from behind me. Initially, I didn't respond, or even look behind me, as I thought I might have been hearing things. But there it was again. I heard my name called out, this time a bit louder.

I turned towards the house and looked for the source. As I scoured the patio area, I spotted Uncle Phillip, still seated by the television on the upper patio and surrounded by the elders of my family and the neighborhood. He gestured demonstratively to me, signaling for me to come over. I took a quick glance back over at the horseshoe pit and instantly heard the sharp chime of another horseshoe clashing against the steel stake.

"Son of a bitch!" I blurted out loud to myself, upset that I had missed Dad's latest throw. Despite the alure of the horseshoe match, I couldn't resist the beckoning from Uncle Phillip, so I darted to the upper patio to answer his call.

"Hey, what's going on?" I asked, as all eyes of the elders shifted to fix on me. "Come here. I want you to see this, Michael," Uncle Phillip directed. "Are you guys still watching the parade?"

I wondered. "Yes, and we want you to see this next ship coming in," Uncle Phillip answered.

"Oh Phillip, he wants to watch his father playing horseshoes, for God's sake!" Aunt Polly proclaimed. "Polly, this is important. He should see this!" Uncle Phillip countered. "That's okay, Aunt Polly. I want to see it," I responded. "You see, he wants to see it. Attaboy! Here, come closer so you can really see," my uncle said, directing me to sit on the patio and up close in front of the TV screen.

"What is it? What did you want me to see?" I asked. "The Vespucci. It's the next ship to come in. Wait until you see it. It's the most beautiful ship in the world!" my uncle claimed. The whole bunch gathered there by the TV nodded their heads in agreement.

I, of course, thought this was a typical and predictable overstatement that was prejudiced by national pride and drenched with bias. But then, as the camera angle on the television transitioned, I saw it. And it was amazing! I couldn't believe my eyes. I instantly deliberated with myself, searching for the word or words to best describe the sight. All I could come up with was … majestic. I wasn't even sure if I was using "majestic" in the right context, but it felt right and I resolved that it was, without question, majestic.

Everyone inched forward in their seat to get a better look at the massive ship. The Italian made vessel was extraordinary. The hull of the ship was coated in black with two brilliant white stripes outlining the ship's entire body and highlighting the hull's many portholes. Gold accents, particularly at the bow of the boat, completed the ship's striking appearance. There was at least a couple dozen distinctive, grey canvas sails in full display, hanging from the ship's three towering masts.

And if the awe-inspiring visage of the ship alone wasn't impressive enough, the icing on the cake had to be the couple hundred Italian sailors, dressed in full navy regalia, that lined all sides of the ship's surface. And the most incredible sight of all was the groupings of Italian sailors, stacked neatly in an optical pyramid, proudly stationed atop the riggings of each of the three massive ship masts. It was an incredible scene, and I was happy that my uncle had called me over to witness it.

"What do you think, Michelino?" my grandfather asked. The obvious care and sincerity in his voice surprised me. "It's awesome," I said, with a huge smile. "Can you believe that our brother, your uncle, once served on that ship?" Uncle Phillip asked. "No, I can't. That must have been so cool!" I answered, emphatically.

"It's such a beautiful boat," Aunt Gray chimed in. "It's a ship, Grace. Not a boat," Uncle Phillip answered, with a wry smirk on his face for all to see. "Sorry Phillip, it's a beautiful ship. Better?" Aunt Gray responded, sharply. "Much better," he replied. "Nano, have you ever been to see the ship … when your brother was on it?" I questioned. "No, I was already here in the States when Pietro was on the ship. But someday, I'm going to go see it in person. Maybe go on board. Someday," he answered. "That'll be the day, Mike. And I'll go with you," Uncle Phillip asserted.

The two brothers looked at one another and nodded their heads to each other, seemingly cementing the vow to one day visit the ship together. We continued to watch the ship make its way gracefully into New York Harbor, as our group of spectators grew to include my two younger brothers and the Padovani boys. We watched quietly seated beside the older generation, who seemed to collectively take in and appreciate the wonderment that the younger generation shared with them in watching the Italian Naval Academy's stunning entry into our country's Bi-Centennial Celebration and Tall Ship parade.

XXXV - Giochi Pericolosi
(Dangerous Games)

After taking in the Tall Ship parade, I decided to head back to the pool for a quick dip. The horseshoe battle that had been ongoing while I was in front of the TV screen had already ended. It was surprising how the boisterous sounds from the lively match had simply melted away as I got engrossed watching the Vespucci sail into New York Harbor.

The yard had now become largely vacant as many hands were hard at work getting the final preparations ready before we were all to sit down to eat. I glanced over at the pool and hesitated mid-stride, as I saw the only occupants included my brother Bob, Marco, and Ricky. Unsurprisingly, they were goofing around, taking turns trying to knock one another off an old, pitch-black tire tube.

The tube was over-sized, most likely from an old truck tire, with a large, extended air valve jutting from one side. Bobby was floating on the tire in the shallow end of the pool, with both hands firmly grasping onto the tube's side, as Marco and Ricky took turns trying to overturn him from beneath. I thought better of taking a dip and, instead, slinked off to the side and opted to take a seat at the patio table.

Marco and Ricky continued their attempts to displace Bobby from the tube but with little to show for their efforts. At one point, Bob actually looked over at me and flashed a quick smile, clearly enjoying his reign atop the inner tube. A moment later, Marco, abandoning his conventional approach, pulled himself from the side of the pool and onto the pool deck. He then quickly launched himself high in the air and towards Bob and the tube.

He angled his body and extended his legs in what could only be described as a drop-kick motion and landed with force against the tube. It was a direct hit but with limited effect. Rather than dislodging Bob from the tube, the force from Marco's legs landing hard against the side of the tube simply sent Bob and the tube rushing sideways across the shallow end.

The tube jetted to the far side and rebounded off the pool siding and returned to the center of the shallow end. Bobby, all the while, remained steadfastly secure atop the oval watercraft. The three mischief-makers howled loudly. Marco and Ricky then changed tactics and attempted to inundate Bob, splashing him with wave after wave of pool water crashing against his face.

As Bobby squinted and scowled his way through the onslaught, a booming voice abruptly detonated over the yard and brought the scene to a full standstill.

"Marco Palermo! For crying out loud! What the hell are you doing in that pool!? And where's the bag to cover that cast?" Mrs. Palermo roared. I stopped breathing for a second, waiting for her to notice, and then anxiously awaited his impending response.

"You said I couldn't go in the pool with my cast. Or, unless I put a bag over it," Marco answered, smartly. "Yeah. That's what I said. So, where's the bag?" she shot back." Marco paused a second, all eyes on him, and then he slowly raised his recently broken left arm, revealing a naked and cast-less limb.

"What the hell is that? What happened to your cast?" she exclaimed, her voice rising yet another octave. "You said I couldn't go in without the cast covered, so I cut it off," he responded, nonchalantly. "You cut it off?" she repeated, her volume now at eleven.

"Yeah, I cut it off. It's no big deal, Ma," he answered. "What in god's name would possess you to cut that damn thing off?" she questioned. "Well, you said I couldn't get it wet. Ma, it's fine. I'm fine. Stop your worrying," he pleaded with her, as he climbed from the pool.

"You're like a wild animal. You should really get your head checked, you know that?" she muttered, as she turned and began to retreat from the pool area. "It's fine, Ma … don't tell Dad!" Marco implored her loudly. She just waved him off with her back now to us, as she walked back towards the open gate leading to the driveway.

Once she reached the gate, she turned back towards us and shouted her final command, "I need yous all out of the pool. The food's ready and we're all going to eat together. So, dry off and come sit with us at the tables." With that, Mrs. Palermo exited the backyard. Given her tone, I knew that she was dead serious, and I fully expected the group to comply immediately.

However, as Bobby began to wiggle his butt from his tire tube perch, Marco, by this time, was already airborne and headed straight for him. He struck the side of the tube, landing a perfect cannonball right on target. Instantly, the tube shot from under Bobby and careened off towards the deep end of the pool. Both Bob and Marco sunk and momentarily disappeared underwater. They resurfaced nearly simultaneously a second or two later, both wearing wide grins on their faces, while whisking away any residual water from their full heads of hair.

"I got you! Got you good, Bobby!" Marco yelled excitedly. "Yeah, you got me pretty good," Bob conceded. "That was pretty awesome," Ricky chimed in. "Hey Marco, you got a huge welt on your side. You okay?" Ricky observed, pointing to Marco's right side.

"Whoa! What the fuck?" Marco blurted out, as he inspected the mark on the right side of his rib cage. "Dude, that looks nasty. Does it hurt?" Ricky asked. "Yeah, it does, shit for brains. I must have landed on that dumb ass air spout sticking out of the tube. *Madone*, mother …," Marco gasped, as he winced in pain.

As Marco removed his hand from his side, I caught a glimpse of a purple and red abrasion that immediately swelled into a raised, round contusion. I slowly rose to my feet and discreetly made my way towards the gate leading out of the Palermo's yard. I wanted to make my exit without facing any possible wrath from Marco. As I walked away, I could hear him continue to curse as the trio slowly got out of the pool.

XXXVI - La Festa
(The Feast)

I walked into the Palermo's driveway and was awestruck by what I saw. The area had been entirely transformed from just an hour earlier. A horde of neighborhood moms were scurrying about, bringing out countless platters of food that were carefully wrapped in Reynolds Wrap aluminum foil.

Karen Drive, the dead-end road that fed from Fieldstone and only served as an access way to the Palermo and Raffaelli's driveways, was now converted into an extended, outdoor dining hall. There were at least a dozen farm-style tables lined in a single row with a mishmash blend of folding chairs dotted around the tables. The tables were neatly covered in fresh, white linens that hung nearly to the ground on both sides. It was an impressive spectacle, and I was truly mystified by the speed and complete transformation that had taken place.

It looked incredibly cool and thoroughly inviting. I ambled across the driveway, taking care to avoid the still smoldering clam bake pit, and walked onto Karen Drive to get a better look. Moms kept coming and going to drop off woven bread baskets filled with fresh rolls. A second wave of moms followed shortly behind and dropped off small bowls of melted butter. And then a third pack trailed that group and placed thin, plastic lobster bibs on top of each place setting.

It was like clockwork. Every cog of the assembly line was moving and in perfect timing. As this prep work unfolded flawlessly, a throng of dads hustled in front of an over-sized picnic table. They were focused on getting all their grilled and steamed fare separated and properly plated. It was like watching a group of primal carnivores taking inventory over their collective kill. Occasionally, a brave mom would arrive on the scene, bark out a few instructions, only to be waved off by the men.

There was a lot of chatter, head nodding and an even greater volume of hand gesturing. Seated at the farm table, directly across from the dads' station, was the elder set of relatives and neighbors. They carefully watched over the dads, shouted unwanted instructions – some in English but most in Italian – and sporadically snickered at the men, who were obviously wrestling over the task at hand. I walked over to get a closer look.

"Mannaggia, che casino!" Nano shouted from his seat, seemingly targeted at Dad. "Enough from you!" Dad answered. This got a big chuckle from all at the seniors' table. "Your grandfather really knows how to push your dad's buttons, huh?" Uncle Ray asked. "Yeah, I'd say so," I answered. This got an even bigger laugh at the table. "You eating quahogs?" I asked, pointing to a couple of big, empty clam shells sitting on the table. "What, these? Yes, I brought them for your grandfather and uncle. We saw it yesterday, it's their favorite. I have a whole bunch of them right here," he answered, pointing to a cooler at the side of the table.

"You want one, Michelino?" Nano asked. "No, I don't think so," I answered, as Uncle Ray brought the cooler onto the table. "C'mon, have one. We'll have one with you, right boys?" Uncle Ray urged. "No, that's okay. I don't think so," I replied quickly, leaving little doubt that I wasn't interested.

Uncle Ray wrestled three more clams from the cooler and placed them in front of him on the table. "Well, you don't know what you're missing," Uncle Ray went on, as he grabbed a short, stubby knife with a wide, wooden handle. "Open them up, Ray," Uncle Phillip encouraged him. "I'm going, I'm going, Phillip. Hold on to your horses. Ladies would any of you like to join us?" Ray asked my aunts sitting at the table. This was met with immediate head shakes from the gallery, indicating no dice.

"I don't know how you eat those huge clams, like you do, just raw and right out of the shell," Aunt Polly responded, crinkling her nose, and signaling her repulsing disapproval. "Raw is the best way to eat these. Are you kidding me, Polly?" Uncle Phillip shot back. "That's fine. It just means that there's more for us," Uncle Ray reasoned.

Ray took the shucking knife, placed it on the rear of the clam and with a thrusting and twisting motion he popped the top of the shell off. The clam revealed inside was enormous and extremely gooey looking. It looked utterly disgusting to me. However, beauty is truly in the eye of the beholder and both Nano and Uncle Phillip gushed over the same site that simultaneously turned my stomach.

"Woo, that's a nice one," Uncle Phillip exclaimed. "Okay, it's yours," Ray said, handing the now open quahog to my uncle. Ray then reached for the next clam, which was of equal size. He again made quick work of detaching the top side of the shell, revealing another super-sized gelatinous slop and handed it to Nano. "Oh perfecto! Thank you, Ray" Nano responded. "Last one! I think I'll keep this one for myself," Ray declared, with a smile on his face.

In a flash, his quahog was also free from its upper shell. Ray then reached back into the cooler and retrieved a small glass vessel that held a light-yellow colored milky looking substance. "What's that?" I asked, pointing to the tiny bottle nearly lost in his massive hand. "This is lemon juice. I squeezed it myself using lemons from a lemon tree that I keep in my yard in Nahant," he answered, proudly.

"Michael, you at least have to try the lemon juice. It's home-made and out of this world," Uncle Phillip urged. "You want to try it?" Ray asked, as he shook the bottle mildly in his hand. "I guess. But just a little bit, not a lot," I answered warily.

Uncle Phillip gestured down the table towards my aunts and, without a word spoken, a white and yellow dixie cup was passed forward. Uncle Ray took the cup and carefully poured a small amount of juice into it. "Here … sip it … a little at a time," Uncle Ray directed, as he handed it to me. I slowly raised the cup to my mouth and did just as he said.

I took a modest swig of the juice and swallowed. I was instantly surprised. The juice was smooth and milky with a clean citrus aftertaste. It wasn't what I expected as it was entirely free from that harsh acidic quality that I had known from store bought brands. I immediately went in for another sip.

"He likes it! Look, he likes it. Hey Mikey, he likes it!" Uncle Phillip exclaimed with a huge smile on his face, parroting the Classic "Life Cereal" commercial of the time. Of course, his version of the catch phrase came with a heavy dose of Italian inflection. I nodded my head in agreement as I finished what was left of the juice and handed the paper cup over to Uncle Ray.

"It's good, really good," I said. "Thank you, I'm glad you liked it," he answered. Uncle Ray then got right back to business, pouring a small portion of his homemade lemon juice on top of his exposed raw clam. He then handed the small juice bottle to Nano, who did the same and then passed it over to Uncle Phillip.

With the trio now having all properly seasoned their quahogs, they paused and raised their clams toward one another. "Salute!" Nano toasted, the other two men then quickly echoed. "One, two, three … Forza!" Nano enthusiastically shouted. The three men, with a distinct slurping sound, sucked in and then swallowed the large clams whole.

In response to this horrific sight and its equally awful glugging sound, I felt my face contort in disgust. I quickly glanced around the table and spotted my Aunt Polly's matching look of pure dread. The three men let out a great collective and agreeable sigh, "Ahhh!".

To cap things off, they each plopped their now-empty clam shells atop the table and reached for their respective juice glasses that had been neatly topped off with Nano's homemade wine. This dining ritual would undoubtedly be repeated for the rest of the day and night.

"Time to eat!" Mrs. Palermo barked for all to hear, as only she could. "Everybody, come on over and make your plates while everything's hot! We have everything from the clambake at this table. And the hot dogs, hamburgers, and cheeseburgers over at this table!" she yelled, pointing at the respective tables.

No one waited to be told a second time and everyone rushed

into place. I wasn't much of a seafood eater, especially after seeing the quahogs up close, so I darted right for the dogs and burgers table. Although I skipped the seafood station, I couldn't help noticing, and appreciating, the extent of the clambake spread. That table was staffed up front by Mom and Mrs. Padovani, with Dad and Mr. Limone working behind them. They worked cohesively, like clockwork, with the moms dishing out portions and the dads insuring all items were fully stocked.

The lobsters were a blistering red and you could still see steam lifting from their shells. The steamers were sitting atop the table in a massive caldron that Mrs. Padovani stirred with an oversized ladle. There were huge, roasted potatoes, piles of green beans, tons of corn on the cob, skewers of vegetables, a mountain of coleslaw and a bubbling vat of clam chowder. Everything, and more, that you would hope for at a clambake.

My table of choice, however, was simpler and more classic Fourth of July fare. I couldn't decide if I was leaning towards a hot dog or cheeseburger, but then decided, why not go for both. This table was manned by Mr. Palermo and Mr. Padovani, with Mr. Desanto out front, cattle calling out for customers.

"Don't wait, get your burgers and dogs right here! Fresh off the grill! Make sure you leave a generous tip for your servers! Hey, hot dogs here! Hey, get your burgers here!" he shouted loudly.

I was about a dozen kids deep in line and anxiously waiting for my food. As each kid stepped forward, Mr. Desanto had something witty and entertaining to say. This table was dominated with burgers and dogs but also had plenty of corn on the cob, green beans as well as tubs of macaroni and potato salad as side options.

I finally reached the front of the line, where Mr. Desanto greeted me. "Okay, here comes trouble! What, you get a release from reform school today?" he kidded. "Ha, ha. Very funny," I quipped back at him, slightly embarrassed.

"What'll you have today?" he asked. "I'm going to go with a hot dog and a cheeseburger," I answered. "One of each? Good for you. You're a growing young man, you should feed the body. I like it! One of each for the still growing young man!" he shouted out, like a short-order cook.

"And don't forget your vegetables. You need those too to

grow healthy bones. Take some green beans and a piece of corn," he directed me. Mr. Padovani handed me my plate with my burger and dog as well as a piece of corn and some green beans. "Another happy customer! We aim to please! Who's next? Step on up. Don't be shy. What will you have, short stack?" he asked my brother Steve, who was right behind me in line. I quickly grabbed an ice cold can of Pepsi from a large tub that was filled with ice and an assortment of soda cans and headed for a seat at the table.

I sat with the usual crew, which included my brother Dave, the Padovani brothers, Matteo Palermo, Lou Limone, and Tommy Ferraro. We were all starving, I guess from being active all day, and couldn't eat fast enough. Nearly every one of us had chosen to dine from the burgers and dogs table, except for Lou Limone.

Lou was apparently a huge fan of lobster, and he was diving right into it like a pro. His sister, Lisa, who was seated one section of table over from us, did Lou a favor and also took a lobster. Lisa, however, wasn't as much of a lobster fan as her older brother was and only wanted to sample a single claw. So, after using her nutcracker to detach the larger of her lobster's two claws, she promptly delivered the rest of her lobster onto Lou's plate. Lou barely paused to acknowledge the gesture and simply muttered, "Keep'em coming," which got some laughs.

"Wow, you really love lobster, huh?" I asked Lou. "You know it. I've always loved lobster," Lou declared. "Do you eat the whole thing?" I followed. "Well yeah, but just the normal parts. Not like the old country folks down at the far end of the table who will likely be digging into the head and shit," Lou scoffed, as he pointed towards the last section of table.

We all quickly glanced to the end of the tables that were stringed together. Lou then picked up the body of his lobster and forcibly twisted his hands in opposite directions. The torque from his grip broke the shell in two and exposed a stringy orange and green goop from the head half of the lobster. This was met with a chorus of retching and gagging sounds from our table. Lou held up the innards for all of us to see, "You see this. Right here," he said, as he pointed to the insides of the lobster. "Well, this here is a no go for me. But, for the crowd at the other end of the tables, they'll eat this shit right up. It's like some sort of delicacy or something. Whatever we want to toss in the garbage, they're down there fighting over it!" he exclaimed.

There were a few more mimicking sounds from the table to emulate someone puking, followed by some giggles. And, although I knew that Lou's ridiculing was largely in jest, I also knew, as the person who sat closest to Nano at our own kitchen table, that he was pretty much spot on.

I took another long look down the row of tables and, sure enough, I caught a glimpse of Nano with one of the narrow lobster legs in his mouth. Although disturbing, this wasn't an unfamiliar sight to me, as our family had a tradition of serving lobster at every Christmas Eve dinner. The slurping sound that would emanate from Nano, while he siphoned what he could from the narrow leg of the lobster, was actually far worse than the mere sight of this ritual.

And, of course, this would be repeated eight to ten times, or, at least, for whatever number of legs that a lobster has. Nonetheless, I had firsthand experience and knew that Lou's mocking certainly had some truth to it. And, as I looked back over to Lou, sure enough, he had a lobster leg hanging from his mouth and was pretending to use it as a straw. This again got good laughs from everyone at the table.

As we were finishing up with dinner, I peered down the span of tables that covered nearly the entire street. I spotted that the seating was largely divided into three segments. I was sure that there hadn't been any kind of seating chart organized for the outing, as no one had instructed us where to sit. But it was striking enough for even me to notice that that there were three distinct areas.

The first stretch at the far end of the street, where I was sitting, is where all the kids had come to be. Our section was further split by boys and girls, with the majority being boys in the neighborhood. Though a couple of girl cousins of the Palermo's helped even out the odds.

The middle seating area is where all the parents had gathered. Unsurprising to me, this group was by far the loudest, but they were also the hosts for today's celebration, so if anyone had earned the right to relax and blow off some steam it was this group. And by the sounds of the whooping and hollering, there was a lot of steam being released.

The third section, nearest to the Palermo's driveway and the serving tables, is where the grandparents and great aunts and uncles were located. The volume of this cohort was only fractionally lower than the parents' area. That was in large part because Nano was there and actively holding court with his people. Overall, the neighborhood was buzzing across generations, and it was just a great day.

My table, as you'd expect, was in a big hurry to finish our meals. Day light was burning, and everyone wanted to get back to the pool and to resume goofing off. On my way back to the Palermo's backyard, I had to walk past the full length of dining tables neatly arranged on Karen Drive.

As I strode up the street, I was amused as I noticed the table-top of the kids' section was littered with a massive stockpile of empty Pepsi cans. This was in stark contrast with the parents' section, where I found an equally immense number of empty cans. Except these empties weren't of the soda variety but instead were empty beer cans, predominantly Budweiser.

The "adults'" table was still in rare form and Mr. Desanto and Mr. Palermo were leading the way. The duo, whom I had named the "Cabana Boys," from the earlier horseshoe game, stood in front of the other parents gathered at the table. They were seemingly acting out some kind of scenario or encounter that they had experienced and had the table hanging on to every word and gesture of their story.

Just as I reached them, their captive audience let out a resounding roar. The entire crowd just exploded with uncontrollable, wholehearted, full belly laughing at the apparent punchline. Clearly, they were enjoying themselves.

The last section of tables was home to the grandparents. There weren't very many empty soda or beer cans in their area, but there certainly were a handful of empty wine bottles. This crew, notwithstanding Nano's presence and impact, weren't quite as loud as the parents' area but they were still uncharacteristically boisterous. The grandmothers and great aunts were the most notably out of character. I chuckled as I walked by and observed the senior ladies cackling at the tales being spun from the table. Without question, this group of partygoers were enjoying the day as much, if not more, than anyone.

XXXVII - Evitare l'Alveare
(Dodge the Beehive)

I sped into the backyard and found the pool already half full. The sun was beginning to slip lower in the sky, so I scrambled to get more pool time in. I quickly ripped off my tank top and then looked for some open water. I found an open area just outside of the shallow end, where the pool's bottom sloped most steeply towards the deep end.

I leapt firmly from the coping and quickly shaped my body into a cannonball. I pierced the crystal blue water, sending an unimpressive and meager wave of water in my wake. The water had that familiar and welcoming late afternoon or early evening warmth that only came after hours of sunlight beating on the pool's surface all day.

I turned and headed for the pool's ladder in the deep end. I wanted to get a couple turns off the diving board before the pool got too crowded. I swam over to the ladder and began to hoist myself out of the water.

"Michael, what are you doing in the pool already? You just ate!" my mom shouted to me. "What's the big deal, Ma? Everyone's in the pool already," I answered back. "I don't care about everyone else. You know that you need to wait an hour after eating before you swim," she countered. "Are you kidding me!? That's not even a thing. How does that even matter? Does some kind of magic happen in an hour? Plus, there's like a hundred people around … nothing's gonna happen," I declared, defiantly.

"Don't make a scene about this, Michael. Those are our rules," she responded. "C'mon Ma, are you serious!?" I pushed a bit further. There was a good four or five second pause, as we stared each other down. "I'll let you go in the shallow end for now, but no deep end until it's been an hour. Do you understand?" she bargained with me. But I wasn't having it.

"You're seriously going to ruin the day, Mom," I warned. "That's it … take it or leave it. Either get in the shallow end or get out of the pool. An hour will pass in no time," she finished. "Yeah, it will … in about an hour!" I sniped back. "Michael … That's final," she cautioned me one last time. "Fine!" I shouted, as I slammed my fist into the pool water, punching her imaginary face. I immediately pouted, ducked under water, and swam off towards the shallow end of the pool. The matter was closed, and not in my favor.

I was now in the shallow end of the pool with all the young kids and the neighborhood girls. My brother Dave and the Padovani brothers took a seat on the coping near the pool stairs, allowing their feet to hang in the water. They had just witnessed my banishment to the shallow end and chose not to bother getting into the pool themselves.

"This sucks! It's like a hundred degrees out here and I have to stay in the shallow end with all the girls. What the fuck!" I cursed. "I can't believe that she said it was okay to be in the pool at all," Dave confessed. "It's just insane. What does eating something have anything to do with your ability to swim. It's fucking stupid," I went on. "Well, if she hears you swearing out here, she's not going to let you in the pool at all," said Dave. This was a reasonable observation by Dave as I was known to have a bad mouth and had been disciplined regularly for similar outbursts.

I continued to simmer over my "timeout" in the shallow end when Matteo Palermo approached us. "Hey, we were thinking about getting a dodgeball game going over on the court. You guys in?" Matteo offered. "Who's playing?" I asked. "Right now, it's me, Lou, Tommy, Kevin, and if you guys play, we'll have eight. So, four a side. What do you think?" he asked.

Considering my plight in the shallow end of the pool, I only needed to mull it over for a half second. "Yeah sure, I'm in!" I answered. "How about you guys?" Matteo asked the other three seated at the edge of the pool. "We'll play," Dave quickly answered for the trio.

I promptly left the pool, grabbed my towel, hastily dried off and got my shirt and shoes back on. We raced over to the rear of the yard, where, a year earlier, the Palermo's had installed an asphalt, dual purpose court for tennis and basketball. The court was massive. It was at least forty feet deep, and it ran the full width of the backyard, which had to be nearly a hundred feet across.

The tennis net wasn't out today, so we were able to use the full open court to rifle dodge balls at one another. We gathered at the center line and set out to make two teams.

"Me and Tommy will be the two captains and pick the teams," Lou Limone announced. "I'll pick first," Tommy declared. "Okay then, who's your first pick?" Lou asked. "I'll take Michael," Tommy answered, pointing at me. I was happy to be the first guy picked.

"Okay, let's see. I'll take Dave and Matteo then," Lou responded, picking the next two guys. "Mario and Kevin, you're with us," Tommy quickly followed. "Okay Johnny, that means you're on our team. We'll take this side," Lou finished, as he palmed one of the medium sized, red jelly balls. "Okay, we're over here then," Tommy shouted, as he bounced a matching red jelly ball and ran into place. Matteo had the third and final jelly ball and placed it directly in the middle of the center line.

The objective of the game was to get all the players from the other team "out" by striking them with one of the jelly balls. To be a good "kill," however, the ball had to strike the player in flight and couldn't hit the ground or any other object first. Additionally, a player would be out if he threw a ball that was caught by an opposing player.

So, a player could be removed from the field of play by either being struck by a thrown ball or by throwing a ball which is caught by an opposing player. Once a player was ruled out, they had to move to the far end of the court and were "jailed" there. That player could not leave the "jail" area but could still make throws at opposing players, if any game balls came into the confined area. Jailed players were, otherwise, out of the game, unless or until a teammate caught a ball thrown by an opposing player. Any such player catching a ball would not only get the thrower out of the game but could also "free" one of his jailed teammates and have them re-enter the action. The game basically ends and is won by a team once they have jailed all the players from the opposing team. It was a very simple, and purely brutal, game that was loved by boys of all ages.

The two captains each held a ball in hand and the third game ball rested at center court. "It's on … game on!" Lou shouted, excitedly. Everyone began to move around, opting not to be a stationary target. I feinted a run and an attempt to swipe the loose ball at center court. Lou fell for my head fake and whipped his ball right where he anticipated I was headed. The ball missed its mark and whistled above my head by nearly a foot. This allowed me to race up to the midcourt and pilfer the free, third ball.

Knowing that my team now possessed all three game balls, I was safe to stand right up to the center line separating the two teams. I cocked my right arm high and faked a couple of throws, as I searched out a target. Much like lions hunting a herd of antelopes on the Serengeti, I sought out the weakest member in what was our own form of natural selection. In this game, that was usually the youngest, so I fixed my aim on Johnny Padovani.

And, just like an inexperienced herd member, John loitered, wandering in the middle of the court like a lost deer. I made one mock throwing motion, causing John to leap in the air from a phantom ball toss and then let the ball go as he landed awkwardly. The ball struck John's shoulder, as he turned away to protect both his head and face from the projectile. The thud from the ball crashing against his body announced to everyone that John was "out".

"Got you!" I screamed. John dutifully made his way to the jail area on our side of the court, as Matteo raced to retrieve the ball that had careened off his teammate. Tommy then rushed forward and hurled his ball at Matteo. Matteo, as he reached for the loose ball, dove to the court's surface. Tommy's volley soared just inches short and struck Matteo on the bounce, so it wasn't a clean hit and Matteo was still "alive" in the game. The rubber ball ricocheted from the ground, off Matteo's leg and high into the air.

Kevin then sprung forward and took another attempt at the now prone Matteo. But, to Kevin's surprise, Lou had taken the rebounding ball from Matteo's leg out of the air and instantly converted it into a fastball that struck Kevin directly in his mid-section.

Red rubber balls continued flying in a relentless fire fight, as players were sent to jail and later called back after a team-mate won their release. It was wildly fun, and after about fifteen minutes into the game, I was a sweaty mess. I managed to stay out of jail by keeping my throws low at my opponents and then retreating quickly when I wasn't armed with a ball in hand.

We were about twenty minutes into the game and both teams had two players live and two imprisoned. I was still active on the main court with Tommy on my side, with Lou and Dave facing off against us. I was armed with a ball, as were Lou and Tommy who were squared off against one another. As those two egged each other on, attempting to lure their target to take an ill-advised shot, I decided to attack Dave.

I took two big strides forward, telegraphing my shot, and hurled the ball towards Dave's feet. My throw drifted wide of Dave and then spun wildly on the ground, ultimately bouncing to my teammate, Mario, who was playing from behind the line at the far end of the court. But I had made the critical error of fixating on my failed toss and, consequently, lost focus of my most dangerous adversary. I had left myself entirely vulnerable, and Lou pounced on it.

I barely had a second to react as Lou rifled a shot that simply exploded against my face. He nailed me! I had expected that Tommy would be able to keep Lou at bay, as he was mirrored across from him. But he hadn't and I paid the price. I'm not sure what was louder, the sound of the rubber ball pounding against my face or the chorus of "oohs and aahs" from everyone who saw it.

The force of the blow caused my legs to buckle underneath me, and I collapsed to the ground like a crumpled beach chair. I instantly reached for my face and immediately knew that I was bleeding. Lou was the first to rush over to me to ask if I was all right.

"You okay, man? I'm so sorry, I didn't mean to catch you in the face," he apologized. A half second later, he got a good look at my face. "Oh shit. Fuck! Holy shit, you okay? Dude, you need to get a towel or something," he exclaimed, with real worry in his eyes. "I'm fine. It's just my nose. My nose bleeds all the time. Any kind of bump and I get a nosebleed," I assured him, as I got back to my feet.

"Yeah, but this was no bump. I pummeled you with that ball … right in the face," he continued. "Yeah, it's fine. I'm fine," I answered, as I took my towel from Dave, who had quickly grabbed it for me. "You should go get some ice or something," Tommy chimed in. "Yeah, I think I will. It's fine. Maybe you can get someone to take my place," I went on, as my ears were still ringing loudly from the impact.

"You sure, you don't mind?" Lou asked. "Yeah, I'm sure. It's not a big deal," I claimed. "Man, again, I'm sorry. I didn't mean to plunk you in the kisser like that," Lou repeated. "I know. Really, it's no big deal," I said, as I walked away, the towel firmly pressed against my face.

I walked towards the Palermo's house, looking to get some ice for my nose. I was unfortunately met by the "elders," who had returned to their perch on the upper patio of the backyard.

"What happened to you!?" Aunt Gray asked, concerned. "He hurt himself playing that stupid game," Nano interrupted. "I didn't hurt myself, Nano. I got hurt in the game," I shot back. "Well, it's a stupid game," Nano insisted. "It's just a game, Nano. It's not stupid. It's fun," I countered.

"I don't know, Michael. We were watching from here and it does look like a stupid game. What kind of game is it when the objective is to hit someone in the face with the damn ball?" Uncle Phillip argued. "It's not someone's face, it's just to hit the other team with the ball," I clarified.

"Do you lose points if you hit someone in the face then?" he pressed. "No, but …," I began. "And where were you hit with the ball?" he interrupted. I paused and followed with a minor eye roll. "In my face," I conceded. "Good, then we agree. It's a stupid game," Uncle Phillip determined. "Okay, whatever. It's a stupid game, I guess," I admitted.

"Stupid!" Nano shouted, coming over the top to get the last word. "Leave the poor boy alone, you two. For god's sake, give it a rest! Let me see your nose, Michael," Aunt Gray came to my rescue. I took a step closer to her and lifted the towel away from my face. "They got you good, huh? It actually looks like it's stopping, but it's a bit swollen," she declared. "Let's get some ice on it," Aunt Polly chimed in.

"Here, I've got some right here," Uncle Ray offered. He reached below his seat and lifted the medium sized cooler onto the patio table. "I've got plenty, right here," he said, as he lifted the lid to the cooler.

"Isn't that the cooler that you had the quahogs in?" I asked. "Yeah, so what?" he questioned back. "You want me to put quahog ice on my face? "No thanks," I shot back. "Why, what's wrong with it. It's not going to bite. It's just ice," he responded. "It had quahogs all over it. It's gross. And it's going to smell," I argued. "Don't be silly, it's not going to hurt you. We were eating those quahogs and we're all fine. You're just going to use the ice to stop the swelling. Now come on," he finished, ending the debate.

"Here put some in this, Ray," Aunt Gray directed, as she handed Ray a few sheets of paper towel. Uncle Ray pulled a half dozen cubes from the cooler and neatly wrapped them in the paper towel. He folded the sheets twice over the cubes to give an extra layer between the ice and handed it to me. "Here you go. Keep this on it, ten to fifteen minutes ought to do it," he instructed me. I thanked everyone at the table and took my quahog ice, swollen nose, and injured pride back to the court and the dodgeball game.

I walked back to the court, holding the wrapped ice to my nose while dragging a pool chair with me. I positioned my chair on the grass beside the pool and tuned in as the dodgeball game was going strong. Rob Schaefer had been tabbed to replace me and was now serving time in dodgeball jail. The teams were the same, albeit with Rob replacing me, but it looked like a new game had gotten underway since Rob was now the only player who was "out".

I watched as several wild throws sailed far and wide from their intended marks. Lou, as usual, was loud and obnoxious, taunting his opponents tirelessly. I could tell by his facial expression that Tommy had had enough of Lou's mouth. He hustled, scrambled, and picked up two loose balls bouncing on his side of the court. He raced to the mid-court line, straight towards Lou, and whipped the first ball wildly.

His toss was a bad one and missed by a mile. But in the excitement, Lou tripped and fell only a few feet from mid-court. This time, Tommy didn't rush his throw. He homed in on his fallen target, sprawled out on the ground, and hurled a BB at him. This one was on target and struck Lou directly on his butt!

There was a resounding "thump" when the shot found its mark. The ball rebounded high in the air and then spun away, coming to rest beneath a shrub on the far side of the court. The two Padovani brothers, on opposing teams, rushed to lay claim to the displaced ball. They arrived at the shrub at the same time and scuffled to gain possession of it.

Suddenly, both brothers made an abrupt about-face and, with panic stricken looks, raced away from the bush. Both were screaming and flailing their arms wildly. Mario, while in mid-stride, began to rip his shirt off his back. The rest of us, although we had no idea what was going on, instinctively began to flee the area.

Johnny was about two steps behind when Mario reached the pool deck. Without any hesitation, Mario ran straight off the deck and right into the pool. Johnny hit the water less than a second later. We had all retreated far from the court and hovered over the pool around the deep end. Mario resurfaced above the water.

"What? What the hell is it?" Lou asked. Mario paused and caught his breath, "Bees, fucking bees! They're still on me!" he screamed. Johnny then resurfaced as well, "Bees!" he screeched.

Mrs. Schaefer and Mrs. Ferraro, who had been setting up the dessert table, saw the commotion and rushed over. "Is everyone all right? What's going on?" Mrs. Schaefer asked. "They chased a ball under a bush over there. And there was a beehive and they both got stung," I answered. "I got stung about a dozen times!" Mario shouted. "So did I!" Johnny added. "Oh boys, you're all right. Are either of you allergic?" she followed. "I don't think so," Mario replied. Johnny just shook his head, no.

"Okay, let's get you boys out of the water and make sure all the stingers are out. Come on and we'll get something on those stings that will help. The two brothers paddled over to the ladder and climbed out of the pool.

"All of you stay clear from that side of the court, please. We don't need any trips to the emergency room. Come on, boys," Mrs. Ferraro added. The Padovani brothers followed the two moms to the house. As they rose from the pool, I got a good look at the raised, red welts on both their chest and arms. It made me appreciate that a bloody nose wasn't all that bad.

There was something uniquely special about swimming in a pool at night. I don't know if it was the resonating glare from the pool light or just a sense that you've cheated the day out of some extra life, but it was dreamlike. It just gave me an incredible sense of freedom and satisfaction. And this night was like no other.

We had the entire neighborhood together; we had the pool after dark and we had fireworks still to come. Once again, we impatiently waited in line to leap off the diving board. This time it was in the dark of night and into a fully illuminated pool which somehow made the water appear even more inviting and crystal clear. One after another, we took turns launching from the board to dive and flop back into the water.

After my third or fourth dive, I spotted two figures who had arrived and taken seats at the far end of the pool. I wasn't sure but I thought it could be the Padovani brothers, so I decided to swim down and check it out. I swam most of the pool's distance underwater, at least to the point where I could now touch the bottom in the shallow end. I quickly confirmed that it was Mario and John. They were sitting together on a bench beside the pool watching the mayhem.

"Hey, you guys all right?" I asked. "Yeah, we're okay now," Mario answered. "That was insane ... and scary," I said. I got a better look at the guys, and I spotted loads of odd, white splotches smeared all over them. "What the hell is that all over you?" I asked.

"What this? This is a paste of baking soda that Mrs. Palermo made. She said it would help with the bee stings. And then she put it all over us," Mario answered, with a somewhat defeated tone in his voice. "What does baking soda do? I mean, did it work?" I followed. "I don't know, I guess. I mean I feel better than before but who knows. That could be from the Benadryl that Mrs. Schaefer also made us take," Mario responded. "Okay well, at least if something's working then I guess that's better than nothing," I reasoned.

We began to hear a smattering of fireworks off in the distance. We were all pretty hyped for the adults to get our own show started. "Can't be long now, before we light off our fireworks," I offered. "No, shouldn't be too long. We saw them getting set up outside on the street before we came out back," Mario responded. "You guys gonna come back in the pool at all?" I asked. "I don't think so. She told us to keep this gunk on for a while. It'd just wash off if we jumped back into the pool," Mario reasoned.

"Yeah, I guess that makes sense. I'm gonna get out in a couple minutes. I kind of want to watch them set up for the fireworks anyway," I stated. With that, I turned and headed back to the deep end. I wanted to get one more turn off the board before leaving the pool. As was the case before, I was going to be at least six or seven divers deep in line before getting my turn off the board.

XXXVIII - Sta Per Iniziare Lo Spettacolo
(Show Time)

After getting out of the pool, I rushed from the Palermo's backyard, intent to get an up-close look at this year's fireworks stockpile. I immediately ran into Dad and Mr. Limone who were stacking and organizing fireworks at a table stationed in the corner of the driveway.

"Whoa, can I see what you have there?" I asked. "Okay Michael, sure you can. Step right up, but no touching," Mr. Limone answered. "Are you wet, Michael?" Dad then asked. "No, I'm dry. Got out of the pool a while ago," I fibbed a little.

They returned to the task at hand and continued pulling sets of tube cannisters, with brightly colored imagery, from an oversized carboard box. "I honestly don't know where Cos finds these things," Mr. Limone stated. "He gets all of it in the North End," Dad replied. "No, I know where he gets it all, I just don't know how he knows what to get," Mr. Limone responded.

These weren't your average, everyday fireworks that you might find in a typical suburban neighborhood on the Fourth of July. These fireworks were completely legit; like you might find at an organized, public show that a small town would put on for its residents. There weren't any bottle rockets or Roman Candles here, only serious aerial fireworks that would shoot barrages and batteries of flaming shots into the air, exploding in vibrant flower or star-like shapes.

My favorite was the type that fired multiple shots high into the air and then exploded in bright, gold layers with simultaneous and thunderous crackling sound effects. After detonating, the glimmering gold ash would seemingly hang in the air for a second or two. The gilded cinders would then arch and slowly cascade downward, resembling the fullness of a willow tree's branches. Accompanying the gold-lace visual effects were distinct sizzling and crackling pops and bangs that would resonate through the air. They were awesome and I could only hope that a few of the canisters being lifted from the box included some of those.

I stood back a few feet from the table and watched as the last canister was pulled from the box and put onto the table. "Is that it?" I asked, curiously. "'Is that it? Is that it?' Did you hear that, Bobby? He thinks that's all we have tonight!" Mr. Limone joked. "No, we have more coming. Mr. Desanto is heading back over with his contribution to tonight's show," Dad added.

"Oh, cool. I just thought there'd be more than that, that's all," I replied. Dad shot me a quick look and smirked. "We aim to please over here, Michael. So, get ready to be pleased!" Mr. Limone teased. "Ahh, here he comes now," Dad exclaimed, as he pointed to a large figure crossing the Palermo's side lawn.

"That's right, here I am!" Mr. Desanto shouted, drawing all eyes to him. "Well, you've kept me and Bobby waiting over here! You know we don't like to be kept waiting," Mr. Limone joked back. Mr. Desanto was carrying a large cardboard box of his own and placed it down beside the table.

Mr. Desanto's booming voice, and all the activity around the table, had now drawn a crowd, as I was joined by a swarm of other kids. "Do you know what we call the contents of this box in my business, kids?" Mr. Desanto asked, rhetorically. "We call this contraband! And it's been confiscated. Me, and my crack team of assistants here, are going to put it to the test and make sure that what's been seized is actual illegal contraband!" Mr. Desanto yelled, with most of us kids missing the joke.

The contents of Mr. Desanto's box were added to the inventory on the table. There was a chorus of "oohs and aahs" as each item was pulled from the carton and revealed on the table.

Mr. Limone hammed it up for the crowd and made a game out of displaying each firework as it emerged from the box. "What do we have left to do, Bobby?" Mr. Desanto asked. "I think we're all set here. We just have to make sure the ignition team is ready to go," Dad answered, pointing to the far end of Karen Drive where the kids had been seated for dinner just a couple of hours earlier.

"And who do we have working things over there?" Mr. Desanto asked. "Cos is over there with Tony Ferraro," Dad answered. "Good. Good men for the job. Okay then, if you and Jimmy are going to be running the shots over to those two, then I guess I'll be crowd control!" Mr. Desanto yelled. "That works for us, Nick," Mr. Limone answered, enthusiastically.

"Okay kids, you heard them! I'm crowd control. So, you better be ready to be controlled! Everyone back … back … back … back. Everybody get back. I'm crowd control and I want everyone back! At least one hundred feet from here. All the way across the street. Right about where we parked the old folks!" Mr. Desanto shouted, as he spread his arms out wide, corralling and waving us away from the Palermo's driveway and further from Karen Drive.

We had been shepherded across the street and now sat on the curb in the front corner of my house that directly faced Karen Drive. The moms, grandparents, aunts, uncles, etcetera, were sitting in a row of lawn chairs directly behind us. In the median strip of grass separating the street from our front yard, a half dozen or so tiki torches had been staked out. The torches were now ablaze, in hopes of warding off any unwanted mosquitoes. In terms of that goal, they didn't seem all that successful to me, as I needed to repeatedly shoo away the irritating pests.

Nonetheless, it was certainly a cool look that just added to the night's already rich atmosphere. We were all super excited and anxious for the show to get started. Some of the moms, however, were not big fireworks fans and appeared to be in full countdown mode for something imminent and catastrophic to go wrong. But they were surely in the minority, as the rest of us were psyched for the show to get started. Oddly enough, it was the older crew that began to jeer and chastise the organizers of tonight's event. They were having fun with it and were loudly impatient and calling for them to "get the show on the road!".

Mr. Limone, trying to appease the angry villagers, appeared from his station in the driveway to give an update. He shouted from the Palermo's lawn and asked that the kids keep the grandparents in-line. He then announced that we were in the final two-minute countdown and suggested that we both "hold our horses" and "buckle up" for the start of the show. This got some laughs and infused even more buzz and excitement amongst the crowd as things were about to get underway.

Although we knew the first shot was only moments away, the thunderous sound from the mortar still caught many of us off guard. There was an immediate cheer from the crowd that followed the massive "boom" that announced the show's opening.

The first firework was a shell that left a silver tail in its wake and then detonated into a bright green floral shape. "Oh, I like that one," Aunt Gray announced loudly. There was a smattering of "whoas," "oohs," and "aahs," from the gang and even some light clapping.

The second launch only trailed the first by a few seconds. This variety was a multi-shot barrage that launched numerous shells, in short succession, that exploded at their peak into orange stars. Clearly, another favorite of Aunt Gray's, as she clapped passionately from the edge of her seat. The bright auburn flashes revealed small residual clouds of expended gun powder that immediately drifted south and vanished as quickly as they had appeared.

There was a slight pause in between the second and third firework launches. But the wait was worth it, as the third mortar shot turned out to be my favorite, a "Golden Willow". It was a huge explosion with the full display of golden trails that seemingly hung in the sky for a full ten seconds. It was incredibly cool! And by the resounding response of everyone gathered, it unquestionably was the hands-on favorite.

While waiting for the next volley, I spotted Marco, Ricky, and my brother Bob slither out of the house across the street and park themselves on the corner of the Palermo's lawn. Of course, this was a privilege that I couldn't let rest unchallenged. But, before I blew the whistle on it, I decided to try and benefit myself from that group's complete inability to follow the rules. So, I opted to do some slithering of my own.

I waited for the launch of the next firework and, as all eyes were cast upward tracking the shot's flight, I quietly made my way across the street. I knew enough to give this group a wide berth, so I roamed over to their general area, but did not get right on top of them. Naturally, my move across the street did not go unnoticed. In just a mere few seconds, I was joined by at least a half dozen other kids. I guess there was strength in numbers, but our cover was clearly blown.

The question now was simply whether Dad would send us all back over across the street or allow us to stay put. Honestly, we were still a good one hundred feet or more away from where the fireworks were being set off, so I crossed my fingers that we'd be allowed to stay where we were. A moment later, the next missile took off with a deafening "boom"! At a height of about two hundred feet, it exploded in a spherical ball of brightly colored lights. It was super cool. And yes, it was even better, now being closer to the action. But now came the test.

Dad and Mr. Limone returned to the stock table to assist and reload for the ignition team. Dad spotted us immediately. "How'd you guys make it over here?" he asked. This was met with a bunch of shoulder shrugs. "We're okay over here. We're far away from the action. And we're just around the corner of the house here," Lou Limone answered for all of us. Dad and Mr. Limone quickly glanced at one another.

"Okay look, if you stay right where you are, around the corner of the house and away from everything, then fine. But we have a lot going on here and we can't constantly be checking on you. So, will you stay put?" Dad asked the group. We shook our heads, signaling yes, and we had an accord.

We were now a good thirty minutes into the fireworks show. The air in the neighborhood was full of the unmistakable smell of spent gun powder. But I loved it! It just triggered something in me that spelled out summer in all capital letters. It was also crystal clear to me that everyone present, the entire neighborhood, was having the time of their lives. And I had this overwhelming feeling, a sort of innate understanding, that we were sharing something very authentic and special. It was very much in-tune with the historical significance and spirit of today's celebration across the country.

Through this point of the night, the sheer assortment of fireworks was remarkable. I don't believe a single variant had been repeated. Our group seated on the Palermo's lawn had gathered closer together, all eager to get the fullest view of the show. And we didn't have to wait long before the next pyrotechnic took flight.

This next firework, known as a barrage, fired multiple shots, nearly at once, hurling a cluster of bomblets that exploded in a flurry of gold and silver sparks. It was extremely loud with a seemingly endless supply of explosive punch. Everyone in our group began to cackle at the breadth and extent of firepower that this one device held. We were impressed and amazed at its considerable staying power.

"No way!" someone shouted, as the explosions seemed to gather pace. "Awesome!" someone else yelled. We were shaking with excitement and delight as the device rattled off one detonation after another. Just as the canister emptied its final few shots, we were startled to hear an ear-piercing siren, shrieking from somewhere behind us. It was immediately assumed by all that the local police had been summoned to investigate and quash the illicit fireworks show.

Dad and Mr. Limone had obviously heard the blare of the siren as well, as both leaned forward from the driveway to get a look around. "It's the cops! The cops are here! We're busted!" Marco blurted out. We all whipped our heads around to look for an approaching patrol car. Mr. Limone shouted to the ignition team, which now included Mr. Desanto, and signaled to halt operations.

Dad climbed onto the Palermo's lawn to survey the area. The siren continued to fill the air and sounded as if it were getting closer. Suddenly, Marco rose from the lawn and sprang into action. "We got to get these fireworks outta here!" he exclaimed, jumping from the lawn onto the driveway.

It was pitch-black dark out now and I quickly lost sight of Marco as he scurried away. My heart began to race, pounding in my chest as the earsplitting siren grew even closer. But still, there was no police car to be found. And then, suddenly, it revealed itself. We hadn't caught sight of a cop car because there wasn't one at all. Instead, it was Herb Schaefer who was pulling a prank on all of us. Herb emerged from behind the shrubs of the Palermo's house sporting a huge grin on his face and a bullhorn in his right hand that, obvious to all of us now, had a siren feature on it.

Herb was cackling and snickering, proud of the ruse that he had successfully carried out over the neighborhood. The response he received, however, was far less cordial than he likely expected. He was met by a cascade of boos immediately after he emerged from the shadows. There were even a handful of crumpled up paper cups thrown his way in protest.

Of course, Herb just ate this all up, especially after being duped earlier in the day at the lawnmower race. "Herbie, what are you doing? You scared the wits out of us!" Mrs. Palermo yelled. "Sorry Lillian, just having some fun with everyone," Herb answered, still belly laughing.

But the good-natured fun didn't last very long as it was interrupted by Marco, who had returned from his driveway and was now squawking loudly. He was holding his right wrist securely in his left hand, supporting it as he walked towards us. He was hot under the collar, completely pissed off, and shouting.

"Are you fucking kidding me!?" he yelled. "Marco! Your language. What's wrong with you!?" his mother responded. "I'll tell you what's wrong. This jack ass joker had to goof off and scare the shit out of everyone, making us think the cops were here. And I ran to stash the fireworks and tripped over a god damn boulder that they left in the middle of the fucking driveway after the clambake!" he cursed, at the top of his lungs.

"It was a joke, Marco. That's all. Herb was just being funny," she answered. "Well really funny. I think I broke my fucking wrist!" he continued to curse. "For crying out loud, let me see it. Show it to me," she demanded. Marco used his left hand to help extend his right wrist for his mom to inspect. She extended her thumb and index finger so that she could check his injury.

"Does it …," she began. "Ahh, fuck! That hurts. What are you squeezing it for?" he interrupted her examination. "Oh, good lord … Let's go," she answered. "Go where?" he asked. "It's broken, Marco. We have to go to the hospital so they can do whatever the hell it is they have to do," she shouted, now clearly angry herself.

"Lillian, I'm so sorry. I didn't mean for anyone to get hurt. I was just trying to have some fun with everybody," Herb pleaded. "I know, I know. It's always this one. It's a day, just like any other day," she sighed.

"Ma, can't we just go in the morning? I'll be fine until then," Marco tried to bargain. "Do you see what I mean!? This is what I'm dealing with, he has a broken wrist but wants to wait until the morning!" she screamed. "I'm fine," Marco said softly. "You're not fine and we're going now," she exclaimed.

"Lil, I'll get my things and come with you," my mom offered. "No, no. You's all stay here and continue with the show. I'll take him myself. What are the chances that they'll be busy at the emergency room on the fourth of July?" she barked, sarcastically.

Mrs. Palermo ran into her house to retrieve her pocketbook and car keys. A few dads, including Mr. Palermo, now encircled Marco in the middle of Fieldstone Drive. I, and about a half dozen other kids, made a ring around the dads and looked in with nosy, prying curiosity.

"You always have to be running around like a wild animal, don't you?" Mr. Palermo chided Marco. "Dad, this wasn't my fault!" Marco shouted. "He's right, Cos. This is on me. It was a stupid prank and I'm sorry," Herb interjected.

Mr. Palermo took a good, close look at Marco's wrist. "Well, it's broken for sure. I hope you enjoyed your full five or so hours outside of a cast," Mr. Palermo teased. "We might have a bigger problem," Marco then confessed. Mr. Palermo slowly raised his eyes from Marco's wrist and fixed them directly into his son's eyes. "Oh yeah, what's that?" he asked Marco tersely. "When I tripped over the rock, I had some of the fireworks in my hands and dropped them," Marco answered. "And?" Mr. Palermo asked, just waiting for even worse news. "And one of the canisters rolled into the clambake pit," Marco admitted.

"Into the pit? Or did it land on top of the tarp covering the pit?" Mr. Palermo followed. "It fell INTO the pit," Marco replied, strongly emphasizing the word "into". The pit had been securely cordoned off by using the eight brightly colored orange police barricade horses and then covered by the heavy industrial tarp. It was still an open hole, however, and undoubtedly still hot from its use earlier in the day.

"Into the hole that had a raging hot fire in it all day, that pit?" Mr. Palermo pressed. "Yeah, that pit," Marco replied, smartly. "And that wasn't the first thing you decided to tell us, huh?" Mr. Palermo wondered. There was a slight, uncomfortable pause. "Are you sure it was just one canister?" Mr. Palermo then asked. "I'm positive. I picked up three, tripped, dropped all three and saw one roll into the pit. I know the other two are still in the driveway," Marco answered definitively.

Just then, Mrs. Palermo reappeared from her front door. She had her pocketbook tightly gripped in her left hand and held her car keys in her right. "Okay Marco let's …," she began to shout but was harshly interrupted by a resounding "boom". My eyes were immediately drawn skyward as a cascading shower of bright gold sparkles fell in full shape over the Palermo's house.

"Hey, it was my favorite … a Golden Willow," I thought to myself. I quickly glanced back at Mr. Palermo, equally interested to see his reaction. Would he explode, like the Golden Willow that was now raining flaming ash over his house, or would it be something else, I wondered. I was stunned to see that he had no reaction at all. He didn't flinch. He didn't turn his head to look. He just stood there, stoically like a statue, as if he expected and knew what would happen. Mrs. Palermo, on the other hand, was far less subdued.

"Jesus, Mary, and Joseph! What in god's name is that!?" she shouted. "That, that's your son's contribution to the fireworks this evening," Mr. Palermo answered. Luckily, the tarp on top of the pit restricted and captured a good amount of the firework contents within the hole.

After the shot had fully expended, Dad and Mr. Limone quickly rushed to the area to assess the damage. There they found the other two cannisters that Marco had dropped on the driveway. They also found the remaining fireworks unscathed and moved them far from the area. The only damage seemed to be to the tarp which had extensive burn marks scattered across it. Given the possible outcomes, I thought this could actually have ended a whole lot worse.

Believe it or not, the show went on, and without any further hitches. Everyone felt badly that Mrs. Palermo had to leave with Marco, but that empathy seemed to fade once the fireworks started to fly again. Once again, we were all positioned on the grass in front of my house, safely away from any danger.

The extent and caliber of the fireworks continued to wow and thrill everybody. We even saw some families from a few streets away that had come to watch the show from a distance. By any measure, this was the biggest production and display in our neighborhood, and perhaps even in the town. And, as a huge fireworks fan, I couldn't have been happier.

Following a clear lull in the activity, we all realized that the show was over. This was confirmed once the dads emerged from the clouds of smoke hovering over Karen Drive. They were immediately welcomed onto Fieldstone Drive with a rousing round of applause. The elder crew even rose from their seats to show their appreciation. The dads clearly enjoyed the attention and basked in the limelight for a moment. "We did it! That's the show! And, with only one small injury, and a minor fire hazard … we pulled it off!" Mr. Desanto shouted.

This was instantly met with another round of boisterous cheers. "Thank you, thank you everyone. Let's do it all over again next year!" Mr. Palermo quipped. "Good night, everybody!" Mr. Limone shouted.

I was about to turn and head for my house when Matteo approached me. "Hey, you guys up for a late-night swim?" he asked. I turned and looked at Dave and Mario. "Not me, I'm way too tired," Mario answered. "I don't know, I don't think my mom and dad are going to be okay with it," Dave added. "Come on, it's not a big deal. It'll just be us in my backyard," Matteo pressed. "Well, I'm not going to ask them," Dave said, looking straight at me. "All right, so If I ask and they say it's okay, are you in?" I followed. "Yeah, I guess but only for a little while. It's really late," Dave reasoned.

I spun around trying to search out the whereabouts of my parents. I spotted Mom first. She was carrying a load of dirty platters and a stray lawn chair back towards our house. By the looks of it, I could tell that asking her would be dicey at best, so I passed. I then zeroed in on Dad, who was still exchanging good-byes with the Limone's, as they stood in the middle of the street.

I slowly approached them, hesitating slightly, as I wondered if this was a good idea. Dad spotted me and beat me to the punch, "What is it, Michael?" he asked, as if he already knew that I had planned to ask for something more. I was quick to read the situation, though, and decided to call an audible and abort. "I just wanted to say that today was awesome. And thanks!" I replied. Dad smiled at me, but also looked right through me, just as a poker player would at his opponent.

"Good night, Michael," he answered, with a wry smile. "Well, that was nice, huh Bobby? Certainly, makes it all worth it!" I heard Mr. Limone going on, as I turned and slunk back to my crew. Matteo was first to ask, "Well, what did he say?"

"Sorry, it's a no," I answered. "Really!? Awe, c'mon! That sucks!" he exclaimed. "I know. But it was a long day," I replied. "Yeah, I just didn't want it to end, I guess," Matteo added. With that, we called an end to an awesome day and headed for the tent in my backyard to get some much-needed rest.

Once we got into the tent, we quickly settled into our sleeping bags. We were all entirely spent and thoroughly exhausted. Within seconds, my head barely hitting the pillow, I detected the very faint sound of someone snoring. I immediately assumed that someone was joking and took a quick glance around the tent.

I found that the low and muffled breathing was coming from Johnny, who would be very unlikely to be kidding around. "Is he sleeping already?" I wondered out loud. Mario took a quick glance at his younger brother and, with a healthy chuckle, report-ed that yes, he was already asleep. "I don't know how, but yeah, he is," he said, giggling. "That's unbelievable!" I answered. "Yeah, I know," Mario agreed.

There was a brief pause, which I used to quickly replay all of the day's events in my head, as I stared up at the tent top from my sleeping bag. "It was a pretty awesome day!" I declared. "Yeah, it was," Dave was quick to agree. "All except for those fucking bees. They sucked!" Mario countered, loudly.

I laughed out loud but couldn't disagree with him, "I bet. That must have sucked. But other than the bees, it was pretty awesome," I responded. "Yes, except for the bees," Mario finished, just before we all drifted off.

Lunedi 5 Luglio, 1976
(Monday, July 5, 1976)

XXXIX - Desiderio
(Yearnings)

Surprisingly, I was early to rise the next morning. This was partly due to force of habit given my regular responsibilities to deliver the newspapers in the early morning. But this was Bob's week and not mine, so my early start to the day was more out of curiosity. I was anxious to get a look at the aftermath from last night's show and to see what it looked like in the daylight.

Sluggish, I slowly crept from my backyard and headed over to ground-zero, which was Karen Drive. The early morning sun was already blistering, I could feel the heat radiating from the road in front of me. It was going to be another hot one. I crossed the street in front of the Palermo's and strode on the sidewalk to the corner of Karen Drive.

I was amazed to find a determined and hustling crew already fast at work. There, I found nearly a dozen women, mothers, grandmothers, and aunts fast at work. There was a push broom brigade, all dressed in house coats of varying and colorful patterns, dialed-in and focused on the task at hand. A second unit trailed close behind with kitchen brooms, picking up any small debris missed by the push broom squad.

It was quite a sight to see. My immediate reaction was mixed between mild amusement and genuine appreciation. But this undertaking really was emblematic of the spirit of our neighborhood laid bare in front of me, encapsulated by this simple act. It was a sort of communal work ethic and commitment. A commitment to family, to friends, to neighbors and to values. And I felt incredibly fortunate to be a part of it.

As I stood and watched the bustle of activity, I spotted Marco Palermo leaving his backyard and heading my way. "Hey, ass wipe, what are you doing up this early," he shouted. I instantly noticed that Marco now had casts on both his left and right arms. Though, he acted as if there was nothing there at all.

"You got two casts now, huh?" I asked. "Yeah, you know doctors. They probably charged us up the butt for these. I'm going to have Ricky draw some art on them," he answered, and then walked away. I took another long and thankful glance at the crew feverishly working to clean up Karen Drive.

After a moment, I turned and began walking back towards my house. As I walked back home, I thought about the last couple of days and determined that I had unquestionably just enjoyed the time of my life. And even so, I was now simply looking forward to sitting down at the kitchen table with my family and enjoying the familiar and welcoming sounds and smells of a typical morning at home.

It was an ordinary and seemingly unremarkable occurrence but would become something that I would forever yearn for. It's odd that something so simple, so basic could become our own bit of nostalgia. This is a realization that everyone ought to have while they're living it, rather than miss it when it's gone.

Postface

Every good story needs an antagonist. In this story, and in my early life, that was my brother, Bob, for me. And he was one of the best! Together, we had one epic battle after another, which usually ended painfully for me. It was a sibling rivalry for the ages and got quite bitter from time to time.

But that's only half the story; not nearly half in reality, if measured in years. What would be shocking to many back then, Bob and I eventually became incredibly close and the best of friends. He fast became someone I could trust, confide in and have my back in any circumstance.

Thirteen years after the events of the Bicentennial weekend, as told in this story, Bob served as the Best Man at my wedding. Just a few years later, I returned the favor and served as best man at his wedding. Bob then became godfather to my first-born child, and a few years later, he named me as godfather to his.

So, was Bob a great antagonist to me during my youth? Yes, the best. But, that fact, and those years, are now dwarfed by his kindness, generosity and friendship that he has extended to me ever since.

Acknowledgments

I would like to acknowledge the incredibly supportive, giving, and helpful people who were vitally important to me in putting this life story down on paper. First and foremost is my wife Karen, who provided steady and tangible moral support during this effort. I would also like to thank my kids Samantha, Nicholas, and Justin Sorabella, as well as their significant others Nick, Jennifer and Lauren, for their interest in hearing about my early years.

Vincent and Regina Cuccaro, Tonia Cuccaro-Beer, Giana Beer, and the entire Cuccaro family — I would not be able to get this work done without your assistance, wisdom, translations and incredible artistic skill. Thank you all!

And to my friend Joe Bertagna, I owe a special thank you and acknowledgment for your work, patience, insight, and expertise that unquestionably made this endeavor a possibility.

Lastly and most of all, thank you to my family and old neighbors for providing such a wonderful and caring upbringing; especially my mom, Louise, and my dad, Robert R. Sorabella.

About the Author

Michael Sorabella, a third generation American, and one of five kids in his family, grew up during the 1970's as an exceptionally typical American kid. He and his family had recently moved, from a city on the outskirts of Boston, to reside in a recently developed suburban neighborhood. That neighborhood, comprised predominantly by households of Italian descent, grew quickly into a close-knit community of young families all searching for their slice of the American Dream.

Emblematic of the times, most neighborhood kids spent a great deal of their youth playing outside with siblings and friends, riding bikes, competing in sports, making treks in the woods and occasionally-to-frequently, participating in wide-ranging acts of mischief. Again, an exceedingly American upbringing.

Simultaneously, and quite unwittingly, however, Michael's youth was also surrounded by, and steep in, Italian culture. That culture was completely encompassed with an incredible devotion and commitment to family and to the extended family: your neighbors. Today, as a fully assimilated Italian American adult, he can benefit from the gift of hindsight, and he can both appreciate and miss what was simply part of life in those younger days. And, without question, that multi-generational and multi-cultural upbringing serves as the keystone today to his values and understanding of what is truly important.